ACCLAIM FOR BETH WISEMAN

LISTENING TO LOVE

"*Listening to Love* is vintage Beth Wiseman . . . clear your calendar because you're going to want to read this one in a single setting."

—Vannetta Chapman, author of the
Shipshewana Amish Mystery series

HEARTS IN HARMONY

"This is a sweet story, not only of romance, but of older generations and younger generations coming together in friendship. It's a tear jerker as well as an uplifting story."

—*Parkersburg News & Sentinel*

"Beth Wiseman has penned a poignant story of friendship, faith, and love that is sure to touch readers' hearts."

—Kathleen Fuller, author of the Middlefield Family novels

"Beth Wiseman's *Hearts in Harmony* is a lyrical hymn. Mary and Levi are heartwarming, lovable characters who instantly feel like dear friends. Once readers open this book, they won't put it down until they've reached the last page."

—Amy Clipston, bestselling author of *A Seat by the Hearth*

AMISH CELEBRATIONS

"Wiseman's (*Amish Secrets*) collection of timeless stories of love and loss among the Plain People will delight fans of the author's heartfelt story lines and flowing prose."

—*Library Journal*

HOME ALL ALONG

"Beth Wiseman's novel will find a permanent home in every reader's heart as she spins comfort and prose into a stellar read of grace."

—Kelly Long, author of the Patch of Heaven series

LOVE BEARS ALL THINGS

"Suggest to those seeking a more truthful, less saccharine portrayal of the trials of human life and the transformative growth and redemption that may occur as a result."

—*Library Journal*

HER BROTHER'S KEEPER

"Wiseman has created a series in which the readers have a chance to peel back all the layers of the Amish secrets."

—*RT Book Reviews*, 4½ stars and July 2015 Top Pick!

"Wiseman's new launch is edgier, taking on the tough issues of mental illness and suicide. Amish fiction fans seeking something a bit more thought-provoking and challenging than the usual fare will find this series debut a solid choice."

—*Library Journal*

THE LAND OF CANAAN NOVELS

"Wiseman's voice is consistently compassionate and her words flow smoothly."

—*Publishers Weekly* on *Seek Me with All Your Heart*

"Wiseman's third Land of Canaan novel overflows with romance, broken promises, a modern knight in shining armor, and hope at the end of the rainbow."

—*RT Book Reviews*

"In *Seek Me with All Your Heart*, Beth Wiseman offers readers a heartwarming story filled with complex characters and deep emotion. I instantly loved Emily, and eagerly turned each page, anxious to learn more about her past—and what future the Lord had in store for her."

—Shelley Shepard Gray, bestselling author of the Seasons of Sugarcreek series

"Wiseman has done it again! Beautifully compelling, *Seek Me with All Your Heart* is a heartwarming story of faith, family, and renewal. Her characters and descriptions are captivating, bringing the story to life with the turn of every page."

—Amy Clipston, bestselling author of *A Gift of Grace*

The Daughters of the Promise Novels

"Well-defined characters and story make for an enjoyable read."

—*RT Book Reviews* on *Plain Pursuit*

"A touching, heartwarming story. Wiseman does a particularly great job of dealing with shunning, a controversial Amish practice that seems cruel and unnecessary to outsiders . . . If you're a fan of Amish fiction, don't miss *Plain Pursuit*!"

—Kathleen Fuller, author of the Middlefield Family novels

LISTENING
TO
LOVE

Other Books by Beth Wiseman

LISTENING

TO

LOVE

An
Amish Journey
Novel

BETH WISEMAN

ZONDERVAN

Listening to Love

Copyright © 2019 by Elizabeth Wiseman Mackey

This title is also available as a Zondervan ebook.

This title is also available as a Zondervan audio book.

Requests for information should be addressed to:
Zondervan, *3900 Sparks Dr. SE, Grand Rapids, Michigan 49546*

ISBN 978-0-310-35967-8 (library edition)

Library of Congress Cataloging-in-Publication Data
Names: Wiseman, Beth, 1962- author.
Title: Listening to love / Beth Wiseman.
Description: Grand Rapids, Michigan : Zondervan, [2019] | Series: An Amish
 journey novel ; 2
Identifiers: LCCN 2019013783| ISBN 9780529118714 (softcover) |
ISBN
 9780529118745 (epub)
Subjects: | GSAFD: Love stories. | Christian fiction.
Classification: LCC PS3623.I83 L57 2019 | DDC 813/.6--dc23 LC
record available at https://lccn.loc.gov/2019013783

Printed in the United States of America
19 20 21 22 23 LSC 10 9 8 7 6 5 4 3 2 1

To Sharon and Sam Hanners,
with love and appreciation

GLOSSARY

ab im kopp: crazy, off in the head
ach: oh
boppli: baby
bruder: brother
daed: dad
danki: thank you
dochder: daughter
Englisch: those who are not Amish; the English language
fraa: wife
Gott: God
gut: good
haus: house
kapp: prayer covering worn by Amish women
kinner: children
lieb: love
maedel: girl
mamm: mom
mei: my
mudder: mother
nee: no

Ordnung, the: the written and unwritten rules of the Amish; the understood behavior by which the Amish are expected to live, passed down from generation to generation. Most Amish know the rules by heart.

rumschpringe: "running around"; the period of time when Amish youth experience life in the Englisch world before making the decision to be baptized and commit to Amish life

schweeger: brother-in-law

schweschder: sister

sohn: son

Wie bischt?: Hello; how are you?

ya: yes

CHAPTER 1

Natalie pulled her coat snug as she crossed the yard, hurrying toward Mary and Levi's house. She was anxious to get inside the warm home as she eyed smoke billowing from the chimney. The heat had gone out in her SUV over a week ago, but her class schedule hadn't allowed time for repairs yet.

Her teeth chattered as she knocked on the door. Lucas wasn't here yet, but the icy weather might have slowed him down. Natalie had offered, more than once, to pick up her Amish friend and drive him to Mary and Levi's house for their Friday night dinners—or supper, as the Amish called the last meal of the day—but Lucas always declined and insisted on making the drive from Orleans to Shoals in his buggy.

"*Ach*, hurry, get inside." Mary held the door wide so Natalie could step over the threshold. "You still don't have the heater fixed in your car?"

Natalie rushed to the fireplace, where orange sparks shimmied upward. She pulled off her black gloves, held her hands close to the glowing embers, and breathed in the smell of freshly baked bread. "Not yet, but hopefully soon."

"Lucas isn't here yet. I'm sure you noticed his buggy isn't tethered outside." Mary took Natalie's coat when she was finally warm enough to slip out of it and hung it on a peg by the door.

Natalie pulled off her boots and carried them to the area by the front door where other shoes were lined up against the wall. "Oops." It wasn't the first time she'd forgotten to remove them upon entering the house. She'd worn thick socks, knowing Mary and Levi didn't wear shoes inside. Or socks. "Aren't your feet frozen?"

Mary grinned as she walked barefoot toward the kitchen, motioning for Natalie to follow. A loaf of bread cooled on a rack next to a plate of chocolate chip cookies.

"You've asked me about my feet every Friday since it got cold." Mary shrugged. "We grew up going barefoot all year long, so I guess our feet are conditioned to the cold."

Natalie walked to the stove and lifted the lid off a simmering pot. "Oh, wow. Mashed potatoes." Mary made the best potatoes on the planet. Natalie wasn't sure if it was the amount of butter, the seasonings, or a secret ingredient that made the difference, but they were awesome.

Friday night supper at Mary and Levi's house was the highlight of her week. The food was great, and Mary and Levi were her closest friends. Along with Lucas. He was her best friend—and Levi's older brother. Natalie and Lucas had hit it off a few months ago when she went with Mary to visit

Levi. Lucas had slipped Natalie his phone number when no one was looking. It was a surprise since their family was so conservative compared to most Amish in the area. Many used cell phones, but she wouldn't have thought anyone in the Shetler family would have one. Mary had even stowed hers when she married Levi, compromising with her husband that it would only be used in an emergency. When Natalie asked, Lucas had admitted he kept the phone hidden.

Natalie and Lucas kept their friendship quiet for a while, mostly talking on the phone before they started meeting at the library. Their love of books had drawn them together, but Lucas was also helping Natalie learn about God in a way she could relate to.

"I wish you'd let me bring a dish or something for our meals." Natalie poured herself a glass of tea as Mary waved off the comment, the way she always did when Natalie offered to contribute. Levi and Mary had both encouraged her to feel at home here, and she did. The three of them had nursed her cousin, Adeline, in this house, taking turns caring for the older woman until she died a few months ago. Adeline blessed them all when she left her house to Levi and Mary in her will.

She also left all of her money to Natalie to use for college. As it turned out, their elderly friend didn't have much money when she died. Mary and Levi had sold the Steinway piano that came with the house, and they graciously gifted the proceeds to Natalie so she could pay for college. None of them had any idea the piano would provide enough to support Natalie through four years of school. She had argued that Levi and Mary should keep the money, but her friends wouldn't hear of it, saying Adeline's intent had been to help Natalie with school. And besides, instruments were forbidden in Mary and Levi's world anyway.

Smiling, Natalie glanced around the kitchen and recalled so many fond memories. A lot of meals had been prepared in this room, mostly the best chicken salad sandwiches she had ever eaten. And she couldn't look at the kitchen table without remembering the times she, Mary, and Levi had worked on a jigsaw puzzle with Adeline. Natalie missed their friend but believed she was kicking up her heels in heaven with her husband, Percy. *Maybe she even runs into Mimi Jean sometimes.* Natalie was sure her grandmother and Adeline would have been friends here on earth if they'd known each other.

She was thankful God had brought their little group together. First it was just Levi, Mary, and Natalie, always meeting on Friday nights for supper. But it wasn't long before Lucas joined them. He and Levi were the closest of their siblings, so it worked out well for all of them.

Mary reached for her own glass of tea, and she and Natalie took their seats. Mary always set a beautiful table— white china that had been her grandmother's, white cloth napkins with silver holders that had belonged to her aunt, and always fresh flowers in a vase. Levi bought them for his wife every Wednesday during the winter months. Natalie practically swooned the first time Mary told her the flowers were a weekly thing. *So romantic.*

"Levi is showering and running behind schedule." Mary paused and took a deep breath. "Maybe this is a *gut* time for us to talk, before Lucas gets here."

"What's wrong?" Natalie studied her friend, whose eyebrows had narrowed into a frown.

Mary let out a breath and her facial muscles relaxed, but her expression remained sober. "You know how much Levi and I love you, *ya*?"

Natalie nodded as she wondered where Mary was going with that kind of introduction.

"And we've noticed that you seem to be developing a closer relationship with *Gott*." Mary nervously ran a finger around the edge of her glass. "We're so happy about that."

"Lucas has taught me a lot about God. We even read the Bible together sometimes, and he explains the things I don't understand." She paused, trying to read Mary's expression, but her friend wasn't giving much away, just staring blankly at her. "If there is something you want to say, it's okay. Just say it." She leaned back in the chair and smiled, hoping to ease whatever tension Mary was feeling, but also wondering why she looked so serious.

"You and Lucas have been meeting here on Friday nights for weeks. And we *lieb* having you here. Lucas is Levi's *bruder*, and I consider you like a *schweschder*." Mary took a deep breath and blew it out slowly. Whatever was coming couldn't be good.

"Mary, what is it?"

Her friend locked eyes with her. "Levi and I have noticed the way you and Lucas look at each other. You've also mentioned that you meet for lunches or at the Bedford library." She reached across the table and put a hand on Natalie's. "We're worried that this is becoming more than friendship."

Natalie was surprised it had taken Mary this long to

broach the subject. "I've been expecting this—questions from you and Levi about me and Lucas. Yes, we spend time together, and we're super close. But we know that's as far as it will ever go."

Mary raised an eyebrow. "So, you've discussed your relationship?"

Natalie tucked her blonde hair behind ears that still felt frozen, as she avoided her friend's inquiring expression. "Well, no. I mean, we haven't talked about it." She shifted her weight in the chair. "We don't need to talk about it. He's Amish. I'm not. I'm planning to be a vet, and he will meet a nice girl in Orleans and eventually get married."

Mary began twirling the string of her prayer covering, something she did when she was either nervous or in serious thought. "I know you've said you're just friends, but sometimes we can't control who we fall in love with. It's obvious that you and Lucas care about each other. How do you know this friendship won't evolve into something more?"

"Because we won't let it." Natalie sat taller and shook her head.

Mary let go of the string on her prayer covering and placed both palms on the table. "*Ya*, okay. But for the sake of argument, let's just say that you and Lucas did fall in love."

Natalie slouched into the chair and sighed.

"Just hear me out. You know how differently you and I live. And even though Levi and I are both Amish, we lived very different lives before we were married. I come from an Amish community that isn't nearly as conservative as the one Levi and Lucas are from. Our bishop is more forgiving and lenient, and our interpretation of the *Ordnung* isn't as strictly enforced as it is in the Orleans community. Levi and Lucas come from a world far different even from mine."

She waved a hand around the kitchen, brightly lit with lanterns on the counter and hanging above the table. "I have propane to fuel our stove and refrigerator, a luxury Levi and Lucas's family doesn't approve of." She leaned over the table, closer to Natalie. "Don't you remember the compromises Levi and I had to make in order for us to be happy? And I was already living an Amish life. We adopted some of his ways and some of mine. I take my cell phone with me when I go to town sometimes, to charge it, but otherwise it stays turned off in the drawer of my nightstand. I agreed not to use it unless there's an emergency. We only use drivers in emergencies, too, as opposed to asking someone to drive us to the market in the rain or snow. Can you even imagine what an overhaul it would be to your life or Lucas's if this friendship progressed into something more?"

Natalie held up a hand to gently shush her friend. "I know all of this, and you're worrying for no reason. The Shetlers are very conservative. And I respect that. Even though we're just friends, Lucas and I are never alone together." She looked over her shoulder to make sure Levi wasn't coming, then spoke in a whisper. "We don't kiss or anything like that, Mary. We are just *friends*."

"It's still dangerous. And reckless." Mary spoke with an authority Natalie didn't think she'd heard her friend use before. "We talked about this when you two first started becoming friends a few months ago, and your friendship has grown. Someone is going to get hurt."

Natalie was quiet for a while. The thought of Lucas in

another woman's arms stung a little, but it was something she tried not to think about. "You, Levi, and Lucas have told me that everything that happens is God's will. I'm choosing to rely on God's will for my life. And for whatever reason, my friendship with Lucas is part of my journey. I will keep listening to God and following His lead. If I step onto the wrong path, I'll know." She paused as she recalled the trauma she'd gone through with her parents' divorce. "Even if Lucas wasn't Amish, I'm not in the market for a romantic relationship. Not now, and maybe not ever."

Mary cringed. "Don't say that. You *will* fall in love someday. The right person will come along, and you won't be able to think straight. True love will knock you off your feet. And I'll say it again—you can't control whom you fall in love with. Yes, I believe that all things are *Gott*'s will, but He also gives us free will."

They were quiet as Natalie pondered Mary's comments about God and free will, knowing they must be intertwined. The God she was getting to know wouldn't put her in a situation that would hurt her or Lucas.

A few moments later, they heard the clip-clop of hooves approaching, and it wasn't long before a knock sounded and the door opened slightly. "*Wie bischt?* It's me."

"Come in," Mary said as she and Natalie stood.

After the door closed, heavy shoes fell to the floor next to the others. Lucas crossed the living room in his socks and met them in the kitchen, smiling. "Smells *gut*."

Natalie took in Lucas's broad shoulders beneath his dark blue shirt. He reminded her of a lumberjack. She loved the way his dark hair fell straight against his square jawline, and when he smiled, his cool and confident green eyes twinkled. Lucas was one good-looking guy. But men and women could be great friends without including the complications of a romantic relationship, even if there was a physical attraction. God had blessed them with a wonderful friendship that Natalie cherished.

Love came in many forms. Natalie loved Levi and Mary, she loved her brother, Sean, although she didn't see him much, and she loved her parents, despite what they'd put her through—and what they'd done to each other. She was capable of loving Lucas the same way she loved Levi and Mary. Maybe Mary was right and Natalie would fall in love someday, but it would be a long time before she trusted her heart to romantic love. And that made her relationship with Lucas feel safe, not dangerous or reckless as Mary had said.

⁂

Lucas said hello to Natalie and his sister-in-law, and Levi came into the room a few minutes later.

"*Wie bischt?*" Lucas shook Levi's hand, then went to where Mary was standing by the oven and gave her a hug before he sat down. Lucas had never hugged Natalie, even though he felt closer to her than anyone in the room, including his own brother. He was certain God had sent Natalie into his life to help her find her way to Him. Natalie had a hunger for knowledge about God and the Bible and faith, and Lucas loved watching her grow and learn.

It didn't hurt that she was easy on the eyes with her long

blonde hair and eyes as blue as a cloudless sky. He'd never had a friend quite like her. They weren't encouraged to interact with outsiders unless necessary, but Lucas believed their friendship was necessary for her spiritual growth. She'd recently started attending Oakland City University in Bedford, a faith-based college, but she still had a lot of questions she wasn't comfortable asking her teachers or the other students.

After they bowed their heads in prayer and filled their plates with roast, mashed potatoes, carrots, and buttered bread, Levi wanted to know how things were at home. He and Mary had only been married a few months, so having a house of his own probably still felt new. He asked about the family weekly. It was a twenty-mile ride in the buggy from Orleans to Mary and Levi's house in Shoals, so they didn't see the rest of the family often.

"*Ach*, well, it's the usual chaos. Not much has changed since you asked me last week." Lucas chuckled. "You're barely missed."

Levi scowled until Lucas grinned again. "I'm kidding, *bruder*. *Mamm* misses you the most."

Lucas's brother rolled his eyes. "Probably because I'm the one who took her everywhere in the buggy."

"*Ya*, Eli carts her around most of the time now, and sometimes Miriam." Lucas sighed. "I think Miriam is seeing someone. I've seen her sneaking out of the *haus*. *Daed* will go *ab im kopp* if he finds out."

Lucas reached for another slice of bread and noticed everyone was quiet. Mary's eyes were cast down, and he suddenly felt like a louse. "Sorry, Mary. I-I probably shouldn't have mentioned anything. Is Lydia doing okay? How are she, Samuel, and the new *boppli*?"

Last year, Mary's sister had been sneaking out of their house in Montgomery to meet a guy named Samuel, and she'd gotten pregnant. Their parents insisted they be baptized and married right away, even though Samuel and Lydia weren't happy about it. Lucas prayed Miriam didn't fall into the same kind of trouble.

Mary pushed food around on her plate but looked up at him. "I think they are okay, adjusting to married life and being parents. It's hard to know for sure. I don't see them as often as I'd like."

Samuel had worked for Lydia's father at the time, but he'd accepted a different job after he and Lydia married. Lucas wasn't sure if it was because of the awkward situation or a better job opportunity.

He glanced at Natalie as she took a drink of her tea, then looked at Mary. "They don't live far from my mom, and I try to see her once a week." She spooned more potatoes onto her plate. "I know it's quite a trek in the buggy. I can take you to see them if you ever want me to."

Lucas knew about Natalie's mother, who was a bit on the needy side since she and Natalie's father divorced last year. Looking out for her had taken a toll on Natalie and her relationship with her mother, but she'd said recently that they were making more of an effort to regain the good relationship they once had.

Mary glanced at Levi, then back at Natalie. "I appreciate that, but don't forget the rules. No rides from the *Englisch* unless it's an emergency, remember?"

"Right. Sorry. I still forget sometimes . . . I hate when you refer to me as *Englisch*." Natalie set down her fork. "It makes me feel like an outsider."

Levi laughed. "You are."

"Hey. Take it back." Natalie's mouth took on an exaggerated pout, but it wasn't long before she scooped more potatoes onto her fork.

She looked five years old when she rolled her lip under the way she did sometimes, but it was cute. Lucas grinned as he waited for his brother to respond.

"He takes it back," Mary said. "Our family has a lot of friends who aren't Amish."

Lucas hung out with Natalie a lot, but he'd never mentioned her to his parents. With eight brothers and sisters still living at home, it was easy to get lost in the crowd, as long as everyone kept up with their chores.

Levi finally said, "I take it back."

"Look who decided to join us." Mary nodded to her right at their black cat.

Natalie reached out to pet him. "Maxwell! You sweet boy, I've missed you." Grimacing, she looked at Mary. "What's wrong with him? His hair is standing straight up, and his eyes look wild."

"He has started doing that when a storm is coming."

The cat circled the table and even hissed once before he returned to the living room.

Mary craned her neck until she could see the distressed animal. "He gets on the windowsill. Isn't it odd how he just knows when bad weather is approaching?"

"*Mamm* says her knees ache when a storm is coming."

Lucas laid his fork on his plate. "It didn't look like rain, and *Daed* usually tells us if bad weather is forecast. He checks the newspaper."

As if it was God's perfect timing, a loud clap of thunder shook the windows, followed by a loud neigh of disapproval from Lucas's horse.

"Uh-oh." Natalie pushed her lips into a pout again. "That's not good. You can't take the buggy home if it storms bad." She wiped her mouth with her napkin before she laid it across her plate. "You'll have to make an exception and let me drive you home. It was already a little icy on the roads. If it rains, it's going to be a mess."

Lucas stood, as did Levi. "For now, I gotta get Red in the barn. I just have her tethered to the fence."

They were out the door in seconds, and by the time they reached the horse, another thunderous roar sounded, followed by a downpour that filled the sky.

Uh-oh, indeed.

⁂

Natalie walked to the kitchen window as black clouds hovered overhead, firing lightning bolts and unloading massive amounts of rain. "You have to talk Lucas into letting me drive him home, Mary." She spun around. "I know you all occasionally drive in bad weather, but won't this thunder spook the horse? Not to mention how slick the roads will be. Or he needs to spend the night here."

"I don't think he will stay here." Mary stood and walked to the fireplace in the living room. Natalie followed. "Levi told me Lucas walks in his sleep and that it's much worse when he's away from home. As a young boy, he was allowed to stay with friends sometimes, but it was always a problem. One time he even left a friend's house and headed down the road."

"He still does that as an adult?" Natalie had sometimes walked in her sleep when she was a child, but she'd outgrown it by the time she was a teenager.

Mary shrugged. "I don't know. I don't think Levi knows for sure either. It stands to reason that he must still sleepwalk sometimes since he is so against sleeping away from home." After Mary added a log to the fire, she turned around to face Natalie. "But maybe don't mention that to Lucas. I think it would embarrass him."

"I won't say anything." Natalie tried to picture Lucas sleepwalking.

"Personally, I don't think either of you should travel in weather like this. My family would put each of you in extra bedrooms, or even on the couch, but Levi and Lucas's family has a strict rule about two single people staying overnight in the same house, no matter what."

"That's crazy. They'd rather their son get into an accident than stay safe?"

Mary shrugged again, then stoked the fire. "I just don't think he will stay."

"Well, if that's the case, he's going to have to let me drive him home." Natalie groaned a little. "I couldn't live with some of these Amish rules." She couldn't imagine not having a car, for starters.

"*Nee*, you couldn't." Mary touched her friend's arm. "Lucas is a grown man. He'll do what he thinks is best."

Something about Mary's response made Natalie wonder if her friend was still worried about her friendship with Lucas. She sat on the couch and crossed one leg over the other.

"If this storm doesn't let up, he should stay or let me drive him home. I think bad weather is close enough to an emergency."

Mary looked past Natalie and out the window. "Let's just wait and see what the weather does."

Natalie lifted herself from the couch. She wished she hadn't had that third slice of buttered bread or extra helping of potatoes, but she always overindulged on Friday nights. She followed Mary back to the kitchen to help clean up. Mary would argue that it wasn't necessary, but Natalie would help anyway.

As the wind whistled and howled outside, more lightning and thunder filled the sky, and rain pelted against the farmhouse's tin roof like pebbles.

"I think that's hail." Mary handed Natalie a dish to dry. "I think you're right. We are going to have to convince Lucas not to take the horse out in this. But I don't want you leaving in your car either until we think it's safe."

"No arguments from me." Natalie disliked driving in the rain, even more so in sleet and snow.

"It sounds like a few card games will be in order." Mary handed Natalie another dish.

Natalie nodded. She prayed the storm would end and she and Lucas would both get home safely, but playing cards and spending more time with her friends wouldn't be so bad either.

"*Ach*, remember, no supper here next Friday. We're having both families over on Saturday, and I'll have a lot of food to prepare. You're coming Saturday, *ya*?"

"Yep. My mouth waters when I think about all the good food that will be here." The wonderful meals were always a bonus at an Amish gathering.

A few minutes later, Natalie and Mary rushed to the front door each carrying a large bath towel. Lucas and Levi walked into the living room soaking wet and shivering. Neither had put on a coat before they rushed out the door to tend to Lucas's horse.

Mary wrapped the towel around her husband, and Natalie did the same for Lucas, gently rubbing the towel across his face, neck, and arms. She wouldn't have thought a thing about it if Lucas hadn't abruptly moved away from her, taking the towel with him to stand in front of the fireplace.

She'd never really touched him before, but helping him dry off was instinctive. Did he think it meant something else? They'd never held hands. They were friends. They hadn't hugged because Natalie learned a long time ago that the Amish were not fond of public affection. She supposed a hug in the privacy of Levi and Mary's home would have been fine, but it had just never happened. And she and Lucas were never alone. They chatted in restaurants, libraries, or anywhere other people were. They talked on the phone a lot.

Natalie took a deep breath and reminded herself she had a tendency to overthink things, but she hadn't done so about her friendship with Lucas. She wasn't going to start now. Maybe he was just cold and anxious to get in front of the fireplace.

She shivered as flashes of lightning came closer together, followed by thunderous booms that sounded like explosives going off. She wondered when traveling would be safe.

CHAPTER 2

Helen stared out the window into the darkness. It was almost midnight, and Lucas hadn't returned home from Levi and Mary's house. She turned around when a board creaked behind her, the one outside her and Isaac's bedroom.

"Lucas still not home?" Her husband spoke through a yawn as he cozied up beside her.

Helen shook her head as she hugged herself.

"He's a smart man." Isaac yawned again before wrapping his arms around her. "Maybe he waited out the storm at his *bruder*'s *haus* and is on his way, or he might have chosen to spend the night there."

"You know he won't spend the night away from home." Shivering, she turned to face him and leaned into his warmth.

"Come back to bed, Helen. He'll be here in the morning."

Her husband kissed her gently on the lips, then turned her around and pointed out the window. "Look, car lights."

"Please, dear Lord, let that be Lucas in the passenger seat and not someone delivering bad news." She placed her hands over her pounding heart and peered out the window until the blinding headlights caused her to look away. When she looked back, she saw Lucas walking across the front yard.

"See, he looks fine. Just waited out the storm and hired a driver." Isaac leaned around and kissed her on the cheek.

"We only hire drivers when there is no other option. I hope he wasn't in an accident." Helen leaned closer to the window when her son turned around to go back to the car. "Why is he going back?"

"Maybe he forgot to pay the driver."

Lucas had only taken a couple steps when the driver's door flew open and a young woman stepped out carrying Lucas's hat. She handed it to him and they both laughed before she walked back to the car. "Why does that *Englisch maedel* look familiar?"

Isaac leaned closer. "It's hard to see her." He shrugged. "Probably just a woman he hired."

Helen squinted. "Maybe."

A few minutes later, Lucas walked into the living room, quietly closing the door behind him as he slipped out of his coat and shoes. When he turned around, he startled. "*Ach!* What are you doing up?"

"Your *mamm* was worried. You're usually home much earlier. I told her you probably waited out the storm at your *bruder*'s *haus*."

"It stopped raining over an hour ago. Why did you hire

a driver?" Helen stepped closer to Lucas, picked up the lantern from the coffee table, and held it up. She just needed to see that he was all right.

Lucas took off his hat and placed it on the rack by the door. "Levi and Mary's road had iced over. Even in a car, it was slippery until we got to the main road. Then it was okay. I'll get Red and the buggy tomorrow after the sun is out."

"You could have just stayed at your *bruder*'s *haus*, though I know that wouldn't have been your preference." Helen walked back to the window just as the car pulled out of their driveway. "Who did you hire?" She turned to face him when he didn't answer right away.

"I, uh, didn't hire anyone. That was Natalie, Mary and Levi's friend. You've met her once or twice when she was with Mary." Her son started toward the stairs.

"It was hard to see, but I told your *daed* I thought she looked familiar."

Lucas slowed his stride but didn't turn around. "*Ya*, she is going to stay at Levi's instead of driving all the way back to Montgomery." He finally looked over his shoulder. "It was nice of her to bring me home, and I was glad we didn't hit any more ice, so she should be okay getting back to their *haus*." He gave a quick wave. "Night, *Mamm*." And he disappeared upstairs.

"Can we go back to bed now?" Isaac sighed before yawning again.

"You go ahead. I'll be there shortly."

Isaac ambled back to their bedroom, and Helen carried the lantern to the kitchen. She eased a chair back from the kitchen table, set the lamp down, and slipped into the chair.

A moth that must have followed Lucas inside buzzed around the dim light, bumping it every now and then.

Her heart raced as she thought about all the Friday nights Lucas had been going to have supper with Levi and Mary. She wondered if Natalie had been there all those evenings too. If so, why hadn't Lucas mentioned her?

⁓

Lucas climbed into bed, glad he'd transformed the attic into his own private space not long ago. Otherwise, he'd be forced to share a bedroom with one of his brothers. He lowered the flame on the lantern, fluffed his pillow, and pulled the two heavy quilts up to his neck. He regretted not grabbing a hot water bottle before coming upstairs. His mother always heated water and left it on the woodstove, along with a plentiful supply of hot water bottles for frigid nights. Lucas was too cold and tired to go back downstairs, and he didn't want to miss Natalie's call. He was dozing off when the phone buzzed.

"I didn't have any problems getting back to Mary and Levi's," she said right after he answered.

Lucas breathed a huge sigh of relief. He'd tried to talk her out of driving him home, but Red would have had a hard time on the ice. Mary tried to convince him to stay in their extra bedroom, but visions of himself roaming around their house caused him to politely decline the offer.

"Thank *Gott* you made it back okay. I wish you hadn't needed to drive me, but I'm glad you're staying with Levi and Mary instead of going all the way back to your apartment."

It had been a quiet ride to his house. Natalie drove slowly, and Lucas tried to watch for ice. But there was more to their silence, and they both knew it. Sometimes awkward conversations were easier to have over the phone.

"Yep. No problems getting here, and I'm in the extra bedroom with the propane heater running. Comfy cozy. I could have gone the extra twenty minutes home, but there's a stretch between Shoals and Montgomery that gets really slick during the winter."

"*Gut*." Lucas knew he owed Natalie an explanation for the way he jerked away from her earlier, but if he told her the truth, would it make things uncomfortable between them or jeopardize their friendship?

"Lucas . . ."

"*Ya?*" He swallowed hard, assuming Natalie would get right to it.

"Are we okay? I mean, you and me? I value our friendship. You know that, right? I mean, I feel like I shouldn't even have to ask, but it just felt weird tonight when—"

"When I pulled away from you?" He took a deep breath. His next words could affect the future of their relationship, and he wasn't ready for Natalie to be out of his life. It was bound to happen sooner or later. She'd meet a man who could share her lifestyle. Lucas had already spent time in the outside world during his *rumschpringe*, and he knew it wasn't where he wanted to be. The only reason he hadn't already been baptized was because he wanted to share the experience with the woman he would marry. Eventually he would find an Amish woman to settle down with.

"Yeah, when you rushed to the fireplace after I tried to

help you dry off," Natalie finally said. "There have been so many times I've wanted to give you a hug. You know me, I hug everyone. But I grew up here, and I know the Amish frown on public affection. But it was just Levi and Mary, and I thought I was helping, and . . ."

Lucas sighed. Apparently, he was going to have to tell her the truth, but hopefully in a way that didn't scare her off. "It felt *gut* when you wrapped the towel around me." He cringed, wishing he'd said something else.

She was quiet.

"Are you still there?" A flicker of apprehension coursed through him as he wondered if she'd hung up.

"Yeah, I'm here." She laughed softly. "Well, maybe we need to hug sometimes so you don't get so freaked out by it. There's nothing wrong with hugging a friend and helping him dry off after getting soaked."

If she had any idea how much he'd wanted to kiss her at that moment, she might not think so. But telling her that would surely scare her out of his life. "We just don't hug much." He recalled hugging Mary in front of Natalie every Friday night and flinched.

"Lucas." She paused, and he pictured her tapping a finger to her chin, the way she did when she was thinking. "I look forward to these phone calls every night. I enjoy our lunches and trips to the library. Let's not let things get weird, okay? I've learned so much from you, and my relationship with God continues to grow. Can't we just trust Him to guide us?"

Warmth filled Lucas's heart. It sounded exactly like something he would say to her. "*Ya*, we can."

He knew himself well enough to know that physical

contact of any kind needed to be avoided. He hadn't expected to have such a strong reaction to her touch, and the strange surge of affection he'd felt had rattled him. Now he was having trouble not thinking about her lips. Kissing her would mess up their friendship—or end it. As a couple, they had nowhere to go. He'd stay friends with her until she started dating someone, and then he'd be weaned out of the picture. He'd have no choice but to wish her blessings for a happy life. He'd done what God set him on the path to do— show Natalie the way to Him.

They settled into a relaxed conversation about the ways God works in everyone's lives, and for the first time since he'd known Natalie, she was doing most of the talking about the many ways God was showing Himself to her.

"I hear Him everywhere, Lucas—in my thoughts, in things I read, and sometimes I could swear He was in the room with me."

Lucas smiled again.

"That's the Holy Spirit, isn't it?" She talked with a peacefulness and a calm that came over her in the evenings.

"*Ya*, I believe it is."

They talked a little bit longer about her growing relationship with the Lord, but soon he heard her yawning.

"Maybe we can meet for lunch in two or three days." She sighed. "I have to have lunch with my mother tomorrow. I'll eat while she whines and rants about Dad and his girlfriend."

"So, the move to Mississippi didn't make things any better?" Lucas yawned, too, knowing four thirty would come early. It was well after midnight. Usually their calls wrapped up around nine or ten, but they'd gotten a late start tonight.

"Nope. The distance has not made the heart grow fonder, nor has it stopped my mother's exasperation with him. I keep telling her if she would get a job she could refocus her anger into something productive. But she says she isn't qualified to do anything but be a housewife."

Lucas thought about his own mother. If she had to get an outside job, she wasn't qualified to do anything else either. "Maybe she just needs something to occupy her time, like a hobby or something."

Natalie grunted. "She needs to occupy her time with a *job* so she can support herself."

Lucas wasn't sure how to counsel Natalie about her mother, and it wasn't his place. The thought sounded ironic since his people weren't keen on ministry, and he'd spent a lot of time ministering to Natalie about God. He decided to take a shot anyway. "Don't take this the wrong way, but maybe if you stop giving her money, she'll have to get a job."

"I know. And I'm going to run out of funds for school if I keep giving it to her. She's just always so pitiful, and despite everything, she's my mom, and I love her. I just want her to snap out of this."

"I don't know anything about divorce, but I would think it takes a long time to recover from the heartache." Lucas looked at the clock on his nightstand and yawned again.

"I hear you yawning. I've kept you up too long. I know you get up *way* earlier than I do, even on Saturdays."

"Let me know how it goes with your *mamm* tomorrow."

"I will. Maybe slip in a prayer or two about that. I try to show her compassion. It's hard sometimes."

Lucas agreed to pray for Natalie and her mother's lunch

the following day. After they said good night, he kept his word and prayed for Cecelia—that she would find peace and happiness in whatever way God saw fit.

When he closed his eyes to sleep, he saw Natalie's face. But that wasn't anything new. Like Natalie, he was going to trust the Lord where their relationship was concerned.

⁂

Cecelia strummed her fingers on the table as she waited for Natalie. After a heavy sigh, she picked up her cell phone to check the time. Her daughter was almost twenty minutes late.

Her eyes darted to the door of the small restaurant when it opened, but an older couple walked in and went straight to the counter. Cecelia would have chosen somewhere else for lunch, but Natalie loved Stop N Sea. And since her daughter always paid, it was hard to argue about where to eat. The quaint restaurant served good fish sandwiches, but Cecelia wondered if Natalie chose the eatery because it was run by Amish women. Natalie had developed a fondness for the Plain folks, maybe too much so, in Cecelia's opinion.

Mary and Levi were her closest friends, and she spent every Friday night at their house. Other than that, Natalie stayed in her apartment if she wasn't in class. When Cecelia called, she always said she was reading. Cecelia could remember a time when Natalie never would have been at home on a Friday night. But the girlfriends she used to have had slowly slipped away. Cecelia wasn't sure if that was Natalie's doing or theirs.

An Amish woman pulled her from her thoughts as she

placed a large Styrofoam cup in front of her. "I thought you might like some tea while you wait."

Cecelia shook her head as she looked up at the young woman. "No, I didn't order this." She picked up the cup to give it back. "I don't want to pay for something I didn't order."

The Amish girl waved a hand. "It's no charge, ma'am. But can I get you something else?"

"Diet Coke, please." Cecelia was finally warm enough to unwrap the scarf from around her neck and take off her coat. She set them on the chair next to her, where she'd put her purse. Then she dug through her bag until she found her wallet, deciding that if Natalie didn't show in a few minutes, she was leaving. She'd tried to call her daughter repeatedly, but the calls went straight to voice mail.

Cecelia held up a five-dollar bill when the Amish girl returned with her drink. The girl waved her off again. "It's complimentary. You've been waiting for a long time." She smiled before she left.

Four teenage Amish girls were scrambling around in the small area behind the counter, and an older woman squeezed in and out, often heading to a room in the back. Maybe Cecelia would use the five dollars for a fish sandwich if her daughter didn't show up. Cecelia couldn't imagine what was keeping her.

Natalie burst into the small restaurant and hurried to where Cecelia was sitting. "I'm so sorry, Mom." Her teeth chattered as she pulled off her black gloves, then rubbed her hands together. "I had a flat tire."

Cecelia raised an eyebrow. "Did *you* change it?"

Natalie pushed back the hood of her coat. "No. I was going to try even though I've never done it before, but it started snowing right as I pulled off the road, and I changed my mind. I pulled out my phone to call someone for help, but it was dead. Thankfully, an Amish buggy pulled up behind me, and the man offered to change the tire for me." She chuckled. "I was kinda surprised he knew how."

"Did you have to pay him?" Cecelia took a sip of her Diet Coke. "I mean, you probably should have, but . . ."

Natalie unzipped her coat. "No. I tried to give him twenty dollars. That's all the cash I had on me, but he wouldn't take it. I just got my heater fixed this morning, and I felt guilty sitting in my warm car while he worked out in the snow." She reached for the large cup of tea still sitting on the table and took a few sips. "I'm not surprised though. All of the Amish people I've met are like that, generous and kind."

"There are good and bad in every religion and walk of life, but luckily one of the good guys helped you." Cecelia had been around the Amish folks most of her life with so many Old Order districts in the area. But she'd never gotten close to any of them. She had nothing in common with those people, and they didn't go out of their way to befriend outsiders anyway.

"I'm not surprised your father never taught you how to change a tire. I don't know how either." Cecelia heard the bitterness creeping into her voice and remembered she'd promised Natalie to try to keep her feelings about Tom to herself.

Natalie scanned the large sign across the room that listed the lunch offerings. "Do you know what you want?"

Once they'd both settled on a fish sandwich, Natalie went to the counter to order. When she returned, Cecelia got right to the point. "Natalie, I'm almost completely out of money."

Her daughter hung her head for a few seconds and didn't say anything. If Natalie had any idea how hard this was for her to admit, she wouldn't give her any grief about it.

Natalie lifted her head and sighed.

Cecelia avoided her eyes. "Please don't tell me to get a job. I've tried." She finally looked up at her daughter. "I went to that recruiting agency you told me about. They don't have anything right now, but they have my résumé on file." She rolled her eyes. "If you want to call it a résumé. Helping your troop sell the most Girl Scout cookies isn't really job worthy, nor is maintaining a household, cooking, or any of the other things I spent my life doing for your father."

Cecelia cleared her throat when Natalie narrowed her eyebrows. Her daughter had been known to get up and walk away if a conversation about her father turned sour. Cecelia knew Natalie was mad at Tom, too, or at least hurt and disappointed, but she didn't like to hear Cecelia say anything negative about him. "Anyway, I'll keep looking."

"How much do you need?" Natalie took off her blue scarf and shed her coat on the back of her chair.

Cecelia lowered her eyes, humiliated again that she was in this position. "Whatever you've got to spare, I suppose." She couldn't tell Natalie that she owed almost twenty thousand dollars on her credit cards. After Tom left, her only comfort had been buying expensive things she didn't really need, like a six-hundred-dollar pressure cooker when she had no one to cook for. And the pair of diamond earrings that Tom never would buy her, probably because they cost almost two thousand dollars. The list went on and on, and now the piper had come calling in the way of high credit card installments, and she was behind on her mortgage. She also had utility bills, a car payment, insurance, phone bills, and everything else that totaled a good sum of money. And her measly divorce settlement was long gone.

The worst part about getting money from Natalie—aside from the humiliation—was that she was cutting into her daughter's college fund. She wondered how much Natalie had left. She'd paid her college tuition, bought books for the semester, and already given Cecelia way more money than she deserved. Natalie had also purchased a newer used SUV, an upgrade to the one she'd been driving. This newer vehicle had four-wheel drive, which was almost a must-have in southern Indiana.

Cecelia regretted that they hadn't bought Natalie a better car for the winter weather when she'd turned sixteen. Natalie told Cecelia she'd paid cash for the SUV. Cecelia would have advised her to finance the vehicle and hold on to her cash for school. It was an amusing thought since Cecelia hadn't handled her own financial situation well at all. But Natalie had never managed a large sum of money like what she'd received from the sale of Adeline's piano.

Natalie got out her checkbook, wrote an amount, and handed her a check for a thousand dollars. "Is this enough?"

It wasn't even close, but Cecelia nodded, fighting the tears building in the corners of her eyes, and forced a smile. "How was your Friday night visit with Mary and Levi? The weather was horrible. I heard on the radio that it was pretty icy between Shoals and Montgomery."

"It was good. I figured the roads would be bad, so I took Lucas home after dinner, and I stayed at Levi and Mary's."

"Who's Lucas?" This was a name Cecelia hadn't heard before.

"He's Levi's brother." Natalie left her chair when one of the girls called her name from behind the counter, and after she brought back their baskets of food, she said, "The road from Shoals to Orleans was icy, though not too bad in the car, but it would have been hard on Lucas's horse to make the trip."

Cecelia thought she heard a mild alarm go off somewhere in the back of her mind. "Is Lucas at your dinners—or suppers, as the Amish call it—every Friday night?" The weekly get-togethers had been going on for months.

"Yes, but before you get all wound up, Lucas and I are just friends." She rolled her eyes as she unwrapped her sandwich. "There seems to be concern that we're at risk of becoming more than friends. Can't a guy and girl just be friends without making a thing out of it?"

"I didn't say a word. But who's showing concern?"

Natalie finished chewing a bite of her fish sandwich and swallowed. "Mary brought it up, citing the obvious—that he's Amish and I'm not. She thinks one of us is going to get hurt."

Cecelia's chest tightened. If Natalie's closest friend had concerns, then maybe there was reason to worry. "Why would someone get hurt if it's not a romantic relationship?"

Natalie actually smiled. "Thank you. Exactly. That's

what I had to explain to Mary, that Lucas and I are just friends."

Cecelia nibbled on her sandwich. There was something about the way her daughter said "Lucas." Did Natalie hear how dreamy her voice sounded at the mention of his name?

There was no way Cecelia would be okay if Natalie fell in love with an Amish man, nor did she want her daughter distracted by a silly crush that had nowhere to go. Even if Natalie ran out of money before Cecelia got her act together, she'd find a way to get her daughter through college somehow. Neither Cecelia nor Tom had a college degree. She wanted Natalie to have a career income so she could take care of herself and not end up like Cecelia—unqualified to do much of anything and borrowing money from her child.

Knowing her money situation threatened to destroy Natalie's education more than anything else, Cecelia's heart ached. Natalie thought she was selfish, she was sure. But if her daughter had any idea how much Cecelia loved her, she'd know that Cecelia was plagued with regret and depression. Each morning, she awoke with a plan to change, to better herself, even if it was for Natalie's sake. But she was failing.

"Maybe Lucas is looking for a way to leave his people?" Cecelia finally said. "A relationship with an outsider would make that easier, unless he's been baptized already. Then he'd be shunned. Just be careful he doesn't become attached to you for the wrong reasons."

Natalie shook her head. "No, he hasn't been baptized, but he would never leave his district. His family is really conservative. His mother doesn't even have a propane oven.

She still uses a wood oven to cook in. No cell phones allowed. For that matter, no phones at all, not even in a shanty." She paused to take a sip of tea. "And no refrigerators. They use blocks of ice to keep things cold. They get the ice from a non-Amish neighbor."

Cecelia dabbed her mouth with her napkin and nodded. "They are Swartzentruber Amish."

Natalie tipped her head to one side, her eyebrows narrowing. "No, they're Old Order."

"Well, yes, they are Old Order, but Swartzentruber Amish normally don't even mingle with other Old Order districts who are more liberal. A former Amish woman explained that to me years ago. I'm surprised Levi's family was okay with him getting married to your friend Mary."

"It was going to happen with or without Levi's family blessing the union, so I'm glad they didn't balk too much. I think they fell in love with Mary, too, but I hear what you're saying. Mary's family isn't very conservative. They use solar panels, allow cell phones, and use propane for their ovens and refrigerators."

Cecelia shook her head. "I know, and I think that's hypocritical. They brag to the world how they are detached and living the simple life, but they've brought modern technology into their homes."

"They're just changing with the times, Mom." Natalie glared at her a little. "And it's not our place to judge. Only God can do that."

There had been a lot of mentions of God lately. The college she chose could explain Natalie's new interest in religion, but Cecelia suspected some of it had to do with Levi and Mary, or this Lucas fellow. Cecelia and Tom hadn't raised Natalie or her brother in church. They hadn't been brought up in families who went to church either.

As Cecelia grew older, she regretted that she hadn't gone to church or taken her children when they were growing up. Without that foundation, she now found it difficult to have a relationship with God. Maybe if she had been introduced to Him when she was a child, she wouldn't feel so awkward when she prayed. Maybe if she knew more about God, He would show her how to make some sort of sense out of her life. She wondered if Natalie also struggled with that and was searching for answers.

Her daughter could be vulnerable when it came to God, and an Amish person might not be the best to show her the way. Their religion was rigid and filled with rules uncommon to other denominations. Even though Natalie had chosen to attend Oakland City because it was less expensive than other colleges—and closer to home—the theological exposure might be the saving grace that kept her from being lured into the Amish world. Cecelia's son was grown and too far away for her to have much influence on his decisions, but in a recent phone conversation with Sean, he told her he'd been going to church. She was pleased with that news. If he'd said he was attending an Amish worship service, she would have been concerned.

"Anyway," Natalie said, "Levi and Mary's families are making it work. Levi and Mary made a lot of compromises when they got married, each giving up or accepting some things the other wasn't comfortable with."

Cecelia took a deep breath and stifled the urge to grumble

about Tom not making any concessions when it came to their marriage.

"Actually, they're having both families to their house next Saturday so they can all get to know each other better. And it makes sense to have the gathering in Shoals because it's right in the middle of Montgomery and Orleans. I love being around Mary's family. I've only been around Levi and Lucas's a couple of times. Mary invited me to come to the get-together on Saturday." Natalie chuckled. "Mary only has one sister, but Levi and Lucas's family is huge. There are ten kids, if you include Levi, and apparently they're bringing some other family members as well."

An opportunity had opened up, a chance to see who this Lucas fellow was, and to learn more about Natalie's relationship with her Amish friends.

"Maybe I could go with you." Cecelia looked down at her plate and pinched a piece of fish from her sandwich, deciding the bread was too heavy today. When she looked up, she expected Natalie to be frowning and plotting ways to tell her no. Their relationship had been rocky throughout the divorce, and Natalie kept Cecelia at arm's length most of the time, only seeing her for the occasional lunch. There was a time when they had been close, and she wished they could get back to that place. Cecelia braced herself for rejection, but her daughter smiled.

"I think it would be nice for you to come. You don't get out enough. And there will be tons of good food." She paused, and then the frown came. "You're going to be nice, right? In the past you've made fun of the Amish people."

"I don't make fun of them." She didn't agree with their

backward ways, and she didn't condone the rule breaking by some who tried to portray themselves one way but acted another, but she wouldn't do anything to embarrass Natalie. "Of course I'll be nice. They are your friends." Cecelia laid her napkin across her plate. "Speaking of . . . What happened to your friends from school and work that you used to run around with? You practically grew up at Monica's house and she at ours. I haven't heard you mention her in a long time."

Natalie shrugged. "All they want to do is party and shop. I don't care about going to bars and drinking. And I don't feel the need to buy a designer purse I can't afford."

Cecelia swallowed hard as she thought about the expensive items she'd purchased since the divorce, which included a designer purse she couldn't afford.

"I like being around Mary. She likes me for the person inside, and she couldn't care less if I had a dollar store purse or a Michael Kors." She paused, slumping in her chair. "I'm not saying there is anything wrong with my old friends choosing the lifestyle that works for them. It just wasn't working for me. As for Monica, I still see her sometimes, but she has a boyfriend now, so she spends most of her time with him."

They were quiet for a few minutes.

"Mom, there's been so much turmoil in my life the last couple years. I need some peace. I'm more relaxed when I'm with my Amish friends."

Cecelia could use a little peace in her life, too, but she wasn't sure being overly friendly with the Amish was going to help her in that effort. But being closer to Natalie would. "I'll be looking forward to spending time with you and your friends."

"Great. I'll pick you up at eleven thirty next Saturday."

Maybe Lucas was an unattractive young man whom her daughter would never see as anything more than a pal. It would set her mind at ease if that were the case. Even if looks didn't dictate a person's feelings, an initial attraction was usually present in some way.

But Cecelia saw the way Natalie lit up at the mention of Lucas's name. She had a bad feeling about this. Natalie had said herself that her new friend would never leave his family and church district. But love had a funny way of manipulating logic.

CHAPTER 3

Lucas made his way through the crowd of family at Levi and Mary's house, but he couldn't find Natalie.

"Psst."

He turned in the direction of the sound just as Natalie poked her head around the corner and motioned for him to follow her. She looked so pretty. Her blonde hair was curled and hanging just past her shoulders, and she was wearing black slacks and a long-sleeve dark blue shirt. Lucas glanced around, then moved quickly behind her until they were about halfway down the hall. She looked over her shoulder before she opened the door to her left and pulled him into the guest bedroom, closing the door behind them.

Lucas had never been alone in a room with Natalie, and there was a tingling in the pit of his stomach as he tried to keep his eyes from drifting to her lips. He wondered if he would have been so nervous if the towel incident hadn't happened. Now he knew what it was like to have her touch him, even in the most innocent way. He shivered as his thoughts took him to a place he shouldn't go.

"Nice outfit," he said as he looked down at his own black pants and dark blue shirt, willing his pulse to get back to normal.

"I'm trying to blend." She put her hands on her hips. "Don't look so scared. I'm not going to keep you in here long. I feel like I haven't seen you in forever, and I didn't want anyone to interrupt us."

"At least we got to talk on the phone during the week and last night." Lucas stood taller, trying to figure out how she'd picked up on the fact that he was nervous being alone with her. *Because she knows me better than anyone.*

"I know. But it's not the same as seeing you. Like I said on the phone, my class schedule was kinda messed up the whole week." She rolled her bottom lip under in the familiar pout Lucas used to think was so cute. Now all he could think about was kissing her. "No lunches, and I missed the four of us having supper last night." She paused to take a deep breath. "I know we have to hurry. Your folks wouldn't like us being in a bedroom by ourselves."

That's an understatement. "What's wrong?" He kept his eyes fused with hers and hoped they wouldn't stray back to her lips. This was Natalie, his best friend. He needed to harness this new and unexpected warmth that surged through him when he was around her.

"My mom is with me, and I can't leave her unattended for too long. She doesn't know anyone but Levi and Mary, and she's only been around them a couple times." She rolled her eyes. "I never know what might come out of her mouth." She took another deep breath. "I lost my phone somewhere this morning. I've called it, used my phone locator thingy, and nada. I'm sure it's dead, wherever it is. I can't find it anywhere. But can you meet me at the library Tuesday? I wanted to ask you now in case I don't find my phone."

"*Ya*, I'll meet you at the library Tuesday. Same time, around three?" She nodded as Lucas looked past her at the closed door. "But find your phone. I look forward to our talks at night." Hearing her voice helped him sleep.

She groaned as she pressed her gorgeous lips together. "It's got to be somewhere, but if I don't answer tonight—or tomorrow night—or Monday night—that's why." She reached for the doorknob. "You're going to have to meet my mother." Sighing, she said, "I hope she behaves." Then she thrust the door open, stepped into the hallway, and bumped right into Lucas's mother.

"Oh, Helen. I'm sorry." She inched around her and scurried down the hall, leaving him to stand off with his mother.

He was a grown man, but as his mother's expression twisted into a look she used to get before he got a spanking, he didn't feel even half of his twenty-two years.

Lucas waited for her to say something about the inappropriate meeting, but she continued walking to the bathroom at the end of the hallway.

Her silence was usually worse than a scolding.

Lucas sighed and headed back toward the crowd.

Cecelia felt like a butterfly among the moths in her pink slacks and pink-and-white sweater. Black slacks for the men. Black aprons for the women. Black shoes for all. And a dozen black buggies with horses tethered to the fence outside. As she breathed in the aroma of freshly baked bread and a host of other offerings that smelled delicious, she knew the day wouldn't be a complete bust. There was a nice fire in the fireplace, and she'd introduced herself to a few people since Natalie had disappeared not long after they arrived, but she'd yet to meet anyone named Lucas.

"Sorry, Mom." Cecelia jumped when Natalie whispered in her ear.

"Where've you been?"

"I had to find Lucas to let him know I can't find my phone."

Cecelia crinkled her nose. "I thought the Amish weren't supposed to have phones."

"He's in his *rumschpringe*, Mom. That's when—"

"I know what it is. But isn't he a little old to still be in his running-around period? I mean, it starts at sixteen, right? Shouldn't he be baptized by now?"

"I wondered about that, too, but he said it would be nice to share the experience with his future wife. Guess he hasn't found the right person yet."

"Well, his future wife might already be baptized. It sounds to me like maybe he just wants to indulge in forbidden activities as long as he can, before he has to give those things up for good."

When Natalie glared at her, Cecelia wished she'd kept the thought to herself.

"It's his choice when to be baptized. There probably aren't a lot of women to choose from in his small district."

As long as he doesn't choose you. "Well, I've introduced myself to some of these people, although I doubt I'll remember all of their names. I usually attach names to what a person is wearing, to help me remember, but they're all dressed the same."

Cecelia wasn't sure her daughter even heard her. Natalie nodded at a man coming toward them. "Well, here is my good friend Lucas now." The radiance in Natalie's eyes matched the dreamy way she sounded every time she said the boy's name.

Uh-oh. Cecelia blinked a few times. If not for the Amish clothing, suspenders, and cropped hair, he could have been on the cover of a magazine. He was tall with dark hair, broad shoulders, and gorgeous green eyes. When he smiled Cecelia was happy to see his teeth weren't perfectly straight. But it didn't take away from his stunning looks. *This is trouble.*

"Lucas, this is my mother, Cecelia." Natalie nodded at her just before Lucas extended his hand.

"Nice to meet you, Cecelia." His voice was deep and steady.

"Likewise." Cecelia glanced at Natalie, and once again her daughter's face was aglow. Her friend was harder to read. His casual stance suggested confidence, but his inability to keep his eyes from drifting all over the room made him seem nervous. "I'm happy to meet another friend of Natalie's."

Her daughter pointed across the room. "There's Mary's sister, Lydia, with her new baby I haven't seen yet." She motioned for her mother and Lucas to follow, but Cecelia waved them ahead. "You two go." She pointed to the bathroom at the end of the hall. "I'm just waiting my turn."

Natalie and Lucas walked away chatting, and Cecelia wanted to push the worry from her mind. She had enough problems to focus on. But she wasn't convinced her daughter wouldn't get too cozy with a man she couldn't be with.

Finally the bathroom door opened at the end of the hallway. An Amish woman limped toward her, and Cecelia didn't think she'd met this lady yet. Maybe she could slide by without an introduction. The woman had a scowl on her face. But just as Cecelia gave her a courteous nod and moved to her right to walk around her, the woman stopped to face her.

"Are you Natalie's mother?" The woman's eyebrows knitted into a frown, her expression tight with strain.

Cecelia really needed to get down the hallway, but she leaned forward a little and raised an eyebrow. "I'm sorry, have we met?"

"*Nee*, but I asked *mei sohn* Levi who you were earlier."

"Yes, I'm Natalie's mother, Cecelia." She wasn't sure whether to extend a hand to the woman or not, so she waited, hoping to get the introduction over with before someone beat her to the bathroom. If there was a second powder room, Cecelia hadn't found it.

"I'm Helen." The woman leaned slightly to her right, peering around Cecelia, enough that Cecelia looked over her shoulder. Natalie held the baby as Lucas leaned down and smiled at the child. A fog settled around Cecelia like a warning cloud that might not lift.

When she returned her eyes in the direction of the bathroom, Helen caught her gaze. "I think our *kinner*—children—have become *gut* friends."

Cecelia liked to think she was good at reading people. Helen made the statement as if it were poison on her tongue. Cecelia forced a smile, glancing down the hallway again. "I suppose a person can't have too many friends."

"As long as they remain *friends*." Helen raised her chin a little, her lips set in a thin line.

Cecelia stood taller when she sensed a confrontation coming on. She was tempted to defend her daughter, to ask Helen if she thought Natalie wasn't good enough for her son. But as Helen kept her eyes locked with Cecelia's, she decided to go a different route.

"I couldn't agree more." Cecelia folded her arms across her chest, and as Helen's expression softened, Cecelia realized she had an ally, just in case Natalie and Lucas stepped across the friendship line.

"A pleasure to meet you." Helen gave Cecelia a conspiratorial smile before she moved around her, still limping.

Cecelia scampered down the hallway to the bathroom. Finally.

~

Natalie helped Mary replenish empty snack trays. As she spread pickles and olives on one platter, Mary laid out her homemade pretzels from this morning and refilled a bowl with her special cheese sauce. Natalie was sure she could eat the entire plate of pretzels slathered in the yummy cheese, but she'd already had two and was trying to use some restraint.

"Lydia's baby is beautiful." Natalie placed the jar of pickles back in the refrigerator. The crowd was gathered around the food on the dining room table, so this was the first time Natalie had been alone with her friend. "Do you think Lydia and Samuel are doing okay?"

"*Ya*, they seem better. I guess they are making it work. Being forced into a marriage because you're pregnant isn't ideal, but a *boppli* needs two parents. Thankfully neither of them ran away." Mary turned around and leaned up against the counter. "It happens, people leaving our district when things didn't happen the way they planned."

Helen walked into the kitchen but quickly turned around when she saw Natalie.

"I don't think Helen cares for me." Natalie leaned against the opposite counter as Lucas's mother walked away. "It feels weird to call her Helen. But when I called her Mrs. Shetler the first time I met her, she told me to call her Helen."

"Why do you say she doesn't like you? You've been around her a couple times, and she's always been pleasant to you. We even ate supper in their home before Levi and I got married last year."

Natalie hung her head for a few seconds, then bit her bottom lip as she looked up at Mary. "It might be because she caught me and Lucas coming out of your extra bedroom earlier."

Mary winced before taking a deep breath. "Was the door closed?"

Natalie nodded. "Yep." Flinching, she said, "I lost my

phone today, and I wanted to let Lucas know in case I don't find it, so he can meet me at the library on Tuesday."

Mary slammed a hand to her forehead. "Why did you close the door?"

"I don't know." Natalie shrugged. "Privacy, I guess. We weren't in there very long, and what are the chances that Helen would walk by right at that moment?" Natalie squeezed her eyes closed before she looked back at Mary. "I know I boo-booed. Helen probably thinks I'm trying to seduce her son."

"Natalie, this is nothing to play with. My mother-in-law is a kind and loving woman, but she is fiercely protective of her family. If she thinks you and Lucas are getting too close, she might encourage him to end the friendship." She paused. "It would be sad, but possibly for the best."

Natalie tossed her head back before she looked at Mary. "Are we back there again? I thought you understood that Lucas and I are just friends. We don't have any romantic notions at all. And more and more people are getting worked up about nothing when it comes to me and Lucas."

Mary tipped her head to one side. "Who else is worried about your relationship with Lucas?"

Natalie pressed her lips together. "Can we please use the word *friendship* and not *relationship*?" She paused, sighing. "My mother seems a little concerned about it, but my mother worries about most everything."

Natalie walked to the pretzel tray and took one, then dipped a corner into the warm cheese. *So much for restraint.*

Mary waited until one of Lucas's sisters passed through the kitchen. They exchanged pleasantries before Mary spoke in a whisper. "Does it not worry you that several people have concerns about your *friendship*?"

Natalie stared into her friend's eyes. "Mary, you know I love you like my sister. You, Levi . . . and, yes, Lucas, have taught me how wonderful a relationship with God can be. And you've instilled in me that everything that happens is God's will. So why aren't you trusting God now?"

Mary folded her hands in front of her before she shrugged. "You're right." After a few seconds, she went on. "But we are human, and we have fear and worry like everyone else. I don't want to see anyone get hurt."

Natalie smiled gently at her friend. "Fear and worry are sins, designed to throw us off course." She walked to her friend and put a hand on Mary's arm. "I learned that from you. Just trust in the Lord, and all will be well."

Someone cleared their throat, and Natalie turned around to see her mother. "I hope I'm not interrupting anything important between you two, but, Natalie, I need to speak with you for a moment." She looked at Mary. "Could we borrow your extra bedroom to speak privately?"

Natalie grinned.

"Of course," Mary said, smiling back at Natalie. "It's very popular today."

Mary picked up the pickle tray and winked at Natalie before she left the kitchen.

"Mom, if you are going to question me about Lucas, then—"

"This has nothing to do with your friend." She spun around on her heel. "Follow me."

By the time they reached the extra bedroom and her

mother had closed the door, Natalie was ready to unload on the next person who said something about her and Lucas, but maybe her mother was upset about something else. Or had done something.

"Mom, did you upset someone here? I asked you to be nice." Natalie folded her arms across her chest.

"Why do you assume that I did something or upset someone? Did it ever occur to you that someone might have acted inappropriately to *me*?" Her mother raised both eyebrows as she lifted her chin.

Natalie was used to drama from her mother, though it was usually directed at something to do with Natalie's father. "And what exactly happened to you?"

Cecelia walked closer to Natalie as her eyes widened. Then she spoke in a whisper even though no one was around and the door was closed. "There is an Amish man flirting with me."

Natalie pressed her lips together so she wouldn't laugh. "Mom. I'm sure that's not the case. Most of the people here are from Levi and Lucas's side of the family, and I assure you that any man here wouldn't flirt with an outsider. There are a few relatives, a couple of uncles, and maybe a few cousins who came, but they are all super conservative."

"Natalie, it hurts my feelings when you always assume that I am in the wrong or identify things or actions incorrectly. You did that with your father and me throughout the course of our divorce, always siding with him and not seeing him for the cheater he is, and . . ."

Here we go. Natalie let her mother ramble on for a few minutes before she interjected. "Do you see how you go full circle and everything, no matter what it is, ends up back at Dad?"

Her mother clamped her mouth closed and stood silently for a few moments before she spoke. "You're right, Natalie." Her bottom lip trembled a little. "I'm sorry."

Natalie was still getting used to this new side of her mother, a woman who apologized and admitted her mistakes. It was an improvement, and Natalie was trying to better her relationship with her mother.

"It's fine." Natalie turned to go, but her mother reached for her arm, halting her.

"Don't you want to hear what happened?"

Natalie lifted a hand to her forehead and forced her lips to turn upward. "Sure, Mom. What happened?"

"This *man*"—her mother took a deep breath—"has been following me around the house. Every room I'm in, he's there."

"I'm sure it's a coincidence." Natalie still had her hand on the doorknob and hoped this conversation would wrap up soon so she could get back to her friends.

Her mother shook her head defiantly. "No, it wasn't. He finally approached me and struck up a conversation." She pointed a finger at Natalie. "And before you say that he was just being friendly, he wasn't. He was hitting on me." Her mother's indignant tone was almost comical as she raised her chin. "He's *Amish*, for goodness' sake."

"So you said." Natalie decided to play along since her mother was in such a tizzy. "Who was it?"

"He said he was Helen's neighbor, that his wife had died recently, and that Helen invited him to come along." She squeezed her eyes closed and shook her head. "It was so awkward and unsettling." When she opened her eyes, she pointed to herself, first at her boots, then her pants, and finally her blouse. "Couldn't he see that I'm not Amish and that flirting with me would be inappropriate?"

Cecelia Collins rarely lost her composure even when she was being dramatic, but with every word, she became more unraveled. Even her neatly combed and sprayed shoulder-length blonde hair was tousled from shaking her head so much.

Natalie took her hand off the door handle, deciding this was going to take longer than she'd hoped it would. "What exactly did he say?"

Her mother took a couple deep breaths. "He told me I was pretty and . . . and that I smelled nice."

Natalie covered her mouth with her hand to keep from laughing. It didn't sound like something a conservative Amish man would say.

"Go ahead and laugh." She pointed her finger at Natalie again. "And his wife only died a few months ago!" She spoke in a loud, hysterical whisper.

"Mom, he was probably just being nice. And even if he was flirting, maybe he was just practicing since the Amish are encouraged to remarry quickly after the death of a spouse. I'm surprised you don't know that since we've lived here forever." Natalie put her hand back on the doorknob. "You're overreacting."

"Natalie Marie Collins, it's been a long time since a man has flirted with me, but I can still recognize it, whether he's Amish or not."

"Well, I think that in this case you misread the man's intentions." Natalie opened the door, only to have her mother push it closed.

"Oh, really? Did I? Then why did he ask me to dinner—or supper as he called it—for next Saturday night?" She raised her chin even higher as her eyes widened. "Isn't that against their rules or something, dating a non-Amish person?"

Sometime during the past few seconds, Natalie's jaw had dropped, so she slowly closed her mouth.

"Now what do you have to say, smarty-pants?"

Natalie opened her mouth to speak, but she was at a loss for words. Finally she said, "Well, what did you say?"

Her mother huffed. "I'm surprised you even have to ask me that." Then she opened the door and stomped down the hallway, the heels of her white boots clicking against the hardwood floors.

Natalie was too stunned to move.

CHAPTER 4

Helen slipped her dress over her head Sunday morning, glad it wasn't a church day. She needed the Lord more than ever right now, but she'd overslept after not sleeping well. At least the temperature had warmed up some.

"You tossed and turned most of the night, *lieb*." Isaac sat on the bed and slipped on his shoes.

"I'm just worried about Lucas. The *Englisch* girl, Natalie, seems to have a hold on him." Helen tied her black apron and breathed in the smell of bacon cooking. One of the girls had beaten her to the kitchen this morning.

Her husband ran his hand the length of his beard. "Have a hold on him? What do you mean?"

Helen pulled her long hair, mostly gray now, into a bun, then pressed in the pins to hold it. "They're too chummy." She reached for her *kapp* on the nightstand. "She is a pretty girl, and Lucas is a handsome boy." Sighing, she placed her prayer covering on her head and tucked loose strands of hair beneath it. "I watched the way they were with each other." She picked up her shoes and walked to the bed, then sat beside her husband. "Out of all our *kinner*, I thought Lucas would be the last one to ever think of leaving us."

"Leaving us? Lucas isn't leaving us. I worry more about the girls being lured into a world where glamour and fancy things might tempt them." Isaac grumbled underneath his breath. "Lucas might be attracted to this girl, or even have a special friendship with her, but you are losing sleep for no reason."

Helen turned to face her husband. "I love you, Isaac, but you are being dense if you didn't see the spark between the two of them." The possibility of losing her son to the outside world tore at her insides. "And I won't have it, I just won't." She threw her hands up and slapped them to her knees. "I even caught them coming out of a bedroom together at Levi's *haus*, and the door had been closed. Lucas knows that is inappropriate, so I'm sure that girl initiated the meeting."

Isaac rested a hand on Helen's knee. "*Mei lieb*, it would pain me greatly if Lucas left our community, but he is a man, not a boy, and we always agreed that our *kinner* must experience a little bit of the outside world so they understand why we cherish our lives and relationship with the Lord. None of them have strayed far, and half have already chosen baptism even before they selected a spouse."

"Lucas isn't baptized yet, and he's twenty-two. I'm just worried that . . ." Helen swallowed back a lump in her throat. "That he's keeping his options open."

Isaac didn't say anything, and despite his words, Helen could see the concern seeping into his soul through his souring expression. She hadn't meant to upset him. Her husband had enough to worry about—keeping food on the table for their large family, running their household in a strict manner without being too overbearing, and even helping Helen with chores when the *kinner* were busy and her arthritis was acting up.

"Did you meet the girl's mother, Cecelia?" Helen laid a hand over Isaac's on her knee.

His mouth twitched with amusement. "The flashy woman who looked like an azalea in bloom?"

Helen chuckled, which felt good. "*Ya*. That would be her."

"She was hard to miss wearing those bright colors."

Helen thought about her exchange with Cecelia in the hallway. "I don't think she wants her daughter involved with an Amish boy." She sighed. "I mean *man*." She paused, thinking back. "When I briefly spoke with her, we both caught sight of Lucas and Natalie carrying on over Lydia's *boppli*. I could tell Cecelia didn't like how cozy they looked." Helen crossed her arms and rubbed her shoulders. "I shiver to think what I would do if one of our *kinner* shamed our family in such a way, getting pregnant before marriage."

"It happens," Isaac said, too casually for Helen's liking.

"It's the parents' fault when something like that happens." She dropped her hands to her lap and huffed. "They are too liberal down that way, near Montgomery and Oden. No *gut* can come from having mobile phones and fancy technology that keeps them attached to the outside world."

Isaac stood, tucked in his shirt, and pulled his suspenders over his shoulders. "I agree. But it isn't our place to judge." He held out his hand to her. "I smell breakfast. Let's go give praise to the Lord for our many blessings and not let worry creep into our lives over things that haven't happened."

Yet. Helen took her husband's hand, and he pulled her to her feet. She pushed through the pain in her hip, wishing the herbal remedies she used were working better. Her mother and grandmother had battled arthritis from the time they were in their late forties, and Helen hadn't been spared.

She followed Isaac out their bedroom door, longing to free herself of worry about Lucas. He was a smart boy. But in Helen's eyes, he would always be a boy, and she wanted him to make wise decisions.

⁓

Lucas tried not to rush as he walked through the Bedford Public Library Tuesday afternoon, but he was anxious to see Natalie. She obviously hadn't found her phone since he hadn't heard from her.

He rounded the corner of the religious aisle, and his heart sank when he didn't see her. He kept going and found the Christian fiction section, his pulse picking up when he spotted her sitting cross-legged on the floor, her head buried in a book. She didn't look up until he sat beside her.

"This is an amazing story." She closed the book as her eyes captured his. "I've missed you."

"I missed you too." The words came easily, and Lucas wanted to hug her. But he recalled his feelings when she'd wrapped the towel around him, and his eyes drifted to her lips again. He cleared his throat. "What are you reading?"

"*Redeeming Love* by Francine Rivers." She had that

dreamy look in her eyes like she did after she'd finished a good book. "Have you read it?"

Lucas glanced at the cover with a woman in a low-cut, long red dress. "*Nee.*" It didn't look like a book he would choose, and he looked away.

"I've read it several times, and each time it feels like a new story. I always notice something—or learn something—I didn't during my last read of it." She handed it to him. "Read the back cover. It isn't a girly book. The man in the story is front and center, and he's one of my favorite heroes ever."

Lucas started to read the back cover but raised an eyebrow and didn't get past the first paragraph before he handed it back to Natalie. "It's about a scarlet woman." He felt his face warming as he avoided Natalie's eyes, surprised she'd read such a book.

"Read the rest of the description, all the way to the end." She pushed it away and pointed to the words on the back. "See, the author is retelling the story of Gomer and Hosea. It's about God's all-consuming love for us, and it's cool how this woman finds her way to God, despite the odds. It's a story of true redemption, and the hero believes he has been called by God to help her." She closed her eyes for a few seconds before she looked back at him with a sense of enchantment in her expression. "I love this book."

Lucas read the rest of the description. "It might be okay." His mother would have a fit if he brought such a book into the house, but their shared love of reading was one of the first things he and Natalie realized they had in common. So far, neither had recommended a book they didn't both enjoy, but he wasn't sure about this one.

"Just trust me. Read it." Natalie twisted to face him. "I'm not a prostitute and you're not saving me, but in some small ways, the story reminds me of us." She blushed, which was unusual for Natalie. Not much embarrassed her. "Maybe not the ending or even the journey really, but Michael—the guy in the book—his faith in God is almost enough for both of the characters. Sometimes I feel like that about you, that you carry enough faith for both of us, and that little by little it seeps into my soul." She looked down as she twirled a stand of hair between her fingers. "Sometimes I don't feel worthy of God's love either, like the woman in the book."

Lucas reached for her hand, something he'd never done before, and squeezed it. "None of us are worthy of *Gott*'s love, but He gives it to us unconditionally."

She looked up at him and blinked before she laid her head on his shoulder.

Lucas didn't even look around to see if anyone was watching. He just held her hand and decided to enjoy the moment. He was close to Natalie in a way he'd never been with anyone else. His physical attraction to her had been there since day one, but it seemed to intensify the closer they became emotionally. Warning bells were going off in his head, but he chose not to hear them right now.

He looked at the book again and decided he would read it. His mother wouldn't approve based on the cover alone, but Lucas wasn't a child—even though his mother treated him like one—and he could choose what he wanted to read. Still, he had no plans to let his parents, or even his siblings, see the book.

After not nearly long enough, Natalie lifted her head,

reached into her purse, and held up a new phone. "I picked this up on the way here, but I need to charge it. Do you want to go find an outlet and charge both our phones?"

Lucas nodded and they stood.

"I've missed talking to you every day, but I haven't missed my mother's lengthy calls." She sighed. "I probably need to call her, though. She knows I don't have my phone, but I'm sure she's going nuts not being able to get hold of me. And I do worry about her, even if she drives me crazy sometimes." She smiled at him.

Natalie had an odd relationship with her mother. Sometimes, she seemed to act more like the mother and Cecelia was the child. Lucas couldn't picture that type of role reversal in his family.

Natalie picked the most out-of-the-way spot she could find near a power outlet. After she and Lucas plugged in their phones, she gave him her new number, and they settled in on the floor by a window. Natalie pretended to focus on another book she'd picked out while Lucas opened *Redeeming Love* and started to read. She wondered how he would feel about the story. It wasn't as clean and wholesome as the books they normally read, but the message was so strong. She wanted him to feel the emotions that went along with such redemption, the way she had.

Her mind drifted to what happened while they were talking about God's love—the hand holding and the way she'd laid her head on his shoulder. He hadn't stiffened or gotten weird about it. He actually initiated it by reaching for her hand.

Was everyone right? Were she and Lucas in dangerous territory? What would happen if their friendship tried to take the form of a romantic relationship? There was no denying her attraction to him, which had drawn her to him the first time they met. But Lucas was different from anyone she'd ever known. He was comfortable talking about God and his relationship with Him. Natalie found that to be an attractive quality as well.

She forced herself to shake free of the thoughts. *I trust You, God. And You've blessed me with Lucas, my friend. Please help me continue to grow in my faith and to make good choices about my life.* Natalie refused to overthink things right now. She enjoyed her time with Lucas, even when they were just quietly sitting together. A calm seemed to settle over her in his presence, and when she was at peace, she felt more open to hear God's voice.

After about thirty minutes, the peacefulness began to slip away, replaced by concern about her mother. She whispered to Lucas, "I need to call my mom. I'm going to go outside for a few minutes." She put on the coat she had folded in her lap.

Lucas nodded but didn't lift his eyes from the book.

Outside the building, Natalie called her mother twice, and the second time she left a voice mail with her new phone number. She'd needed the few days of space without talking to her mom, but now she was starting to worry.

Natalie tapped her mother's number again, and for the third time it went to voice mail, so she left a second message.

"Mom, I left you a message with my new number, but I meant to ask you if you want to meet for lunch Saturday. Let me know. Bye."

She walked back inside the library, her stomach churning a little. Her mother always answered the phone, as if Natalie was the only person she ever talked to. *Maybe she just forgot to charge it and the battery's dead.*

Natalie hoped that was the case as she settled in beside Lucas again. She picked up her book and tried to concentrate on the story—without much luck.

∼

On Saturday, Cecelia sat drumming her fingers on the table at a small diner in Shoals. She'd been there twice with Tom over the years. Neither time was stellar, but once again, she wasn't the one footing the bill, so she hadn't argued about where to eat.

She pulled her compact mirror from her purse, and before she applied lipstick, she caught a glimpse of the dark roots showing along her part line. *Ugh.* She'd tried to use a box of dye just last night, but it hadn't helped much. Sighing, she touched up her lipstick, a shade of pink Natalie said made her look younger. Since she'd stepped into her forties, she'd take whatever help she could get. She was sure the divorce had aged her another ten years.

"You don't need that, you know."

Cecelia jumped and hurriedly stuffed the lipstick and compact back in her purse.

Moses Schwartz slipped into the booth seat across from

her. "I wasn't sure you would show up." He grinned as he took off his straw hat and set it on the seat beside him.

"You've left a message on my phone every night since last Saturday." Cecelia raised her chin, folding her hands in her lap and willing them to stop shaking. "I decided if I didn't meet you, I'd burn up my minutes listening to all your messages."

One side of his mouth lifted, and it was equally as unnerving as it was last Saturday. Cecelia had turned down lunch with Natalie to meet this flirty and persistent Amish man. She hadn't lied to her daughter. She just said she couldn't make it. Natalie seemed to find it odd that Cecelia would decline the invitation, but Cecelia's curiosity about Moses's intentions had gotten the best of her.

"*Ach*, well . . ." He was still grinning, and Cecelia's hands continued to tremble in her lap. "I'm glad you're here."

"A girl's got to eat." She avoided the twinkle in his hazel eyes and ignored the set of his square jaw and the way he'd swaggered into the restaurant like he owned the place. He probably wasn't even really Amish. Vanity and pride were frowned upon in their world, and this man seemed full of himself. She wished he would wipe that smug grin off his face. But this would be good practice at dating, if and when someone ever asked her out.

"*Ya*, a girl's got to eat," he repeated. "And what will you be having?"

Cecelia had opened her menu when she first arrived, but she hadn't looked at it. "I'm not sure." She couldn't see it, to begin with. But she didn't want to use her reading glasses in front of him, so she picked up the menu and held it out far enough to almost see the offerings, but she couldn't quite make out the words. She pulled it closer again, pretending to scan the entrées, then closed it, deciding to follow his lead.

"What did you choose?" Cecelia met his eyes, surprised to see that he'd slipped on a pair of glasses while she was busy trying to see her menu.

He clicked his tongue a couple times. "Hmm . . . maybe the liver and onions."

Cecelia's stomach rumbled. She'd been too nervous to eat breakfast, and even though she was still anxious, she was hungry. But there was nothing worse than liver and onions. "I'll probably just have a salad."

"What kind of salad?"

Cecelia cleared her throat as she pretended to study the menu. "Um . . . the Caesar salad."

Moses took off his reading glasses and handed them to her. "They don't have Caesar salads here."

Cecelia's heart pounded as she took the glasses but didn't look at him. After she'd read the menu, she handed the gold-rimmed spectacles back to him. *Who cares what he thinks anyway?* And she was hungry for more than a salad. "I'll have the meat loaf."

The waitress showed up as if on cue, and they ordered. Afterward, Moses's smug smile returned. "Why do you keep smiling at me?"

"I'm hoping it will be contagious and you'll loosen up a little."

Cecelia gritted her teeth for a few seconds, hidden by a fake smile. "Loosen up a little?" She raised an eyebrow. "I'm not even sure why you asked me out." She pulled her eyes from his and shrugged. "I mean, I suppose it's not a date, but . . ."

She lifted her eyes to his and lowered her hands back in her lap when they became shaky again.

Moses leaned forward a little. "Cecelia, relax. Maybe just try to have a *gut* time. We are two adults sharing a meal and getting to know each other."

Cecelia straightened. "I *am* relaxed."

"I'd hate to see you when you *aren't* relaxed. I bet you're scary." He chuckled softly.

She took a deep breath and reminded herself she would likely never see this man again after today. So, she took in his over-the-top good looks and stared at him for a long while. She figured she had nothing to lose, so she said, "I haven't been to dinner with a man besides my husband in"—Natalie was nineteen, and Cecelia met Tom three years before she was born—"in twenty-two years."

"I've got you beat. Twenty-nine for me." His snarky smile had vanished and was replaced by a much softer expression.

"I'm sorry to hear about the recent passing of your wife." Cecelia lifted a slightly shaking hand and took a sip of water.

"*Danki*—I mean thank you. That cancer just latched onto her and never let go. And I'm sorry to hear about your divorce. It must have felt like a death after so many years of marriage."

"It did," Cecelia said before she took another drink of water. "I don't know why people don't understand that. Especially my daughter, Natalie, whom I tried to explain that to. She still has her father. But my husband is gone."

"How do you busy yourself these days?"

"I-I . . ." She laughed. "I don't do much, I guess. Unless cleaning house counts."

Moses had wavy dark hair, flattened on top from his hat, and a lengthy dark beard, almost to his chest and barely starting to speckle with gray. He had the traditional cropped bangs the Amish boys and men wore. His ruggedness made him even more attractive. She could almost see him in cowboy boots atop a horse, herding cattle. Maybe she did need to relax and absorb some attention from a nice-looking man, even if he was Amish.

"*Ya*, I work during the day, but my mind wanders in the evenings when I don't have much to do. Do you have a job? I mean a job outside of the house?"

Cecelia shook her head. "No. There doesn't seem to be a market for someone with my skills." She rolled her eyes, something she'd gotten on to Natalie about time after time, yet here she was doing the same thing. "I was a housewife. I kept the household afloat, I guess. I took care of paying the bills, making sure the pantry was stocked, and I cooked and always kept a clean house. I still do, but the workload isn't like it used to be when Tom and Natalie lived there. Tom, that's my ex-husband's name."

Moses nodded but was quiet as the server returned with their meals.

"Running a household is a job. It takes skill and balance." Moses cut into a slice of liver flanked with onions, and just the smell made Cecelia's stomach queasy. "Don't underestimate yourself."

There was something different about this Amish man.

The Plain people only went to school through the eighth grade, but Moses seemed more educated. "Have you always been Amish?"

"*Ya*."

That voided Cecelia's theory that he'd had more education than the rest of them.

"Do you want a job outside of the home?" Moses forked another piece of meat and put it in his mouth, chewing while he waited for her to answer.

"I need to work." If she had a job she wouldn't have to keep asking Natalie for money. She could get caught up on the mortgage before the bank foreclosed on her house. She'd stopped using her credit cards since they were maxed out. In time, perhaps she could start paying down the balances.

"Marianne—that was *mei fraa*—she paid our bills too. She did everything related to our finances, and I'm struggling to keep up with it on top of my work."

"And what do you do?" Cecelia cut into her meat loaf, keeping one eye on him.

Moses swallowed the bite in his mouth. "I break and train horses."

Of course you do. Cecelia covered her mouth so she didn't lose her meat loaf as she started to laugh. Once she'd downed the bite, she still couldn't help her grin.

Moses smiled. "What's so funny?"

"I'm sorry. Nothing." She waved a hand. "I just . . ." She tugged on her ear, realizing she'd forgotten earrings. "So, you're like a cowboy?"

"I guess you could say that."

"My daughter loves animals. She's going to school to be

a veterinarian." Cecelia was proud of Natalie, for her compassion for animals and her determination to go to school and fulfill her dreams.

"What about you?" Moses was nearly finished with his food, and Cecelia had finally relaxed enough to enjoy her meat loaf. "Do you like animals?"

Cecelia crinkled her nose. "I don't dislike them. But to be honest, I'm a little afraid of animals. I was bitten by a neighbor's dog when I was a young girl. When I was a little older, maybe eleven or twelve, I came across a feral cat at my grandmother's house, and it tore me up." She raised her bangs to reveal a small scar on her forehead. "I was left with this, and since then I've stayed away from animals. I always felt bad because Natalie grew up wanting a pet, and my fear prevented her from having one."

"It sounds like she will make up for it by being a vet." Moses smiled, and Cecelia's insides swirled. She couldn't remember the last time a handsome man had paid her any attention, and it felt good, even if she never saw Moses again. A man was attracted to her.

"I have a confession to make." Moses grinned.

Cecelia lowered her gaze and blinked a few times before she looked back at him. Was he going to tell her she was pretty? Maybe even confess to stalking her last weekend, wanting to be near her? At this moment, Cecelia didn't care if this guy was Amish or not.

"I followed you around at Levi and Mary's *haus* last Saturday." He smiled as Cecelia batted her eyes.

"I know." She faced off with him.

"And I asked around about you, to see what your situation was. Levi told me you were divorced, but he wasn't sure if you were working or not. He said you'd been looking for a job. But since you aren't employed, how would you like to work for me?"

The wind went out of Cecelia's sails as her heart sank like the *Titanic*. This wasn't a date. He didn't ask her out because he thought she was attractive. *Of course, he didn't. He's Amish.*

Cecelia's cheeks were on fire, and she was tempted to run out of the restaurant. She silently lambasted herself for saying it was her first time out with a man since her husband. Her ego had just taken a punch in the gut. Still, she did need a job.

"What would this job entail?" She scooped up a bite of mashed potatoes even though she'd lost her appetite.

"It sounds like something you'd be *gut* at." Moses laid his fork across his plate. "I need someone to pay the bills, keep track of deposits and checks on my ledger, run the occasional errand, and I'd pay extra if the person stocked my kitchen with something other than the cans of food I buy." He grinned. "I'm sure there are some easy-to-prepare meals that don't come out of a can, but I'm not finding them. My neighbors drop off more food than I deserve, but I'd like to be able to make myself a simple meal."

Cecelia shook her head. "You shouldn't be eating anything out of a can. I've developed a few bad habits myself since my husband left . . ." *An occasional drink here and there.* She'd never consumed alcohol before Tom left her. It was a crutch she wanted to give up entirely, but one she still leaned on from time to time. "But I do eat healthy most of the time." She eyed her meat loaf, buttery mashed potatoes, and carrots glazed with enough sugar to make them taste like dessert. "Most of the time." Looking up at him, she smiled when he did.

"I don't think that's eating badly." He eyed Cecelia's plate.

"It's a lot of carbs for me. But I tend to bend my own rules when I'm out to eat."

"So, any interest in helping this old guy get his finances in order?" He winked at her, but she didn't take it the way she had when he winked at her last weekend. Moses was just friendly and charming. Cecelia had misjudged him by assuming he was flirting with her. "It wouldn't be full-time." He held up a palm. "And I probably can't pay you what you're worth, but it might serve two purposes. It would occupy your time and ease my mind." He raised a shoulder and lowered it slowly. "You could set your own hours."

"Where would I do this work?" The thought of making any kind of money was causing adrenaline to shoot through her veins. She imagined telling Natalie she had a job. Would her daughter be proud of her, instead of always looking at her like the pitiful, broken woman she was?

Moses wiped his mouth with his napkin. "Marianne used to spread everything out on the kitchen table and do it while she was baking, but there's a small room in the back of the house that she used as a sewing room. You could have that room."

"I don't sew," she said quickly, hoping that wasn't part of the job. She recalled the treadle sewing machine her grandmother used when she was a child. Cecelia didn't function well on an electric sewing machine, so she doubted she'd do any better on one with a pedal. She thought about the no electricity issue—no air-conditioning—and how she'd seen Amish women sweltering in the summer heat. But it was only March. Warmer temperatures wouldn't be upon them for at least a couple months, although the weather could be unpredictable.

"No sewing necessary." Moses stroked his beard. "I don't need a *fraa*, just a bookkeeper."

Cecelia tore at the napkin in her lap, fidgeting like a schoolgirl, and feeling silly that she'd ever thought this man found her attractive. She came for an ego boost, but she might leave with a job, so all wasn't lost.

"What about your . . . your people? Would they approve of me being in your home working since I'm not, um, one of your kind?"

Grinning, he said, "We're not teenagers with raging hormones. I think it will be okay.

"I only have one concern," he said before she had time to reply.

Cecelia straightened as she realized she didn't have the job yet. "What?"

"Sometimes I need help with the horses."

Cecelia's eyes widened. "But they're so big."

"This isn't a deal breaker if you aren't comfortable with the horses, but maybe you could spend a little time with them and see if you can conquer your fear."

She stared at him for a moment. He barely sounded Amish when he talked. Most of the Plain folks had a unique accent and used the Pennsylvania *Deutsch* dialect more frequently.

She snapped back to attention and thought of being near

an animal as large as a horse. *Conquer your fears*. Cecelia was afraid of everything these days—of failing at any job she took on, of sabotaging any future relationship that might come her way, not to mention the way her finances kept her in a constant state of turmoil. Maybe tackling her fear of animals would be a good start. "I would like the job if you're offering it to me." She pinched her lips together. "But maybe baby steps with the horses?"

Smiling, he lifted his glass as if to toast her, so Cecelia did the same.

"Welcome to my world," he said, a soft smile spreading across his face.

Fear and apprehension swirled in Cecelia's mind, but another emotion fought for space, one she was happy to cling to. Hope.

CHAPTER 5

Lucas had overslept. Again. He was the last one at the breakfast table Wednesday morning, so he grabbed what was left of the eggs, snatched two pieces of bacon, and piled his plate with the three remaining pancakes. One by one, his siblings left the table to start their days. Even the youngest, Abram, left the room and returned with his book bag before Lucas finished eating.

As he stuffed the last bite of bacon in his mouth, his mother began to clear the table. Lucas thought about his conversation with Natalie the night before. Their phone calls were lasting longer and longer. He was halfway through the book she'd recommended, so they talked about it in depth, though she was careful not to give away the ending. Lucas was enjoying the story, but the male character was hindered by so many obstacles and even resistance from the woman he loved. He struggled with how he could trust that he was following God's will and not his own desires, both physical and emotional.

Lucas couldn't help following Natalie's train of thought in comparing their situation with that of the characters in the book. Had God really called Lucas to teach Natalie about Him, or was it his own interpretation based on his feelings for her? They lived in a different era from the characters, and their circumstances were different, but love was universal and timeless. He hadn't gotten into all of that with Natalie yet. He wanted to think and pray on it some more.

He pushed back his chair, stood, and reached for his hat and coat on the rack by the kitchen door. "Have a *gut* day, *Mamm*."

"Lucas, wait." His mother set the plate she was holding into soapy dishwater before drying her hands on her apron. "I want to ask you something."

"What is it, *Mamm*?" He was anxious to apply a final coat of stain to the dining room table he was working on before he went to meet Natalie at the library. She'd said last night she would have to meet him earlier than their normal three to three thirty time.

"Where do you go in the afternoons on so many days?" Her eyes expressed more challenge than curiosity, and even though he didn't think it was any of her business, he'd never been disrespectful to his mother. Since he still lived at home, maybe she had a right to ask.

"I go to the library in Bedford." Lucas turned to leave and was almost out the door when his mother spoke again.

"That's a fairly long ride in the buggy. Do you meet the

Englisch girl there—Natalie?" Her voice was clipped as she spoke his friend's name.

"*Ya*, I meet her there." Lucas looped his thumbs beneath his suspenders and shifted his weight. "We are friends, and we both like to read."

His mother took a step toward him. "*Sohn*, there are reasons why we are detached from outsiders." She paused, her eyes darkening like angry thunderclouds. "And Natalie is very pretty." Shaking her head, she said, "There is no *gut* to come from this."

"*Ya*, she is very pretty." He walked closer to where his mother was standing and kissed her on the cheek. "But we are only friends. We like to read and talk about books."

"That's fine, but we can't always control our feelings, and getting involved romantically with that girl will only cause problems."

"Me and Natalie are trusting *Gott* to guide our path, *Mamm*. We're just friends." Lucas did trust God to guide his path, but again he questioned his interpretation of what God wanted from him.

"And the Lord *will* guide you on your journey. But too often we step onto the wrong path without realizing it's not *Gott*'s plan for us. Or we recognize that we've sidestepped but don't have the courage or strength to back up and walk alongside *Gott*."

Lucas had thought about everything his mother said and more, but until the Lord showed him otherwise, Lucas chose to believe Natalie was in his life for a reason—so he could teach her about God. Everything wasn't crystal clear, and maybe it never would be. But one question lingered in his mind more than any other. Even if his interpretation of God's calling was correct, was his time with Natalie temporary? Would they stay friends after Lucas felt like he'd done God's work? These jumbled thoughts were exhausting and causing more and more doubts to fill his head.

"I've helped Natalie grow in her faith," he said. "She has a relationship with *Gott* that she didn't have before. I don't see how that can be wrong."

His mother raised her chin and met his eyes. "We don't make a habit of ministering to others, especially the *Englisch*." She pointed a finger at him. "Someone is going to end up with a broken heart if you get too close to that *maedel*."

"You are worrying for nothing." Lucas turned and walked out the door. As he strode to the barn to apply the stain on the table, he wondered if everyone around him saw something he and Natalie didn't. He loved her, and he was pretty sure she loved him, but it wasn't the kind of romantic love everyone seemed to be worried about. It couldn't be. God wouldn't allow that. Their goals for life were set. Natalie would become a veterinarian, and eventually Lucas would settle down with an Amish woman he hadn't met yet.

He began to apply the stain to the dining room table in the barn, but an uneasiness settled around him. And angered him. His time with Natalie was precious, and he felt calm and at peace with her, as she'd said she felt with him. Why did others have to stir up trouble and make it more complicated than it needed to be?

By the time he finished the project and made it to the library, his thoughts were beyond scrambled and full of doubts that caused him to wonder if his friendship with

Natalie wasn't a good idea. Despite his convictions, maybe he should try to look at their friendship from an outside perspective. *Would things look different?*

A few minutes later, he found her in the same spot as before, sitting on the gray carpet by a window. She smiled when she saw him, but despite the warm glow that filled Lucas, his worries and confusion assaulted him from every direction, dimming the feeling.

Natalie had pondered Mary and her mother's warnings about she and Lucas becoming too close. But today, she refused to focus on anything except the happy news she had to share with her friend. "Guess what?"

Lucas sat on the floor beside her and grinned. "What?"

"My mom started a new job yesterday. For the first time since she and my dad divorced, she sounded happy on the phone. She's doing bookkeeping for a widowed man she calls 'the cowboy.' I don't know his real name, but he trains horses, and Mom is terrified of horses. She isn't a big fan of smaller animals either." She paused as recollections from her childhood surfaced. "We never had any pets when I was growing up. I think she was attacked as a child by a wild cat or something. But she said she doesn't have to be around the horses." She pressed her palms together, smiling. "I feel like this is a big step toward her getting her life together."

"That's great." Lucas plugged his phone cord into the outlet where Natalie's was already charging.

"You know how much I love my mother, but I've been hoping she would regain the confidence in herself that she lost after my dad left. Having a job gives her a sense of purpose. And she certainly needs the money. It's not full-time, but I'm so happy she found something."

Lucas nodded, but his eyes were somewhere else, staring past her. Natalie waved a hand in front of him. "Hello?"

He came to attention. "Sorry. I was just . . ." His mouth took on an unpleasant twist.

"What is it? What's wrong?" She found his eyes and held his attention.

Lucas rubbed his chin as he stared back at her. "*Mei mamm* pinned me in the kitchen this morning and wanted to talk about you."

Natalie sighed. "No, not her too? Don't tell me. She thinks one of us will get hurt, right?"

Lucas's jaw tensed. "Has someone else said something?"

Natalie had hoped to avoid this conversation today. She hung her head, tucked her hair behind her ears, then looked back at him. "My mom and Mary both told me they were worried about our friendship. They think we have feelings for each other and one of us will get hurt." Pausing, she sighed. "Mary even said it was dangerous and reckless."

"*Ya. Mei mamm* is of the same opinion."

She searched his eyes as she tried to figure out how upset he was about the conversation with his mother.

He held a blank expression, keeping his eyes fused with hers. "Are they right that one of us will get hurt?"

Natalie chewed her bottom lip. "I thought we weren't going to buy in to any of that or worry about it, that we were going to follow God's lead and listen to Him." She swallowed the lump forming in her throat. "Are you changing your mind about our friendship?"

"I don't know."

Natalie's jaw dropped as she placed a hand on her stomach, feeling like she'd just been sucker punched. "What are you saying?"

Lucas glanced around the area where they were sitting. No one was around. "I just don't want to ever do anything to hurt you, not ever."

Her stomach pain subsided a little bit. "And I don't ever want to do anything to cause you pain either." She paused. *Because I love you.* She couldn't tell him that. He'd take it out of context and possibly end their friendship. "I feel like everyone is complicating a situation that doesn't involve them, and I get that they love us and are worried. But my trust in God is stronger than my trust in our family and friends. And, Lucas . . ." She waited a few seconds until he was really looking at her, the way he did sometimes when she felt like he could see inside her thoughts. "I trust *you.*"

"Maybe you shouldn't." He unplugged his phone, stood, and waited as she got to her feet.

Natalie fought the tears trying to form in the corners of her eyes. "You can say that, but I *do* trust you."

He stared at her for a long while. "I can't stay. I've got a couple errands to run. But I'll see you at Levi and Mary's Friday night, *ya?*"

She nodded. Did that mean he wasn't going to call tonight or tomorrow night? It seemed likely since he'd barely charged his phone. She didn't ask before he walked off. She wondered if he actually would be at Levi and Mary's Friday night. *God, where are You?*

Whatever Helen said must have really hit him hard.

Natalie picked up her purse and coat, took the books she'd pulled back to the shelves, and left the library. As she started her car, she realized the warnings were true.

We are already hurting each other.

᪇

Lucas didn't know his brother's work schedule, but when he pulled into Levi and Mary's driveway, he was happy to see Levi's buggy. He dreaded the conversation he was going to have with his brother, but he needed to talk to someone, and Levi was the most likely to understand how he was feeling.

"*Wie bischt?*" Levi swung the door open and stepped aside for Lucas to come in. "What brings you here today?"

"Where's Mary?" Lucas slipped off his shoes, hung his hat on the rack, and took a couple steps toward the kitchen, but he didn't see his sister-in-law.

"She's in the sewing room doing some mending, mostly to *mei* socks." Levi grinned. "But I can go get her if you need to talk to her."

"*Nee.* I came to see you." Lucas sat on the couch, propped his elbows on his legs, then held his head. "I'm so confused."

Levi sat next to him and faced him. "About what?"

After Lucas rubbed his temples for a few seconds, he looked up at his brother. "Mary told Natalie she's worried about us, where our relationship is headed. Natalie's mother apparently has the same concerns. This morning, *Mamm* got hold of me and gave her opinion loud and clear." Pausing, he searched his brother's face for a reaction, but Levi just scratched the back of his head and looked down. "I know you and Mary had to compromise on some things to be together since her district is so different from ours, and—"

"It's not the same." Levi shook his head. "I've been worried about you and Natalie too, *mei bruder*. It's not hard to see how much you two care about each other. The obvious difference is that Mary and I are both Amish, no matter how different our districts might be."

Lucas leaned his head back against his brother's couch and closed his eyes.

"That fact that you're even bringing this up must mean things are moving in a more complicated direction."

Lucas raised his head and sighed. "*Nee*, not really. Everyone just seems to have an opinion about it, so now I can't stop thinking about it."

Levi stared at him, squinting. "Thinking about what?"

Lucas grumbled under his breath, wishing he hadn't come. "You know, if everyone is right."

"Right about what?"

Lucas stiffened as he turned to face his brother. "Why are you doing that? Questioning everything I say."

"Because I'm not sure what you want me to say. Are you asking me if you should stay friends with Natalie? Or are you trying to tell me that you're thinking about leaving our faith?"

"*Nee*. Never. I'm not living like the *Englisch*." Lucas surprised himself by how quickly and earnestly he responded.

Levi ran his hand over his short beard. Lucas was still

getting used to seeing his younger brother with facial hair, even though he and Mary had been married for months now.

"I feel like *Gott* wants me to show Natalie the way to Him. She is a *gut* person, but she didn't really know how to have a relationship with our heavenly Father. And we've become close friends. But since everyone has all these concerns about our friendship, I'm trying to put myself on the outside and look in."

"And what do you see?"

Lucas stared at his brother, who was three years younger but seemed much older right now. Levi was married, and Lucas knew the compromises he and Mary made to be together. Since they'd married, Levi had taken on a maturity Lucas felt he was lacking right now, and he hoped looking in from the outside might shed some light.

"I see two people . . ." He paused, sighing. "Who care a lot about each other and are aware there is no possibility of being together as anything more than friends."

They were both quiet for a while.

Levi cleared his throat. "Our family never knew much about *mei* love of music. Mary had a fondness for it too." He waited for Lucas to look at him. "*Mamm* tanned *mei* hide when she caught me playing a piano at an *Englisch* family's *haus* when I was little. Somehow, I just knew how to play it." His brother seemed to recoil as he avoided Lucas's eyes. "I used to play the piano all the time for Adeline before she died."

Lucas's mouth fell open. He knew they'd sold Adeline's piano after she passed, but this was the first time Lucas had heard this. "But you know it's not allowed."

"*Nee*. It's not. I knew I was going against the *Ordnung*, and by doing so I never felt truly at peace playing the piano. But I do believe *Gott* called me to play for Adeline during her last weeks on this earth."

Lucas rubbed his forehead. He wasn't making the connection.

"What I'm trying to say is that I believe *Gott* wanted me to play the piano for Adeline, but only for a season, only to help her passing go smoother and to give her joy and a reminder of what she would have in heaven when she arrived and heard her husband playing the piano the way she remembered."

The light clicked on in Lucas's mind. "I'm being called to show Natalie the way to *Gott*, to teach her the many ways He loves us, how to trust Him, and how to accept His will." Lucas swallowed. "But only for a season."

Levi put his hand on Lucas's shoulder.

Lucas hoped he didn't cry. His brother was right. "How do I know when the season is supposed to end? For you, it ended when Adeline died. With Natalie, how will I know? What will be the determining factor?"

Levi removed his hand and sighed. "I don't know."

Lucas stood, thanked his brother, then left for home, feeling even more confused than before.

CHAPTER 6

Friday morning Helen found herself alone in the house. It was a rare occurrence. Everyone had somewhere to be today. Lloyd and Ben had gone to shoe horses at a farm nearby. Isaac was repairing the fence on the north side of the house. Lucas, Jacob, and Eli were in the barn working on a dining room set. Abram was in school, and the girls had gone to help at the food pantry.

Helen walked upstairs, which she hardly ever did, but she pushed through the pain in her hip. Her joints would hurt even worse going up the steps to the attic, where Lucas's room was. It was a terrible thing to spy on one's children. But Helen had a niggling feeling that Lucas was hiding something, and she was determined to find out what it was.

She flinched as she took each step up the steep ladder, then pushed Lucas's door open. The bed was unmade. No surprise. Her son knew Helen would never come up here.

She'd only been up twice since Lucas converted the attic into his own bedroom.

Other than a pair of black slacks on the floor and the unmade bed, the room was tidy. She walked around and tapped a finger to her chin. What was she looking for? Evidence? She could feel in her gut that Lucas was more involved with Natalie than he let on. The boy just didn't realize his feelings for her yet.

Nervous about what she might find, Helen noticed her hand trembling as she opened the drawer of the bedside table. Her nerves settled when she picked up Lucas's Bible. She smiled. The pages were tattered and worn, a good sign that her son spent time alone worshipping God. As she placed it back in the drawer, she noticed another book. A woman in a low-cut red dress that went all the way to the floor was on the cover. She picked it up and flipped it over to read the description on the back. Her chest tightened as she dropped the book back in the drawer, wishing she hadn't touched it. Her son was reading about a prostitute. Then she noticed a white cord in the drawer. Helen pushed the book aside with one finger and gingerly picked up the cord before she dug around a little more and found instructions for a mobile phone.

Anger rushed through her core until her entire body trembled. She replaced the items as she'd found them, closed the drawer, and sank onto her son's unmade bed, wringing her hands together. Should she tell Isaac? Her husband would want to know, but he'd be unhappy with her for snooping in their son's room.

There had to be a way to end this troubling relationship

between Lucas and the *Englisch* girl. It was a no-win situation. Helen would be devastated if Lucas left them to live in the outside world with Natalie. And she didn't want that girl in her family. It would be impossible for her to become one of them. Children began learning the *Ordnung* when they were toddlers. Natalie's values and ways were already instilled in her. Was she the reason Lucas had a mobile phone?

Her stomach in knots, she ducked her head and went out the small door, closed it behind her, and began the descent to the main floor, praying she didn't fall. After she made it to the second floor, she limped to the stairs and carefully—painfully—walked to the first floor. At the landing, she caught her breath, then went into her bedroom and sat on the bed, her thoughts jumbled.

Helen tried not to meddle in her children's lives, but this situation might need some intervention before things got worse. As ideas rushed in and out of her mind, she could only think of one person who might help her dissuade Lucas and Natalie's friendship. The girl's mother.

Cecelia lived near Montgomery. It was too far to go by buggy, and she didn't even know the woman's address. Helen didn't drive a buggy anymore anyway. She had a minor accident while driving to town one day a couple years ago, and it had shaken her up. Unwilling to confess about the accident, she also hadn't told her family her arthritis had been worse since then. She didn't know if the added pain was related to the mishap, but these days she relied on one of her children to cart her around. They only hired drivers for doctor's appointments that were too far away or if there was an emergency. There had to be another way. Phones, mobile or otherwise, were forbidden, but right now, Helen wished she had one.

By lunchtime, she'd given up hope of contacting Natalie's mother anytime soon. Maybe it wasn't the Lord's will for Helen to get involved. She was already ashamed of herself for snooping in Lucas's room. Lowering her head, she prayed for strength and then lifted herself from the bed to go prepare lunch.

Following the blessing for the noon meal, Isaac and the boys dove into a pot of stew Helen had simmered all morning. Abram was in school, and the girls were still gone. Her sons were talking about going up to Williams to the East Fork of the White River. It was an ideal fishing spot, and she couldn't recall a time when her boys or Isaac had ever returned home without a stringer of channel cat, along with an occasional flathead. There was a long pier at the dam the locals called the catwalk, and it was the one place Helen didn't mind her children mingling with outsiders. The entire family relished the flavor of the fish, which Helen lightly coated with a special seasoning before deep-frying it with potatoes cooked in the same pot.

"We can go get the horses after lunch and head that way," Ben said.

Helen smiled. Her boys had often said buggies were for the girls. She didn't know of any other Amish men who preferred riding horseback, but her boys loved it. They'd found a route from Orleans to Williams that kept them out of traffic they couldn't avoid in the buggy. And they said it was faster to ride the horses. They'd purchased the animals at auctions for next to nothing because the horses had been neglected and were unwell. Helen was proud of the way her boys had nursed them back to good health.

Their family homestead didn't have room for the horses. Their neighbor, Moses Schwartz, had been gracious enough to allow the boys to stable them on his property. Moses broke and sold horses and had a nice setup for the animals. He refused to accept any payment, so Helen took him a meal or freshly baked loaf of bread as often as she could.

"I walked over to Moses's place earlier to let him know we'd be coming to get the horses." Ben snatched the last piece of bread just as Lloyd reached for it.

"I have another loaf." Helen winced as she rose from her chair, limped to the counter, and returned with more bread.

"Moses wasn't there, but he's got an *Englisch* lady working for him. Just started a couple days ago." Ben's eyes turned to Lucas and he smirked. "It's your girlfriend's *mudder*."

Helen's eyes widened as she returned to her seat.

"Natalie isn't *mei* girlfriend." Lucas spoke louder than necessary.

"Cecelia is working for Moses?" Helen couldn't help her need to confirm the information.

Ben nodded. "*Ya*, she's doing his bookkeeping."

God had just presented Helen a window of opportunity. It had to be a sign from above that the Lord didn't approve of Lucas and Natalie's relationship.

After everyone had eaten and left, Helen readied herself for a visit next door. At the last minute, she grabbed an extra loaf of bread to take to her neighbor. He was a kind man. Moses and Marianne had moved to their community only a year before Marianne died. Helen hoped Cecelia wasn't trying to get her claws into the widower. She'd overheard someone say on Saturday that the woman was divorced. Helen would hate to see her take advantage of a good man.

Still, Helen was fairly certain she hadn't misread Cecelia in the hall on Saturday. She was sure the woman opposed any romantic involvement between Natalie and Lucas. That fact alone united them, but were Cecelia's convictions as strong as Helen's?

Thankful it wasn't too far of a walk to Moses's place, Helen closed the door behind her and cautiously descended the porch steps.

Cecelia had spent Friday morning carrying down the balances on Moses's ledgers. Now, as three o'clock approached, she was sorting his bills by due dates. They'd agreed that she would work primarily from ten in the morning until three in the afternoon, with thirty minutes for lunch.

On her first day, Moses showed her the sewing room. An old treadle machine was pushed against the wall next to rolls of fabric. Plastic containers lined a shelf and were filled with needles, thread, quilting squares, ribbons, and various odds and ends. Moses told her to set up the room however she wanted, and he'd pointed her to a box of office supplies that resembled artifacts from the fifties.

She found a few old rubber stamps with ink pads, instead of the more recent pre-inked kind. The stapler was a cumbersome and slightly rusty blue gadget that required a significant slam of Cecelia's hand to staple anything. There were ledger books, pencils, and several small sharpeners, along with an old Remington typewriter and a hand crank adding machine. A desk stood by a window with a view of the pond. Two horses lingered near it, nibbling on the new growth that had pushed its way up through the previously frozen grass.

After Moses showed her to the sewing room and explained a few details about his finances, he announced that he was heading to Indianapolis via bus to attend a relative's funeral and two horse auctions, and that he'd be back Friday evening. When she asked for a key to get in the house, he said he never locked the door.

She'd begun to familiarize herself with Moses's unique bookkeeping system when she started the new job on Tuesday, and it had taken her three days to feel comfortable with his way of doing things, which seemed bizarre. He had four different accounts and all handwritten ledgers.

Cecelia glanced out the window as she piled the ledgers on the corner of the desk. She'd been disappointed that Moses had to go out of town on her first day, but she was proud of the work she'd accomplished and hoped he would be too. She grabbed a piece of paper and wrote him a note.

I hope your travels went well. I left a chicken casserole in the refrigerator and added more ice in the icebox. See you on Monday.

Cecelia

She didn't know where Moses got the big ice blocks to use in the vintage refrigerator, but she'd picked up two bags of ice on her way to his house this morning. Hopefully, the casserole would be a nice surprise when he returned home. It felt good to cook for someone again.

Taking a deep breath of satisfaction, she left the note on the desk, picked up her purse, and headed to the front door, which she'd left open so the nice breeze could blow through the screen. The weather had warmed up some after the last, hopefully, cold spell of the season. A woman raised her hand to knock when Cecelia rounded the corner of the den. It took a few moments to place the woman's face, then she recognized her as Lucas's mother, Helen, the woman she'd met briefly at Levi and Mary's house.

"Hello. If you're looking for Moses, I'm afraid he's out of town, but scheduled to be back this evening." Cecelia pushed the screen door open and stood out of the way so Helen could come in. "I'm just on my way out," she added in case Helen was planning to stay longer than a few minutes.

Helen stepped over the threshold, the screen door snapping closed behind her. She lifted the loaf of bread she carried. "I will just leave this in the kitchen for him, if that's all right. He's so kind to allow our boys to keep their horses at his place."

Cecelia started to tell Helen that the bread would go nicely with the casserole she'd left for Moses, but then thought better of it. Cecelia cooking for Moses might sound a little too cozy for Helen's liking. The woman already had a disapproving scowl on her face.

"Yes, one of your sons came by earlier to say they'd be getting their horses later today." Cecelia waited for Helen to take the bread to the kitchen, but she set it on the wooden coffee table that was in front of a worn tan couch.

"What does Moses have you doing?" Helen raised an eyebrow, the slightest hint of a grin in her expression.

Cecelia smirked and pulled the strap of her purse up on her shoulder. "His bookkeeping."

Helen nodded before lifting her chin. "I see."

"Do you?" Cecelia tipped her head to one side. "Because it almost seems that you're implying there is more than an employee and employer relationship." She laughed. "I assure you that would never happen." She'd been disappointed that Moses asked her to dinner to discuss the job and not because he found her interesting and attractive—but only because she'd been starved for male attention.

"I'm happy to hear that. Moses is a *gut* man. Even though we encourage widows and widowers to remarry quickly, I'd hate for him to fall for someone as pretty as you, but who wouldn't be happy with us."

Cecelia felt herself blushing and softening toward Helen. "Thank you for the compliment. He does seem like a good man, but I'm just working part-time doing his books. However, I don't think a person can have too many friends."

Helen pressed her lips together for a few awkward seconds. "*Nee*, of course not. But . . . a friendship can unexpectedly turn into romance, and"—she stammered, then cleared her throat—"when it's two people who don't fit into each other's worlds, heartache is sure to follow."

Cecelia eased the strap of her purse down her arm and placed her bag on the coffee table by the bread. "Are we talking about Moses and me or my daughter and your son?"

Helen flinched as she shifted her weight. "May I?" She pointed to the couch as she placed a hand on her hip, and

Cecelia recalled the way she'd limped at Mary and Levi's house. "I'd like to talk to you."

"I don't see why not. I just work here." Cecelia grinned, then shrugged before she took a seat in one of two high-back rocking chairs facing the couch.

"And, *ya*, I suppose I was working up to a conversation about Lucas and your *dochder*." Helen cringed again as she placed a hand on her hip. "I'm sorry. I've been battling this arthritis for several years, and the herbal remedies seem to be failing me."

"You look awfully young to have arthritis." Cecelia figured she could repay the earlier compliment even though Helen had dark circles underneath her eyes, sun splotches on her cheeks, and chapped lips. Despite all of that and her graying hair, her features indicated that she wasn't much older than Cecelia. "Do your people not believe in modern medicine?" She didn't intend for the statement to sound as clipped as it did. "I mean, surely that's allowed, right?"

Helen straightened as she lifted her chin again, which was beginning to irritate Cecelia. "*Ya*, we accept traditional medicines, but I've relied mostly on herbal treatments." A pained expression filled her face as a trail of sweat slid down from her temple, even though the temperature seemed comfortable inside Moses's house. It was warmer than usual for the middle of March. But then, Cecelia wore a pair of white capri pants and a lightweight tan blouse, not a heavy blue dress, black apron, black socks, and black shoes. Not to mention the head covering with Helen's hair tucked inside. No wonder the woman looked like she was having a heatstroke.

"So, what do you want to talk to me about concerning Natalie and Lucas?" Cecelia crossed one leg over the other as she folded her hands atop her knees. "I'm guessing you're also worried about their friendship growing into something of a more romantic nature?"

Helen folded her hands in her lap and nodded. "*Ya*, I am. I once had a dream that Lucas would become our bishop someday." She shrugged. "It was only a dream, but I'd hate for anything to prevent him from pursuing the Lord's plan for him."

"Well, if it makes you feel any better, there is no way I see a relationship working out between Natalie and your son." She chuckled as she shook her head. "I can't picture my daughter as a bishop's wife or giving up her dream of becoming a veterinarian."

"You make light of it, but I see the way they look at each other." Helen paused, pressed her lips together again, then sighed. "It would crush our family if Lucas were to leave our district and choose to live a life we don't approve of."

Cecelia felt a little pinpricked at the remark. "I assure you, neither Natalie nor I approve of the primitive way you people live. It's not natural. God would want us to embrace technology."

Helen narrowed her eyebrows at Cecelia. "Are you an expert on what *Gott* wants? Do you even go to church, Cecelia? Was Natalie raised in a church?"

Cecelia stiffened. Helen had hit a nerve. "We believe in God."

Helen's smug expression might as well have said, *Score one for the Amish.* "Within our district and according to the teachings of the *Ordnung*, we do not question each other's faith. *Ya*, some feel the Lord more deeply, but we are all believers and we live by the code set forth generations ago." She took a deep breath. "And we are not in the habit of ministering to outsiders. It isn't our way, but Lucas has been teaching Natalie about *Gott*."

"Forgive me, Helen, but you act as though your people are better than the rest of the world." Cecelia uncrossed her legs and folded her arms across her chest. "I'm sure there are some sinners among you."

Helen stared into Cecelia's eyes. "I could say the same to you—that you portray yourself as better than us—but we are *all* sinners." She looked briefly at her lap. "But I didn't come here to have a debate about our beliefs. I am worried that our children are crossing over from friendship into something more serious, and I don't think you want that any more than I do."

Cecelia wanted to believe that Natalie wouldn't give up her dreams and fall into a life like Helen's. But Lucas was a good-looking young man. "No, I do not want my daughter giving up her life plan to live like an Amish person."

Helen scowled. "Live *like* an Amish person? You're either Amish or you're not."

Cecelia leaned forward and tried to choose her words carefully, even though the time she took to do so left a silence that loomed between them like a heavy mist. She reminded herself that she and Helen were on the same page. "We don't want our children to fall in love and alter the plans they've laid out for themselves. We are in agreement. But I don't know what we can do about it."

"The plans *Gott* has for them." Helen struggled to get to her feet, the lines on her forehead deepening. "I have already caught them alone together once. It worries me that temptation will get the better of them."

Cecelia reached for her purse, dug around for a few seconds, and pulled out a bottle of ibuprofen. She stood and offered it to Cecelia. "God wouldn't want you suffering when there are medicines available to help you. Just keep the bottle. I have more at home"

Helen hesitated but eventually took the ibuprofen. "*Danki.*"

Cecelia draped her purse over her shoulder and followed Helen to the door. They were barely on the porch when a blue van pulled in the driveway. Moses stepped out a minute later, retrieved a red suitcase from the back, and closed the space between them.

"*Wie bischt,* Moses?" Helen nodded over her shoulder. "I left you a loaf of bread on the coffee table. The boys will be by later to take the horses up to the catwalk to fish."

Moses walked up the porch steps and set his luggage beside him. "*Danki,* Helen, but you don't have to bring me bread every time the boys come get the horses." He winked at her, and Cecelia felt silly again for having thought Moses was flirting with her.

Helen blushed as she smiled. "It's no bother." Then she started gingerly down the steps, grasping the wooden handrail, looking over her shoulder to tell Cecelia goodbye.

Cecelia gave a quick wave and forced a smile. She didn't think she could ever be friends with the woman, but a level of civility might come in handy should Natalie and Lucas venture into new territory, although Cecelia doubted they would. Her daughter might be tempted by Lucas's good looks, but surely Natalie wouldn't allow it to turn into a full-blown relationship. Cecelia waited until Helen was out of earshot before she turned to Moses.

"Welcome back. I left you a casserole in the refrigerator, and I also brought two bags of ice." She shrugged, sighing. "Although, I don't know how you'll heat up the food."

"In the wood oven, of course." He smiled and winked at her. "I appreciate the meal very much. It's been a long day."

"Do you do that with all women—that winking thing?" Frowning, she could feel her face warming.

He took a step closer to her, grinning like a Cheshire cat. "Does it bother you?"

Cecelia scowled. "I'm used to men winking at me . . ." That was a lie, but she wasn't going to let Moses get the best of her. "But it seems inappropriate for your kind to do it."

"Then I won't do it again." He picked up the suitcase, eased around Cecelia, and opened the screen door. "Come in. Have supper with me."

Cecelia knew the Amish ate supper around four or five, but she shook her head. "No, I'm fine. Really." The thought of not eating alone was appealing, but Moses was her employer. They shouldn't be socializing outside of work hours.

"Then don't eat and come tell me how you like the job so far." He continued holding the door open until Cecelia finally walked inside, and then he followed her in and set down his suitcase.

Cecelia dropped her purse on the coffee table again and shrugged. "I'm hungry, so I'll eat." It was only three thirty, but she'd had a light lunch. Although, she hadn't a clue how long it would take to heat the casserole in a wood oven.

"*Gut.*" Moses smiled as he motioned for her to follow him to the kitchen. Cecelia felt like she was in an old western movie. She'd been in the kitchen several times since she started the job, and it was hard for her to imagine how people could live this way in this day and time. She'd been in plenty of Amish homes over the years, and a lot of the houses were much nicer than her home, which she considered to be upper middle class. The "fancy Amish," as she had dubbed them, might not have electricity, but their use of solar panels and propane at least kept them in this century. But in this area, near Orleans, these people were stuck in another era. She glanced again at the woodstove and lack of common appliances, like a toaster, can opener, and electrical outlets. And, of course, there were no lights, just a lantern on the counter.

"How do you like the job so far?" Moses lit the oven with practiced ease. Then he walked to the antique fridge and took out the casserole, which seemed lonely as it resided in a refrigerator that held only butter, milk, and a couple eggs. Maybe she'd bring a few items to stock it after she got a paycheck.

"I've carried down all the numbers on your ledgers, and your bills are sorted by due dates." Sweat beads began to pool at her temples as the heat from the woodstove warmed the kitchen. She supposed it would be nice during the fall and winter months, but it wasn't cold enough to enjoy right now. She dabbed at her temples with her finger.

Moses took the casserole, which Cecelia had put in a foil

container, and placed it in the oven. "Let's head back to the den, *ya*? I can tell you're not used to this heat."

"What are you going to do during the summer months?" she asked as she followed him into the other room.

"Cook outside," he said as he lowered himself onto the couch.

Cecelia nodded before she took a seat in one of the rockers.

"That's *gut* that you've got the bills ready. Did you have any problems?" He kicked off his shoes and lifted his socked feet onto the coffee table.

"There weren't any bank statements, so I just carried down the numbers in your ledger. I didn't have any problems, but you have a lot of bills due. I just need to know how you want to proceed. I can write out the checks, then you can sign them, but which account do you want me to use?" Cecelia had been shocked at the balances in two of the accounts— over thirty thousand each. Breaking horses and buying and selling the animals must be a lucrative business. The other two accounts had a few hundred dollars but looked mostly inactive.

Moses took off his straw hat, set it on the couch beside him, and ran a hand through his dark hair, which was flat on top. "I'll add your name to the two larger accounts, and you can just sign the checks. I'd like to have everything paid before the due dates." He grinned. "That's the part I've been failing at. I forget what's due when, and I've been late more than a few times."

Cecelia recalled a late notice from a feed store in town. She watched and listened to him with a growing curiosity.

Moses wasn't just a different kind of Amish man, he was also too trusting. He left his doors unlocked, and he was about to trust a woman he didn't know with his money.

"Marianne used to run the household with the smaller accounts." Moses's gaze drifted past Cecelia as a somber expression settled over him. "I probably don't need those anymore." He recovered with a slow smile that echoed the warmth in his voice. "There isn't much to run around here for a widower. I mostly eat out or open a can of something I can heat up easily, as I mentioned before." He rubbed his stomach. "So, I'm especially grateful for the meal tonight."

Cecelia knew how lonely it was to eat alone night after night.

"Just let me know when the accounts run low, and I'll make a deposit." Moses yawned. "Sorry. Long day of travel. One of the auctions was this afternoon in a town on the other side of Indianapolis, and then the driver hit traffic coming through the city on the way home. And there was the funeral and the other auction the past couple days. Neither auction had horses I wanted to bid on." He shrugged, then winked at her, grinning. "I'm happy to be home." Holding up a palm, he chuckled. "Sorry. No more winking."

Cecelia wished she could control the blush creeping up her neck. And, good grief, how many accounts did this Amish man have if he was going to make deposits from yet another one? She was aware some of the Amish were quite wealthy. They grew most of their own food, butchered their own meat, and canned fruits and vegetables. They had no expenses for cars or insurance, electricity, or even propane in this district.

Many lived in houses that had been passed down for generations, thus no mortgage either. They didn't watch TV or use the internet, and those who lived in this ultraconservative area also had no phone bills. Cecelia was grateful Moses had indoor plumbing. She'd noticed a few outhouses on her way here, and she'd shuddered, hoping her new boss wasn't still using some sort of outdoor contraption. To her relief, Moses's bathroom was quite nice, complete with a lovely, oversized claw-foot tub.

"How long will it take the casserole to heat up in that oven?" Cecelia laid a hand across her stomach when it growled at her, willing it to be quiet.

"Probably longer than your microwave." He pointed at the loaf of bread still on the coffee table. "We can slice into that now if you're hungry, or I can put it in the oven to warm it up. It won't take long for the bread."

"I can wait." Her eyes traveled around the room so as not to meet with his. She hoped it wouldn't always be like this—her nervousness around him. It was uncalled for, but Moses was smug, almost arrogant. Maybe he knew how attractive he was too. Perhaps flirting with women and having them flirt back was the norm for him, even though the Amish supposedly looked down on being prideful.

"Cecelia." Her name slid off his tongue and almost sounded sensual.

She raised an eyebrow. "Yes?"

A huge smile filled his face. "Relax." Then, he grinned and winked at her.

She shook her head and pointed a finger at him. But she smiled the whole time.

Maybe it was possible to have an Amish friend without the complications of romance, and she shouldn't worry so much about Natalie and Lucas. But temptation was already pushing its way to the surface. Cecelia knew she could handle herself and resist the attention of a handsome man who wasn't right for her. She only hoped her daughter could do the same.

CHAPTER 7

Lucas pulled into his brother's place Friday evening and noticed right away that one of their buggies was gone, but Natalie's car was in the driveway. He tethered his horse, washed his hands at the pump outside, and headed across the yard.

He tapped twice on the door before he walked in. Natalie was sitting on the couch with a piece of paper in her hands. She looked up at him, then offered the handwritten note. "Mary left this for us."

> Something is wrong with Maxwell. We are taking him to Big Rudy's. Hope to be back before you arrive, but if not, supper is warm in the oven. Please go ahead and eat. So sorry!
>
> Love,
> Mary

"Who's Big Rudy?" Natalie stood, leaned closer to Lucas, and eyed the note again.

"He's the closest thing to a vet we've got nearby. They call him Big Rudy because there are four other Rudys in our district, and Big Rudy is, um . . . well, he's big."

"I understand Levi and Mary had to compromise on some things, but I really miss Mary having a phone at times like this." She paused, frowning. "And I miss being able to talk to her more, in general."

Lucas nodded but knew he, too, would have to give up his phone after he was baptized. He took off his hat and ran his sleeve across his forehead. It had warmed up in the days following the most recent cold snap, but temperatures were pleasant. He shouldn't be sweating, but his hands were clammy too.

"Well, I hope Maxwell is okay." Natalie rolled her lip into the familiar pout. "He's such a sweet kitty." She tucked her hair behind her ears.

Lucas tried to keep his eyes off her lips. This was becoming bothersome, and now he was alone with her, a situation he'd tried to avoid. He didn't want to disrespect the *Ordnung* or Natalie, but he was becoming more and more aware of her looks. It was getting harder to balance what he knew was right with the feelings and temptations swimming in his mind like piranhas, eating up logic and replacing it with . . . something else.

Natalie cleared her throat. "Do you want me to leave?"

He came to attention and blinked at her. "What?"

She gently tugged on one of her gold hoop earrings as she kept her eyes fused with his. "I know it's against the rules for you to be alone with me, and I don't want you to feel uncomfortable."

He shrugged. "I'm fine, and I'm sure Mary and Levi will be back soon." He took a deep breath and searched his mind for something to change the subject. Natalie usually said what she was thinking, and any more discussion on this topic would feel awkward. Their phone calls the past couple nights had already felt strained. "How's your mom liking her new job?"

She raised both shoulders, letting them drop slowly. "I haven't talked to her yet today, but as of yesterday she said she enjoyed working for 'the cowboy.' She still calls him that since he breaks horses. Mom has this thing for old western movies. But her cowboy has been out of town since right after she started working for him."

Lucas wished his breathing would slow down and his heart rate would get back to normal. He walked over and sat in one of the rocking chairs. "I don't think Moses Schwartz is a cowboy, but he does break horses."

Natalie sat back down on the couch, scratching the side of her neck. "Who is Moses Schwartz?"

"Your *mudder*'s boss." He paused, but when Natalie didn't say anything and tipped her head to the side, he said, "One of *mei bruders* was at Moses's place earlier today. He lives next door to us. He wasn't there, but your *mudder* was."

Natalie's eyebrows raised in surprise. "My mother is working for an Amish man?" She burst out laughing. "You're kidding me, right?"

Lucas shook his head.

"She has always thought the Amish were from another

planet, so the fact that she's working for an Amish man is pretty amusing to me." She giggled again. "But, hey, I don't care who she's working for, as long as she's got a job. And maybe she'll develop a better understanding of your people and be more open-minded."

Horse hooves clomped into the driveway, so Lucas and Natalie went out to the porch. Mary got out of the buggy carrying Maxwell, while Levi took care of the horse.

"What's wrong with him?" Natalie gave the cat's ears a gentle scratch when Mary got close enough.

"He's diabetic." Mary nuzzled the cat with her cheek. "I didn't even know cats could get diabetes." She looked up at Natalie. "Maybe you knew since you're going to be a vet, but I had no idea."

"Actually, I *didn't* know that. But I'm just starting to learn all this vet stuff. I'm having to take a biology class right now." She paused as she scratched her cheek. "Not my favorite."

Levi walked up carrying a small bag. "*Wie bischt, bruder?* Hi, Natalie." He held up the paper sack. "Maxwell's insulin." He gave the cat a quick scratch under his chin. "Two shots every day, probably for the rest of his life."

"Wow." Natalie raised her eyebrows, then eased Maxwell out of Mary's arms and snuggled him. "Adeline would want us to take good care of you." She looked at Mary again. "Will he be okay?"

"I think so. Big Rudy said we have to watch him closely for a while after each shot to make sure his blood sugar doesn't get too low. He said it might take a few days for us to figure out the exact amount of insulin to give him."

Levi motioned for everyone to follow him inside. He looked over his shoulder right before the porch steps. "If he's still drinking a lot of water, we can give him a little bit of insulin. If he looks, uh . . ." He spun around and stopped. "Mary, what was that word Big Rudy used?"

"Lethargic," she said. "Like maybe he's falling asleep for no reason or losing consciousness or seems confused."

"*Ya, ya.*" Levi turned and went up the steps. "If he gets like that, then he's had too much insulin, and we're supposed to give him Karo syrup to jerk him back to life."

Natalie squeezed her eyes closed, then opened them. "That's horrible to think about—jerking him back to life."

Mary huffed a little as they entered the living room. "That's not exactly what Big Rudy said. He said it's hard to determine in the beginning how much insulin he needs. There might be some trial and error." She shivered. "I don't like that part. I wish we knew exactly how much to give him. Big Rudy gave us some guidelines, but we can't establish the exact amount until we see how he reacts. If we happen to give him too much and he looks lethargic, we're supposed to rub a little of the syrup on his bottom lip, and if his blood sugar is too low, it should make him become alert again."

Lucas rubbed his chin, studying the cat in Natalie's arms. "Is the medicine expensive?" Levi made good money doing construction work, but Lucas had watched their mother struggle with the cost of certain medications before, ones the *Englisch* doctor had recommended before she started using herbal treatments.

Mary shook her head before she walked into the kitchen.

"*Nee*. It's around twenty dollars and should last several months." She set a pot she'd grabbed from the stove in the middle of the table, which was already set. When she lifted the lid, Lucas breathed in the aroma of beef stew, his stomach growling.

After they were seated, they bowed their heads in silent prayer. Lucas's heart warmed when he noticed that Natalie prayed longer than anyone. She'd gone from knowing very little about God to building a strong relationship with Him and trusting and worshipping Him.

As Lucas stared at her, he thought about how easily they had become friends. If he tried to picture his life without her in it, a dismal feeling washed over him. He thought he'd done a pretty good job balancing his emotions where Natalie was concerned, knowing they would part ways someday. But the pendulum felt off-kilter lately, and that was beginning to scare him a little.

After supper, they all went to the den. Lucas stifled a yawn, while Mary, Natalie, and Levi watched Maxwell walk back to the kitchen to get a drink of water. It was the third time in the past fifteen minutes.

"Maybe we should give him some extra insulin." Mary looked at her husband. "It's only a tiny bit, and maybe he needs it."

Levi went to the kitchen and came back holding the cat and the small bag. Mary sat on the couch, and Levi placed Maxwell on her lap, pulled out the vial of insulin and a syringe, then filled the latter with a small amount of the medicine. He leaned over the cat, pinched a small chunk of fur, then quickly let go. He turned and walked to Natalie.

"Here, you do it." He handed her the small needle. "It'll be *gut* practice."

Natalie's mouth fell open. "No. Maxwell lives with you and Mary. You both have to know how to give him the shots."

"We do," Mary said before she shrugged. "But you feed him if we go somewhere, like when we had to travel to that wedding last month and stay overnight. You'll have to know how to give the shots too."

Natalie stiffened and didn't take the syringe from Levi at first. After a few seconds, she reached for it, then walked over to where Mary sat holding Maxwell. She pinched the fur like Levi had, but as the needle neared the cat, she began to shake and felt the color draining from her face. She dropped the syringe and shook her head. "I can't."

Then she rushed across the room and out the screen door.

Lucas looked back and forth between Levi and Mary, who appeared as confused as he felt. He went outside and found Natalie sitting in one of the rocking chairs on the porch with her face in her hands.

❧

Natalie uncovered her face when large hands gently eased hers away. She stared into Lucas's eyes and tried to blink back tears as he squatted in front of her.

"I can't give shots." She lowered her gaze for a few minutes before she met his eyes again. "I also don't like blood, and I don't see how I could ever stitch up a wound. The most basic medical tasks unravel me." She clutched the arms of the chair. "I love animals. *All* animals, but I get queasy around blood and needles."

"Why haven't you said anything?" Lucas took hold of her hand.

"I thought I could get past it. I'm doing fine in my core classes like English and math. But I might fail animal biology, my one and only class related to becoming a veterinarian, because I can't do the basics. I almost passed out last week when we had to dissect a frog. In high school biology, I managed to get a passing grade by closing my eyes and letting my lab partner do everything. A college professor won't let me get away with that." She peered over his shoulder into the darkness, then squeezed his hand before she looked back at him. "I'm not sure if my love of animals is enough to help me work through my fears."

Lucas eased his hand out of hers, then gently cupped her face with both hands, his thumb brushing away a tear that had escaped. "I don't like blood or shots either. But I bet you'll get used to it. Please don't cry."

His tender words caused Natalie to cry harder. She'd been holding her fears inside for so long, and they seemed to be spilling out all over the place now. "I've been praying so hard about this. Why would God lead me down this path? He provided me with the money to go to school. He gifted me with you, someone to teach me about His grace and mercy. I feel Him with me all the time. Why am I on this journey to be a veterinarian when it might not work out?"

"You don't know it isn't going to work out." Lucas used one hand to push back a few loose strands of her hair, tucking them behind her ear. "*Gott* challenges us, but that doesn't always mean we are on the wrong path. Sometimes the path of resistance is the right path and will make us stronger, but there are hurdles to getting where we're supposed to be. This might just be one of those hurdles."

Natalie gazed into Lucas's eyes, blinking back her tears. His kind words lingered in her mind, but it was his touch, the feel of his hands on her cheeks that became her entire focus. "I love you," she said softly.

Lucas's lips parted slightly as he leaned closer. She knew what was coming and longed for it in a way that made everything else in her life feel secondary. When he kissed her, it sent the pit of Natalie's stomach into a wild swirl, accompanied by a heady sensation she'd never experienced. It was everything she'd imagined. The feel of Lucas's lips on hers was wonderful, as if all their emotional bonding over the last few months had finally merged into something perfect.

The screen door opened, and Natalie jumped, she and Lucas quickly moving away from each other. Mary's eyes were wide as she clamped a hand over her mouth before turning and going back inside.

Lucas was standing now, his eyes ping-ponging back and forth between Natalie and the door. A few seconds later, he went into the house. The house where his family was.

Natalie wanted to go home, but her purse was in the den.

As she walked inside, everyone was quiet. They were her closest friends in the world, and they were all silent. Mary opened her mouth as if to say something, but she didn't. Lucas and Levi exchanged glances before their eyes landed on Natalie. She picked up her purse and hurried back out the door, all three of them on her heels, asking her not to leave. But she got in her car and pulled out of the driveway.

She'd told Lucas she loved him. And he hadn't said it back. But he kissed her. Would he have said it back if they hadn't been interrupted? And, if he had, then what? When the tears came full force, she found a safe place to pull off the road.

It didn't happen often, but more than ever, she wanted to talk to her mother. She needed her. But her mother didn't answer the phone. Natalie stared at the screen. No calls from Lucas either.

She dried her eyes, forced some composure, and drove home, her heart aching.

⟋

Lucas faced off with his brother and sister-in-law. "It was one kiss," he said as Mary shot daggers at him with her eyes. "Don't overreact."

Mary stepped toward him. She was usually levelheaded, calm, and polite, but right now she looked like she wanted to take a swing at him. "Natalie is *mei* best friend. I thought she was yours too." She lowered her head to her hands. "I knew this would happen."

"How could you know? I didn't even know." Lucas's head was spinning, and the kiss kept playing over and over again, clouding his thinking. He'd heard her loud and clear. She loved him. Her words echoed in his mind, whirling around with the memory of his lips on hers.

Mary uncovered her face, her piercing glare replaced with tears building in the corners of her eyes. "You had to have realized, even if just a little, that you and Natalie were becoming more than friends. She has been through a rough time with her parents' divorce, then Adeline died, and we don't want to see her suffer more." She lowered herself onto the couch, leaned back, and sighed. "And we don't want you hurt either."

Lucas paced, wondering how he'd let the kiss happen. "She was crying and upset because she wasn't comfortable giving the cat a shot. Apparently, she's having some trouble at school with the vet class. I think not being able to give the shot pushed her over the edge. Before now, I didn't know anything about her fears." He shrugged, still walking back and forth. "She was upset, and"—he couldn't tell them what she'd said, so he just shrugged again—"I guess I just wanted to comfort her."

"A hug would have been a *gut* way to do that." Mary folded her arms across her chest, staring at him. After a few minutes of silence, she asked, "Lucas, do you love her?" She held up a hand when he opened his mouth to speak. "And you know what kind of love I'm talking about."

"*Ya*, I know," he mumbled, avoiding his sister-in-law's piercing glare as he also avoided answering her.

Levi walked over to him, halting to place a hand on his shoulder. "*Bruder*, it would crush *Mamm* and *Daed* if you left our district. But you're not baptized. They can't shun you if you want to be with Natalie in the *Englisch* world."

"I'm not leaving our way of life." His heart ached when

he thought about the possibility, and saying his feelings out loud affirmed what he'd really always known. They were right, and he had been foolish to think he could teach Natalie about the Lord, spend so much time with her, and remain only friends. Especially since he'd been attracted to her from the first moment he saw her. But now, he was in love with her, and his heart was taking a beating. When had he lost the balance he'd worked so hard to maintain? He should have stepped back and tried to see things from everyone else's perspective much sooner. Instead, he'd worn blinders and convinced himself he was doing God's work and didn't have feelings for her.

Now he'd done the one thing he never wanted to do. He'd hurt her. She'd told him she loved him, and he hadn't said it back. That would have made things worse. But then he kissed her and hurt her anyway.

Mary stood, tears in her eyes. "I love you, Lucas. And I love Natalie too. But I saw the signs, the way you two look at each other." She dabbed at her eyes, which ripped even more at Lucas's heart. "But I think I know you well enough to know you will never leave our lifestyle. Am I right?"

Lucas glanced at Levi, then looked back at Mary. "I guess everyone saw it but me. I didn't want to see it."

Mary twirled the string of her prayer covering as she paced. "Things never should have gotten this far."

"I know." Lucas rubbed his temples, disappointed in himself.

Mary wiped away another tear. "Natalie is like *mei schweschder*. She didn't represent a threat to Levi and me, to the way we live. I worried when you first started spending time together, but I tried to convince myself that it was your business—and Natalie's. But now everything is such a mess."

Lucas couldn't agree more. He should have stopped seeing Natalie when his attraction to her began to grow. But when had that been? Maybe he'd known all along he was in love with her. But those same emotions had prevented him from letting her go.

⁂

Cecelia sat across from Moses at the small kitchen table after they finished eating her chicken casserole and Helen's delicious homemade bread. "That's the most I've eaten in a long time." She laid her napkin across her plate. "I'll have to diet tomorrow."

"You worry too much about the way you look." Moses wiped his mouth before putting his napkin down.

Cecelia's world seemed to dictate protocol as to how a woman should look. How nice it would be not to have to apply makeup every day and perform facial masks weekly as if her life depended on it. What if she didn't dye her hair and just let the gray come on out? And she could eat those truffles she loved nightly, instead of just binging on the days she thought about Tom.

"I know the women in your world aren't concerned with looks, but the rest of us are." Cecelia put a hand on her belly. She could feel it swelling just sitting there.

"*Ya*, I realize that. But you are a beautiful woman." Grinning, he stood, lifted his plate, and walked around the table to get Cecelia's. He stood looking down at her. "I'll bet you're just as beautiful without makeup."

Cecelia blushed, but she wasn't sure whether to take the comment as a compliment or an insult. She'd hit her forties, and she once read an article that said less was more when it came to women getting older. Still, she hadn't been able to shed her standard makeup routine, which included a lengthy application of the necessary cosmetics—foundation, powder, blush, eye shadow, eyeliner, and mascara.

"Ha," she said as she stood and walked with him to the kitchen sink. "You say that, but you'd feel differently if you saw me in my natural state." She glanced around the kitchen for the dishwasher, then remembered where she was.

Moses plugged the sink and turned the water on. After a few seconds, she ran her hand under it. "You have hot water."

The skin beside his eyes crinkled as he smiled, an expression that was growing on Cecelia. "*Ya*, I have a hot water heater in the basement. It uses propane, which is frowned upon in our district, but it was here when Marianne and I moved in, and we figured no one would see it down there." He grinned as he added dishwashing soap to the warm water. "Nothing like running hot water and a hot bath to soothe the soul."

"Ah, so you're a rule breaker." Cecelia cut her eyes in his direction.

"I can be." He winked, and Cecelia just grinned.

Moses didn't have nice furniture. It wasn't horrible, just broken in. The kitchen was a joke. She wasn't sure how he functioned in here. But his bathroom was amazing. She thought about the oversized claw-foot tub again and pictured herself soaking in it with candles lit around the room, a glass of wine in her hand, and soft music playing.

She picked up a kitchen towel from the counter. "You wash, and I'll dry."

He rinsed the first plate and handed it to her, his arm brushing against hers. Cecelia couldn't recall her and Tom ever doing dishes together. She and Natalie had always cleared the table and loaded everything into the dishwasher while Tom retreated to the living room.

When they were done, Cecelia dried her hands on the towel and laid it back where she'd found it. "I should probably go. It'll be dark soon."

Moses nodded to his right, at the lantern on the counter. "I have plenty of those. Stay." Grinning, he twisted to face her. "Unless you don't like driving at night."

"I'm not an old woman." She thrust her hands to her hips. "I can still drive at night."

"Then stay," he said softly. He didn't wink this time, but his eyes stayed locked with hers in a way that caused her insides to tremble. *Is he coming on to me?* She reminded herself that he'd clearly told her during their lunch meeting that he needed a bookkeeper and not a wife. He wasn't coming on to her. *He's just lonely, like I am.*

"I-I guess I could stay for a little while longer." She felt like a schoolgirl on a first date. Again, she reminded herself that it wasn't like that. She was getting to know her boss, who just happened to be nice looking, even with a beard that nearly reached his middle. She remembered when Tom had wanted to grow a beard, and she'd thrown a fit because she wasn't a fan of facial hair. But it worked on Moses.

They walked into the living room and Cecelia sat on the couch, then scooched over after Moses sat down right beside her.

"Relax, Cecelia. I don't bite." He winked at her as his face turned into the now-familiar expression that caused her pulse to speed up.

She stared at him for a few seconds. "You're not like any other Amish man I've ever known."

He laughed. "I'm wondering how many Amish men you've really known. I think maybe you have preconceived ideas about us."

She raised her chin. "I'll give you that. I haven't spent much time with anyone Amish, male or female."

He twisted to face her. "Tell me about yourself."

Rolling her eyes, she said, "Not much to tell. I married Tom. We had Sean and Natalie. Then we got divorced."

"That's not what I mean. Who is Cecelia?" He tilted his head to one side and fixed his gaze on her, inquisitiveness swimming around in his mysterious hazel eyes.

It had been so long since anyone was interested in her, she had to think for a few minutes. "Um, well . . . here are the things most people know about me." She tapped a finger to her chin, recalling happier times in her life, pre-divorce. "I love shoes, flowers, and watching old western movies."

Moses chuckled.

"I know. Tom used to think it was funny too." Cecelia smiled.

"It's just that you're afraid of animals, especially horses. And I'm not sure you can watch a western that doesn't have horses." He raised a bushy dark eyebrow.

"You're right. But cowboys are usually heroes, or at least one of them is." She thought about the way she'd called Moses a cowboy in her mind and even to Natalie. Then she grinned. "And exactly how many westerns have you seen since TV isn't allowed in your world?"

"A few, in my *rumschpringe*."

Cecelia nodded.

"Now, tell me something else about you, something the general population doesn't know."

"Hmm . . ." She shifted her weight, turning more in his direction as dusk settled in on them, dimming the amount of light streaming through the windows. He hadn't lit the lantern on the coffee table yet. Cecelia would need to go soon. *Not that I have anything to go home to.* She lowered her eyes. "I guess no one knows the ways that I'm trying to change. Even my daughter seems to have planted me in a box in her mind where I'll never grow. I'm just her needy, bitter mom who had a hard time with the divorce, has financial woes, and is a miserable person to be around." She lifted her eyes to his, expecting pity. She couldn't read his expression, but pity didn't seem to be part of it. "I don't want to be that person. I want to be strong, independent, and have joy in my life."

He smiled. "I think your goals are admirable. It couldn't have been easy to go through all that."

Finally. Someone gets it. "It was an ugly mess, but thank you for saying that about my goals. I have a long way to go. Bitterness has a way of attaching itself to a person, and it's hard to shed. But I'm working on it." She chewed on her bottom lip, hoping she wasn't going to cross a line. "Your wife hasn't been gone long. A few months, right?" He nodded. "You must miss her a lot."

"Every day." He looked somewhere past Cecelia, a faraway look in his eyes. She wondered what was harder on the heart—a spouse who passed away or a spouse who cheated, lied, and left.

"I'll admit, I don't know everything about the Amish, but I know large families are common. Why didn't you and Marianne have children? And please don't feel like you have to answer if I'm overstepping."

Moses cleared his throat and reached for a box of matches on the coffee table. He pulled the lantern closer and removed the globe. "It just never happened for us."

"I'm sorry." Cecelia had a complicated pregnancy with Natalie. "I couldn't get pregnant again after Natalie, so I'm especially grateful for her. And, despite the horrible things that happened during the divorce, there was a time when she and I were close. I want to find that again. Sean, Natalie's older brother, is in the army, so I don't get to see him much, but we talk on the phone or video chat about once a week. He was lucky enough to be out of the house when things turned bad for me and Tom."

They were both quiet as Moses lit a second lantern. Cecelia watched the flame flicker and dance, casting shadows across her boss's face.

He sat back, scratching his whiskered cheek, and Cecelia waited.

"I'm not *gut* in the kitchen, but I can whip us up a pot of coffee if you'd like to stay a while longer. I'm enjoying getting to know *mei* new employee."

She thought about her empty house and the bottle of vodka she occasionally got into at night when she was lonely. This sounded better. "Coffee would be great."

She followed Moses into the kitchen, and he lit the lantern on the counter before filling a pot with water and placing it atop the stove. Then he relit the wood inside, which was still smoldering from earlier.

Cecelia leaned against the counter as he took two cups from the cabinet, along with a container of coffee. The smell of the burning wood, the shadows cast from the lantern, the simple table and chairs, the old refrigerator—Cecelia felt like she was in one of the old westerns she loved.

And Moses is my cowboy. It was a comical thought since she'd always assumed the Amish were so different and had never encouraged a friendship with any of them. She decided it was time to rethink her "preconceived ideas" about these people.

CHAPTER 8

Isaac snored, but that wasn't why Helen couldn't sleep at eleven o'clock at night. And this time, her worries weren't about Lucas. Her son had actually come home earlier than usual from his Friday night supper at Levi and Mary's house. Helen was sure Natalie had been there, but right now, the activity next door had her peering at her neighbor's house.

There was a good bit of land between their house and Moses's, but from her bedroom window, Helen had a clear view of lanterns glowing downstairs—and upstairs—along with a car in the driveway. Cecelia's car. Helen recognized the silver vehicle from her visit with the woman earlier. The full moon and a pair of binoculars, which she'd discovered in her husband's nightstand drawer, aided her efforts.

Helen froze when Isaac suddenly stopped snoring. She quickly lowered the binoculars and turned to face her husband as he sat up in bed, rubbing his eyes.

"What's wrong?" His expression wasn't visible with only the light of the moon shining in, but his voice was throaty and hoarse.

She walked to his nightstand, pulled open the drawer, and placed the binoculars back inside. "That woman is at Moses's *haus* at this late hour."

"What woman?" She noticed an edge to her husband's voice.

"I'm sorry I woke you up, but Natalie's *mudder*, Cecelia, is with Moses." Helen walked around to her side of the bed, stepped out of her slippers, and crawled beneath the covers.

Isaac fluffed his pillow and lay back down. "I thought I heard this morning that she was working for Moses."

"Until eleven o'clock at night? I doubt they are working." She turned on her side to face Isaac as he lay on his back, his eyes already closing. "And there are lanterns lit downstairs *and upstairs.*"

"Maybe her car wouldn't start and she had to sleep on his couch." Isaac spoke with his eyes shut. He'd be snoring in a minute.

"If that was the case, she would have called her daughter or a friend to pick her up. That's trouble going on over there, and I'm disappointed in Moses." Helen huffed. "I don't know why either one of them would get involved with an Amish man when it is obvious they disapprove of our way of life."

"You don't know that, Helen." Isaac sighed in the darkness.

"*Ach*, well, I might not know Natalie's thoughts about it, but her *mudder* came right out and said she didn't approve of how we live. She has no business over there with Moses. She's brewing up trouble. Her and her daughter both."

Isaac began to snore. Helen stared at the ceiling, doubting sleep would come soon.

~

Natalie woke up Saturday morning, and before she even got out of bed, she could feel how swollen her eyes were from crying herself to sleep. She forced herself to relive the events of the previous day. She'd told Lucas she loved him, and he hadn't said anything. He'd kissed her. She'd called her mother repeatedly until almost midnight with no answer. But what haunted her most was the way Lucas, Mary, and Levi watched when she left crying.

Outside of her family, the three people she loved most in the world had formed a circle that excluded Natalie, at least for now. She'd thought Lucas, Levi, and Mary were her family, too, and that family stuck together no matter what. Then she remembered her parents and wondered if maybe she should have expected this. When things go badly, families fall apart.

As the pain burrowed deeper inside, it was slowly turning to anger. Lucas initiated the kiss, and Natalie was a willing participant, but why did it feel like she was the only one being ostracized? It didn't seem fair. Mary and Levi wouldn't break the no phone rule, but Lucas could have called her. Or maybe she'd read their reactions and expressions incorrectly before she fled.

She picked up her phone and realized she'd forgotten to

plug it in last night, so the battery was nearly dead. But her mother had sent a text at midnight.

Sorry I missed your calls. I got in late. Love, Mom

Natalie reread the message and stared at the phone. Her mother never went anywhere late in the evenings, and she always answered the phone when her daughter called. Natalie sent her a text.

Call me, please.

She plugged in her phone to charge, set it on the nightstand, and fought the urge to stay in bed all day. Only a few seconds later, her phone rang, and it was her father.

Her mother called a lot, but her dad rarely did. She didn't feel like talking, but her father's calls were usually about something semi-important, even if it was just that he had a new phone number or would be traveling for work.

"Hey, Dad."

"Hey, Nat. You doing okay?"

She hesitated for a couple seconds. "Um, yeah. Why?" She wasn't about to discuss her love life, or lack thereof, with her father—the man who left her mother to run off with someone too young for him.

"I was just checking on you." He sounded like he was calling from another country.

"I'm fine. Where are you? It sounds like you're across the world, kinda fuzzy or something."

"Oh, sorry. Hold on."

Natalie waited.

"Is this any better? Olivia's still sleeping, so I was trying to talk softly in the utility room, but I'd thrown some towels in the dryer. I'm outside now."

"Yeah, I can hear you better." Natalie yawned, waiting for her dad to get to the purpose of his call. He always had an agenda.

"I-I just wanted to tell you that I miss you."

She was wide awake now as she sat up in bed. "What's wrong?"

"Nothing. Can't a father just call to tell his daughter he misses her?"

"Well . . . I guess." She stifled another yawn as she scratched her chin.

"How's your mom?"

Natalie held out the phone, checking the number to make sure this was really her father. Last night's oddities were carrying over into today. "She's fine. You could call and ask her yourself." Natalie rolled her eyes and suspected her father's answer would be the usual, *"I can't. She just gets upset or yells at me."*

"Actually, I did try to call her—twice last night and again this morning—but it went straight to voice mail, like maybe her phone was off or dead."

Natalie ran a hand through her tangled hair. "Dad, what's wrong? You never talk to Mom, and you rarely call me." Her pulse had picked up, and now she was worried.

"That's not true, Nat."

She waited for more, but an awkward silence fell between them.

"Actually, I also wanted to tell you that I love you." Her father spoke softly, and it almost sounded like there was a tremble in his voice. She couldn't remember the last time her father called just to tell her he loved her. Those three little words were being flung all over the place lately.

"I love you, too, Dad." She paused. "You're sure you're okay?"

"Yes, I'm fine."

More uncomfortable silence.

"Well, okay."

"I'll talk to you soon." He hung up.

Normally, Natalie would have rolled her eyes and figured that wasn't going to happen, but after this call, she began to worry even more about her father, which she hadn't done in a long time. She'd focused on nurturing her mother during and after the divorce.

It wasn't long before she snuggled back into the covers and started to cry. More than ever, she needed one of her best friends. Mostly, she wanted to talk to Lucas, but she wasn't going to call him. She'd even accept a little love from her mother at this point.

⌒

Cecelia rolled over and stretched, lifting her arms high above her head as she welcomed beams of sunlight pouring into her bedroom. She was awake much earlier than usual. Coffee sounded good this morning.

Her phone dinged as she walked to the kitchen and began filling up the coffeepot. She read Natalie's text and noticed the battery was almost dead. She reached for the charger cord she kept on the counter and plugged it in, deciding she'd call Natalie later, after her phone charged a little bit more. Right now, she wanted a cup of coffee and a few minutes on the back porch so she could reflect on the lovely evening she'd had with the cowboy.

They'd talked about their marriages and the many differences in the ways they lived. But one thing was universal. Love. It doesn't matter if you have electricity, use a cell phone, or travel by horse and buggy, the human spirit feels love the same way. Cecelia had been surprised how easily she and Moses fell into conversation. Either he was an exception to her thoughts about the Amish, or she'd labeled at least some of them unjustly. It had been quite apparent how much Moses loved his wife, and he seemed to genuinely understand how divorce felt like a death in many ways.

As she settled in on the back porch, she realized she felt different this morning. She had a job, and even though she hadn't had it long, it gave her a sense of self-worth. Her boss was a kind and caring person. His flirting was just part of his charisma. She had a new friend, and she was looking forward to going to work on Monday.

When she walked inside to refill her cup, her phone was ringing, and she answered Natalie's call.

"I thought you'd be glad not to have me bothering you all the time," she said, then chuckled.

"Mom, did it ever occur to you that for once I might need *you?*"

Natalie was crying, and Cecelia almost dropped her coffee cup. "What's wrong? Tell me." Her daughter rarely cried.

Adeline's funeral a few months ago was the last time Cecelia could recall Natalie shedding tears.

"Everything is wrong. Can I come over?"

Cecelia's pulse picked up. She could feel Natalie's pain, whatever was going on. "Of course you can. Are you okay to drive? I can come to you if you want me to."

"No. I'll come there."

After ending the conversation, Cecelia scurried to get dressed. She prayed that her daughter would be okay. Praying wasn't something she did a lot of. But she'd bowed her head when Moses did the night before and thanked God for the meal. Spirituality had become important to Natalie lately as well. Cecelia didn't know much about God, but she felt like He might want her to get to know Him.

⁂

After Lucas attempted to eat some breakfast, he'd left quickly and gone straight to the barn. He hadn't had much of an appetite this morning.

He sat on the stool in front of his workbench, thankful for some time alone to think before the others joined him. He'd tossed and turned all night, wondering who messed up the worst, he or Natalie. She'd said the words they'd both veered away from, and he had kissed her, which was off limits too.

He hadn't called or texted her after she left, and she hadn't attempted to contact him either. A clean break would be the easiest, and that's what he would keep telling himself, even though he felt like his heart might never recover. He

missed her already. But he worried that things would only
get worse if they stayed friends. He would always want to be
with her in a way he shouldn't. The kiss added a new layer
of temptation. They both needed to find someone else.

As tears gathered in his eyes, he mourned the loss of their
friendship. He'd questioned God repeatedly, even though he
was taught to accept all things as the Lord's will. By morning, Lucas's thoughts had been set. Natalie needed a way to
find God, and Lucas had been the person to help her build
a relationship with the Lord. Now, his relationship with her
needed to end. Levi had been right. Lucas was meant to be
with Natalie for a season. He needed to accept that God
doesn't always set us on a path that will be easy. What would
have happened to Natalie if Lucas hadn't befriended her or
shown her how wonderful a life of faith could be?

A tear trickled down his cheek, and he quickly brushed
it away. He needed to pull himself together before his brothers finished breakfast and came outside.

⁓

Natalie fell into her mother's arms the moment she opened
the door. After she'd had a good cry, they walked to the
couch, and Natalie told her mother what happened with
Lucas. She was sure she'd get a big dose of "I told you so,"
but she craved nurturing, and there was a time when her
mother fit that role when Natalie needed her.

She'd detached from the friends she used to have due
to their lifestyle choices. But right now, she wished she had
made more of an effort to get to know some of the people

at school. She only had her mother and her Amish friends. And she wasn't sure where she stood with Levi, Mary, and Lucas. That left her mother, who seemed to be improving but was still on shaky ground emotionally.

"I'm sorry that happened, baby." Her mother tucked her legs beneath her on the floral couch, where they sat side by side. It was ten in the morning, and she was already dressed and on her third cup of coffee. Natalie was glad to see her mother out of her robe, which hadn't been happening by this time of day for a while.

Natalie waited for a lecture about her actions, how she never should have gotten close to an Amish man. Instead, her mother only repeated what she'd said before, that she was sorry about what happened.

They were quiet for a few seconds, then Natalie asked, "So, where were you last night? You said you were out late."

Her mother set the coffee cup on the end table and cleared her throat. "I was having dinner with my new boss." She waved a dismissive hand in the air. "You know, just getting to know him."

Then why are you blushing? "Um, yes . . . I heard your new boss is Amish." Natalie nudged her mother with her shoulder. "That's surprising since you've never wanted anything to do with the Amish."

"He's my boss, not a love interest."

Natalie took a couple moments to recover from what felt like a jab, knowing her mother didn't mean to be insensitive. "Well, just be sure it stays that way."

Her mother laughed. "Oh, trust me. Strictly business. I'm just happy to have a job."

This was music to Natalie's ears. She forced a smile, even though a knot was still in her throat and she was afraid of crying again. Her mother sounded so positive this morning that Natalie decided not to tell her about the phone call with her father. That would only drag her down again.

"I'm proud of you for getting a job." She smiled genuinely at her mother. "He breaks horses, right?"

"Yes." She brought a hand to her chest as she stiffened. "But I don't have to be around the animals. You know how I feel about all things four-legged."

"Oh, I know." Natalie stared at her mother and saw a reflection of their past. Cecelia Collins was a beautiful woman, but she'd been broken for so long that her grief had taken a physical and emotional toll on her. This morning, she resembled the mom Natalie remembered before the divorce. And as awful as Natalie felt about her own situation, she was happy to see her mother starting to make some positive strides. She felt like she understood her mother a little more today—the devastation that follows a broken heart. Maybe she'd been too hard on her. Her parents had been together a lot longer than Natalie and Lucas had been friends.

"I don't have classes Monday." She'd stay home and cry all day if she didn't make some plans. "Maybe I can come visit you at your job and meet your new boss."

"That would be fantastic." Her mother patted her on the leg. "I don't make a lot, but over time, I think I can get myself financially straight. As it turns out, I did learn a few things being married to your father. I ran the household, which included accounting and paying the bills. That's basically what I'm doing for Moses. Can you believe he still handwrites everything in a ledger? And his office supplies are antiques."

"Moses, huh? Before, you called him 'the cowboy.'" Natalie still hadn't lost the urge to cry, but having a normal conversation with her mother was helping. She'd waited a long time for her mother to start recovering. This conversation felt like a turning point in that direction.

Her mother grinned, shrugging. "I figured you would give me a hard time if you knew he was Amish, considering my opinions about them."

"You've always said they were odd, but I wouldn't have given you a hard time. I'm glad you found a job you enjoy."

Her mother was quiet for a few moments. "Moses seems different from the rest of them."

"Mom." Natalie drew her eyebrows into a frown. "Be fair. You haven't really made an attempt to know any other Amish people."

"Okay, I'll give you that. But I still think Moses is different. He doesn't seem as stuffy." Her mother tapped a finger to her chin. "So . . ." She picked up her coffee cup and ran her finger around the rim. "Back to you and Lucas . . ."

Natalie thought she'd covered it all. She'd told her mother how she blurted out that she loved him, how he kissed her, and how she felt out of the circle with her three closest friends right now. Natalie's head throbbed from all the crying and the attempts to analyze her situation. "What about me and Lucas?"

"You said you were crying, you told him you loved him, and he kissed you. But you never said why you were crying."

Natalie lowered her head and chewed on her bottom lip for a few seconds. She was going to have to tell her mother sooner or later. "Mary and Levi had just found out their cat is diabetic, and Levi thought I could give the cat his insulin shot, as practice."

"Makes sense." Her mother kept her eyes on Natalie, her head tilted slightly.

"I couldn't do it." She pulled her hair in front of one shoulder, twisting random strands. "I panicked. And I can't stand the sight of blood, and I don't see how I'll ever be a good veterinarian. It just all caught up with me, I guess, since I hadn't said anything to anyone."

"Honey, you've never liked the sight of blood. Do you think these are things you could get over as you go along?"

Natalie had already thought about that, months ago when she first realized she was having problems with the animal biology class. She whispered, "I don't think so, Mom."

Her mother nodded. "I'm surprised, but not shocked. Moses seems to think I can get over my fear of horses, but I don't see that happening." Her mother scowled. "I wish I could, but I think I've held on to it too long to push beyond it."

Natalie expected her mother to continue talking about herself, pushing Natalie's concerns aside. And, for once, that was okay. She really didn't want to talk about this right now.

"But you're young, so I think you have a better shot at moving past your fears. If you want it bad enough." Her mother stiffened. "You're not quitting school, are you?" She brought a hand to her chest. "Is it because of me, the money I've had to borrow?"

Natalie knew the money she'd given to her mother wasn't

a loan and she wouldn't get it back. Even though her mom had secured a job, it was part-time, and she wasn't making much. Natalie would be happy if her mother could just function on her own, both emotionally and financially.

"No, Mom," she finally said. "*If* I decide to quit school, it won't be about the money." A partial version of the truth. She had gone through a lot of it by going to school full-time. She should've kept her job at Rural King and taken fewer hours. If she'd done that, she wouldn't have had to use Adeline's money to pay for rent, car insurance, her phone, and other necessities.

Her mother stared at Natalie long and hard. "I thought Adeline wanted you to go to college."

"She did. And I know you and Dad do too." She shrugged. "I just don't know what I want to do with my life." A tear slid down her cheek and she quickly swiped it away. "Right now, all I can think about is me and Lucas."

"Pray about it."

Natalie raised an eyebrow.

"Yes, Natalie, I pray." Her mother frowned, but only briefly before a smile filled her face. "And I think God listens."

This admission warmed Natalie's heart. Her mother was growing on so many levels. "I believe God listens too." She nodded over her shoulder at the door. "I heard a car door shut. Someone's here."

Her mother went to the front door and returned with a huge bouquet of flowers. And whether she realized it or not, she was beaming from ear to ear.

"Natalie, don't make a big deal about this." She set the

vase on the coffee table, and Natalie wasn't sure about the grin on her mother's face. "I just happened to mention to Moses that I like flowers. This is probably his way of welcoming me as an employee."

Natalie slouched into the couch and sighed. Her mother said there was no way she'd get involved with an Amish man. "Yeah, well, spin it any way you want." She pointed to a small envelope. "You might want to read the card."

Even as Natalie's heart was breaking, she loved seeing her mother bubbly like a teenager. But Mom was walking into a hornet's nest, even if she didn't think so. She was going to get stung if she wasn't careful. *Just like I did.*

"I'm sure that's all this is." She was still smiling as she took the card out of the small white envelope. "Just an employer sending his new employee flowers."

Natalie rolled her eyes. "Yeah, okay."

The envelope slid out of her mother's hand and floated to the floor as her mom held the card at arm's length, squinting. And she wasn't smiling anymore.

"It's not what you thought, is it? It's more than an employer welcoming his employee, isn't it?"

Her mother blinked a few times as she continued to stare at the card.

"Whatever the card says, don't get involved with Moses." Natalie's voice cracked as she spoke, but her mother didn't seem to notice her daughter's emotions rising again. She kept her eyes on the card, then slowly handed it to Natalie.

Hi CeCe, I miss you. Love, Tom.

Natalie loved watching reruns of *The Twilight Zone*. And she was sure she'd stepped into an episode in the past twenty-four hours. As she handed the card back to her mother, she wondered if this correspondence would be a step back for her mother.

Would she forgive the affair? Would she take Natalie's father back, if it came to that? And where was Olivia? They weren't split up when Natalie talked to her father this morning. He'd mentioned that she was sleeping and he was in the laundry room.

Natalie remembered all the fighting between her parents prior to her father leaving. Since then, her mother had done nothing but stay upset about how she'd never love anyone else, how her life was destroyed. Until recently. The new job seemed to give her hope. Natalie wasn't certain how much the changes had to do with the new job or the boss, but either way, her relationship with her mother seemed to be getting back on the right track too. She didn't want that derailed, and she wanted her mother to be happy.

Her mother was still fixated on the card, then she slowly looked at Natalie and smiled before she ripped the note to shreds and tossed it in the air.

Laughing, she said, "Pigs will fly before I take that man back."

Natalie's jaw dropped. Was her mother infatuated with Moses? That seemed the most likely reason for this change of heart, because before this new job, Natalie always thought her mother would take her father back, despite his cheating and the hatred they'd spewed at each other. She wasn't sure reuniting would be healthy for either of them, but it was their lives and their decision.

Natalie's thoughts drifted back to her own situation. And the fact that Lucas hadn't called or texted. Her journey seemed to be at a crossroads.

CHAPTER 9

B y Monday morning, Cecelia had bitten her nails to the quick, an old habit she thought she'd shed. Moses was out in the arena with the horses when she arrived, and he'd waved and motioned for her to go on in the house. As she stared at the piles of bills, she took deep breaths and tried to focus, even though her thoughts were all over the place.

She'd had time to think on Sunday and was proud of herself for tearing up Tom's note, resolved that she was closing that chapter in her life. But the more she considered the possibility of reuniting with her husband, the more she wondered if she didn't owe it to herself to hear what he had to say. She'd pulled up Tom's number in her contacts list a few dozen times since she received the flowers, but she hadn't called or texted, even though he'd texted her twice asking to talk. Where was his girlfriend—soon-to-be wife, she'd thought? Had he ditched Olivia?

Despite her bitterness and Tom's cheating, Cecelia always

thought she'd take him back if the opportunity presented itself, that she would forgive her husband and they would begin rebuilding the life they once had. Now that the prospect seemed real, Cecelia was more confused than ever.

When heavy steps crossed through the den and rounded the corner to the sewing room, Cecelia turned to see Moses. Smiling, he took off his hat and rubbed his sleeve against his sweaty forehead.

"You have hay in your beard." She offered a weak smile as her stomach grumbled. She hadn't been able to eat more than a few crackers yesterday, and she'd skipped her protein shake this morning.

"Trade hazard." Moses grinned as he pointed to some papers on the corner of her desk. "Those are the signature forms for the two large accounts, so you can sign checks for the business bills."

Cecelia lifted an eyebrow, trying to grin back at him. "Mighty trusting, aren't you?"

"*Ya*, I guess I am." He ran his hand through his beard. "But I'm just going to pay you cash, if that's okay."

Cecelia nodded, though she wondered if he just didn't want to report her income to the IRS. Even the Amish had to file a tax return like the rest of the population.

She signed the bank forms. There were a few others beneath them with her name affixed to the signature lines and highlighted yellow, so she signed those, too, since they both had the same bank name at the top in large print. She was glad Moses had everything highlighted so she didn't have to wear her glasses in front of him. Maybe she needed different glasses since she was so self-conscience wearing the ones she had. She'd worn the hideous spectacles to write out checks while Moses wasn't around. She didn't want to make any mistakes with his finances.

"Is something wrong?" Moses squinted, seeming to search her expression.

"No." She placed her hands on two stacks of bills. "I'm ready to pay these if you are. Everything related to the horses is here." She placed her hand on one pile. "And anything related to farm repairs and maintenance is in this group." She tapped the other stack.

He stepped closer to her and tilted his head to one side. "*Nee*, that's not what I mean. You look like you've been crying."

He was observant, but she wasn't prepared to talk to him about Tom. She and Moses had shared quite a bit Friday night, but Cecelia didn't want to have a conversation about Tom until she decided how she felt about the flowers and note.

"I didn't sleep well last night." She stifled a yawn and forced a smile.

"You could have come in later. Or not at all. Remember, the hours are flexible. We settled on ten to three, but you can change that up anytime you want to." He smiled, but it wasn't his usual complacent expression. "You're sure you are okay?"

Cecelia pulled her eyes from his, nodded, and looked down at the desk. If he kept asking her that, she might burst into tears. She looked back at him when he squatted by her chair. "Even though you have sad eyes, I like the no-makeup look." He smiled. Cecelia's lack of makeup had more to do with the fact that she'd overslept, but she thanked him. Under different circumstances, she would have been self-conscious and felt underdressed without it.

"Let's get out of here," he said. "It's a gorgeous day without a cloud in the sky."

She stiffened. "What? No . . ." She nodded at the piles of bills. "I have a lot to do, and . . ." She hadn't meant to slip up about having financial woes when they were talking last Friday, and she was embarrassed to say that she needed the money.

"You'll still get paid, but I need help with a horse."

Cecelia opened her mouth to protest but didn't get a word in.

"You will be on the other side of a fence, not in the same area as the horse." Moses stood and reached out his arm. "Come on. A little fresh air will do you *gut*."

Cecelia took his hand but let go when she was on her feet. She brushed the wrinkles out of her red T-shirt and looked down at her blue jeans and running shoes. "I guess I am dressed for it today."

"You look beautiful, as always." He winked, and surprisingly she felt a little lighter on her feet.

"Thank you." She followed Moses out of the house and down the porch steps, eyeing the massive horse as they walked toward him. At least he was contained in a large fenced arena and couldn't get to her.

As they crossed the grass, she looked up. "You were right, not a cloud in the sky."

They were quiet, then Cecelia couldn't hold it in any longer. Maybe Moses would have some words of wisdom.

"Tom sent me flowers, and he's also texted me a couple times." She bit her bottom lip when Moses slowed and scratched the side of his face.

"*Ach*, I see. This is what has you looking like you lost your best friend today?" Cecelia thought of Natalie right away and hoped her daughter was doing okay. She'd spoken on the phone with her yesterday but not this morning. Hopefully, Natalie would still come by to see her today, like she'd said.

"It's just confusing." She shook her head as Moses picked up the pace again. "I always thought I'd take him back, no matter what. But now I'm not so sure."

Moses looked her way. "*Ya*, we touched on that subject the other night, and I sensed you might take him back if you had a chance to. But I think sometimes people want what they can't have. Now that the possibility has arisen, he might not be looking as good anymore."

Cecelia thought for a few moments, trying to decide if there was any truth to what Moses said, especially since she'd recently had those same thoughts.

"Pray about it. You'll get answers." He opened the gate when they reached the arena. Cecelia was glad she didn't have to go inside.

She'd tried to pray about it, but she wasn't sure what to pray for, and the whole process of talking to God felt strange to her. Glancing at Moses, she realized she had expected more of a reaction from him, which now sounded silly in her mind. A few compliments from an Amish man she barely knew shouldn't affect her decisions about Tom.

Moses reached for a video recorder that hung by its strap

on the fence post, and he handed it to Cecelia. She hadn't seen one like it in decades. It was big and awkward to hold. "Your job is to video me trying to green break that horse so I can take him to the auction. He's a bit of a monster, but that's because his prior owner didn't treat him well. I'll watch the video several times, I'm sure, so I can see where his sensitive areas are. He seems to favor his left side, and he gets really nervous if I get anywhere near his right side. I had a vet check him out, and he got a clean bill of health."

"I thought you weren't supposed to be in pictures or videos." Cecelia eyed the video recorder, searching for the record button. She'd probably have better luck videoing him with her cell phone instead of this outdated device, but she found the button and saw that it was charged.

"We're not. But this horse has kicked me twice, and I'm going to break the no picture or video rule so he doesn't end up killing me. Besides, it's not a posed picture, and it's related to my work."

"Okay." Cecelia shrugged as she flashed him a fake smile. "But try not to get injured, because I'm not coming in there to save you."

He chuckled before he closed the gate behind him and swaggered toward the horse. Just like a cowboy.

Helen jumped when her husband came up behind her and gently took the binoculars from her. "*Mei lieb*, you've turned into a spy. It's not our business what is going on at Moses's *haus*."

"Look at them." She sneered as she pointed out the bedroom window. "They are carrying on like teenagers, laughing and being silly, and I saw Cecelia put a hand on his shoulder. I feel like she and her daughter are up to no *gut*, even though she didn't seem happy about Lucas and Natalie spending time together." She spun around to face her husband. "And, speaking of that, something is wrong with Lucas. He hasn't eaten much the past couple of days, and he's been quiet."

Isaac sighed as he rubbed tired eyes. He'd been fighting a terrible cold. Helen was glad he wasn't working today. The boys had finally convinced him that they had control of work projects and home improvements, and he should rest. With Helen's tossing and turning all night, he probably wasn't getting enough sleep.

She knew worry was a sin, but it had crept up on her years ago and latched on like a leech when she first started having children. She worried about each of them, and she prayed daily for God to ease the burdens she carried for her family. Those burdens were not hers to carry since each child had his or her own path to travel to reach their destiny. Even so, the boundless love of a parent had kept her up many a night, worrying.

Isaac sat on the bed. "I have noticed that Lucas does not seem to be himself, but I haven't wanted to pry. He will come to us if he needs to."

"I hope so."

Helen stared out the window a few more minutes before deciding to check on the girls in the kitchen. She wanted to see how they were coming along with food preparation for a bake sale that afternoon. Cecelia wasn't one of Helen's children. She wasn't even a friend. Helen was wasting time worrying over a situation she had no control over. If Moses had taken a fancy to Cecelia, it needn't be Helen's concern.

Lucas, however, remained at the forefront of her thoughts.

❧

Natalie grabbed her purse and was leaving to go see her mother when someone knocked.

She opened the door and saw Mary standing on the other side of the threshold. Natalie brought a hand to her chest. "What's wrong? You wouldn't have hired a driver to get here if it wasn't an emergency."

Mary threw her arms around Natalie, which brought on the familiar knot in Natalie's throat. She'd been so hurt that she hadn't heard from Mary since she ran out on them Friday, but she returned the embrace.

"Not having you in my life would be tragic." Mary eased away. "So coming to see you felt like an emergency. I remembered that you didn't have classes today. I wanted to call. Even Levi said I should call, and you know how he feels about cell phones. But *mei* phone was dead. I hadn't been anywhere to charge it, and besides . . . I thought this was a conversation we needed to have in person."

Natalie stepped aside so Mary could come in, then closed the door behind her.

Mary nodded to Natalie's purse hanging on her shoulder. "*Ach.* I caught you leaving."

"It's okay." Natalie walked the short distance to the vintage red couch Adeline had left her. She knew it wasn't everyone's style, but Natalie loved it. She let her purse slip off her shoulder. "I was going to go see my mother, but it can wait."

Mary sat down beside her and gingerly ran a hand along the armrest of the sofa, surely with fond memories of Adeline. She sighed. "You looked so hurt when you left Friday. I just wanted to explain why I waited so long to talk to you."

Natalie pinched her lips together as they started to tremble. She was so tired of crying, but tears filled her eyes anyway. "I felt like it was the three of you against me, like I'd done something wrong. I know I've joked about being the outsider, but I'd never really felt like one until that night." She covered her face as she started to cry.

Mary scooted closer and wrapped an arm around her. "I know that's how it must have seemed, but none of us knew what to do." She paused. "And actually . . . Levi and Lucas had words after you left. I actually thought they were going to get physical."

Natalie uncovered her face and swiped at her tears, sniffling. "Well, that's pretty unheard of. What happened?"

"Levi loves you like a sister, Natalie. He was angry with Lucas for letting things get this far. The conversation escalated with both of them clenching their fists. They both held back, but emotions were running high." Mary lowered her eyes as she fidgeted with her black apron. "And I love Lucas, he's my *schweeger*, my brother-in-law. And we love you. I almost felt like I was going to have to choose between the two of you, at least regarding who would come to supper on Friday nights."

Mary said they loved her. But Lucas hadn't told her that

night that he loved her. "I thought Lucas and I could stay friends without things getting so complicated."

"I know that's what you thought, but Levi and I have seen other instances when an Amish person has become involved with one of the *Englisch*, and it almost never works out. Someone, or both parties, ends up being hurt, which is what happened with you and Lucas."

Natalie thought for a few seconds. "Maybe I should talk to him. He hasn't called, and I haven't called him. Surely there's a way we can still be friends."

Mary sighed as she looked at Natalie, her eyes giving away what she was about to say. "I don't see how. Won't you always want to be with him as more than a friend? And unless you are willing to convert to our way of life, you will only continue to hurt each other." She paused, pressing her lips together. "Lucas will never leave our faith, Natalie. I'm convinced of that, and so is Levi."

"And I don't want him to. I know how important his faith and family are to him." Natalie's shoulders shook as she started to cry again.

Mary waited until she'd regained a little control before she put a hand on Natalie's knee. "But if you want to talk to Lucas, then you should. I just don't want things to get worse."

"I know." Natalie reached for a box of tissues on the coffee table and set it in her lap, pulling one out to blow her nose.

"Lucas is hurting, as I know you are." Mary took her hand back and folded them in her lap. "This is why Levi and I showed concern, because we could tell before you and Lucas that the two of you were falling in *lieb*. You just didn't know it yet." Mary waved a hand around Natalie's apartment. Over the past few months, Natalie had been able to buy a bedroom set, some pictures, and other odds and ends that completed the eclectic charm she'd been looking for. "Could you give up all of this? Electricity—your hair dryer, lights, TV—your car, the type of clothes you wear, and all the other things that wouldn't be allowed if you sought a life with Lucas?"

Natalie let Mary's questions sink in. These were just things, possessions, but it was the only way of life Natalie had ever known. Even though she thought being Amish was more of a spiritual issue, she wasn't ready to dive into a conversation about that right now. She shook her head. "No. But I feel like I will think about Lucas, and miss him, for the rest of my life. And I feel so stupid that I didn't foresee having this much heartache. Logically, I knew we couldn't be together, but I guess I wanted to be close to him as long as I could."

Mary lowered her eyes but looked up when Natalie began to explain.

"I think I know why God put Lucas in my life. Lucas taught me how to have a relationship with God and to have real faith. Without us spending that time together, I'm not sure I ever would have known how awesome it is to know God on such a personal level." Her lip quivered as she went on. "But maybe that's where our friendship was meant to end."

Mary offered a weak smile. "I think you might be right. There's never a way to know why *Gott* allows us to suffer, but in this case, I think it might have been for Lucas to lead you to Him. Knowing what you know now, can you imagine your life without *Gott* in it?"

Natalie shook her head. "No, I can't." She blew her nose again, then got a fresh tissue and dabbed at her eyes. "It changed me. I feel God with me and around me all the time. I talk to Him several times a day, and I can feel when my prayers are answered. But . . ." She swallowed hard.

Mary took a deep breath. "But you're a little mad at Him for allowing you to be hurt like this."

"A little." Natalie folded her arms across her chest. "God is God. You would think He could have managed the end result better." She heard how childish she sounded.

"How do you know this is the end result? You're nineteen years old with your entire life ahead of you. You can't understand His plans for you, and you might not understand what is happening now for a long time. Maybe not until all things are answered when you get to heaven."

Natalie smiled, mostly for Mary's benefit. "Maybe you'll have to take up where Lucas left off. I know ministering isn't normally the Amish way, but I will always be grateful that Lucas showed me the path to God."

"And now you know *Gott* and are building a relationship with Him. But I am here for you, Natalie, if you have questions or if I can help you work through something."

They were quiet for a while.

"There is something else I want to ask you about." Mary twirled one of the strings on her prayer covering, her nervous habit. Natalie wondered what could be worse than what happened between her and Lucas.

"What is it?" She stiffened and drew in a deep breath.

"Lucas said you're having trouble with school, with your class related to becoming a veterinarian." She cast her eyes downward briefly before she looked back at Natalie. "And we saw your reaction about giving Maxwell his shot of insulin. I know becoming a vet has always been your dream. Maybe you just need time to get used to the parts of the job that bother you."

Natalie clutched her hands in her lap and sighed. "My mother said the same thing. I love animals, but I'm not sure I could get used to drawing blood or giving shots."

"You're not going to quit school, are you?" Mary's eyes widened. "Adeline was hoping you would go to college. Even if you decide you don't want to pursue a career as a vet, I hope you'll keep going."

"I think I need to reevaluate my reasons for going to college. I know Adeline wanted me to go, but she knew I wanted to be a vet, the way she once did. I feel like, as crazy as it sounds, I'm in the process of finding myself in a lot of ways. I think Adeline would appreciate and respect that. I'm learning about God. My mother and I are working to repair our relationship. Then there's Lucas and me." She threw up her hands. "I don't know. I might put college on hold for a semester."

Mary stood. "Give yourself time to decide. You're very emotional right now. Pray about it. *Gott* will give you the answers and show you the way." She glanced at the clock on the wall. "The driver is waiting for me, so I should go."

"Thanks for coming by." Natalie reached for her purse and stood, walked with Mary to the door, and hugged her friend. "I can't imagine you and Levi not being in my life." Her voice cracked at the end of the sentence.

"We will always be in your life." Mary ended the embrace with an extra squeeze.

"I'm very thankful for that."

But Lucas won't be.

~

Lucas was charged with repairs on the back fence this week, and from where he was working, he could see Cecelia's car at Moses's house, which made him miss Natalie more. And it had only been three days.

He raised the hammer and aimed for the nail, then yelled when he hit his thumb. He almost cursed aloud, something he'd never done. As he shook his throbbing hand, he kicked the fence post, then threw the hammer to the ground, hard enough that the prongs dug into the dirt.

Would it always be like this? Would Natalie always consume his every thought? When he closed his eyes at night, he saw her face in his mind's eye, and he could feel her lips against his.

"I did what You wanted me to do, *Gott*. I helped her find her way to You. Please release me of this torment that is gnawing away at my heart." He spoke aloud as he held his thumb and paced alongside the fence he was supposed to be repairing.

When his thumb began to swell, he stomped back to the house to get some ice. His mother was pulling clothes from the line.

"What happened?" She dropped a towel in the laundry basket and headed his direction.

Lucas kept walking. "I hit *mei* thumb with the hammer. Just getting some ice." He rushed up the porch steps, found some ice in a cooler, and wrapped it in a towel, then flinched as he pressed his thumb against the cool rag.

His mother joined him in the kitchen. She reached for his hand and studied his thumb. "*Ach*, it might be broken."

Lucas shrugged as he took his hand back. "Nothing I can do about it." It would just slow down his work.

"*Sohn*, are you all right?" His mother lifted her eyes to his. "You haven't seemed yourself lately."

"*Ya*, I'm fine." She would be pleased he was no longer friends with Natalie, but Lucas didn't think he could talk about it without breaking down in her arms. He was a twenty-two-year-old man, and he wasn't about to let that happen. Besides, the open wound would only deepen if his mother said something cliché like, "It's for the best."

She peered at him with eyes that could always spot a lie. But after a few seconds, she went to the den and began folding the clothes she'd just brought inside.

Lucas's throbbing thumb added irritation to the bad mood he'd woken up in. By the time he got back to the fence and picked up the hammer, his temper had worsened even more. He thought about the book still in his nightstand. In the end, the character had gotten the girl. He had to learn he couldn't save her. Only God could do that, and He did. But the woman in the story had to find her own path before she was back in Michael's arms. And it had taken a long time.

Lucas's journey with Natalie had only begun a few months ago. As much as he would like to take credit for saving her, he knew that was all God. But the calling left his heart crushed, and he didn't see that getting better anytime soon. Would Natalie's path lead her back to Lucas's arms? It seemed unlikely.

He positioned another nail and drew back the hammer just as a car pulled into Moses's driveway. He recognized Natalie's silver SUV, and his feet were moving that direction before she stepped out of the car. He'd only gotten a few feet onto the field that separated their houses when he stopped. He knew he could close the space between them in less than a minute, but she hadn't seen him yet, and it was probably better if she didn't. He was about to turn around when she spotted him.

She pushed her sunglasses up on top of her head. Lucas didn't have the strength to walk away if she headed toward him. A clean break was best, but it wasn't going to happen if she took one step in his direction.

He waited, frozen in the moment, his heart thumping wildly in his chest.

CHAPTER 10

Natalie wanted to run across the field and jump into Lucas's arms, to tell him she'd become Amish if it meant having him in her life. But wouldn't she be betraying God if she chose a religion only so she could be with a man? Or would her relationship with God transition no matter how she practiced her faith or whom she loved? Lucas had been building his relationship with God his entire life, but Natalie was just beginning hers. Even if they shared a life in his world, wouldn't they still be unequally yoked, a term she'd heard the Amish use frequently?

She pulled her sunglasses back down and started walking to the front door of Moses's house, but a horse whinnied to her left and she stopped. She raised her hand above her eyes to block the blazing sun piercing through her sunglasses and saw her mother. She turned and went toward the arena where a man, who must be Moses, was working with a horse.

Her mother appeared to be filming with a large camera-looking device propped on her shoulder.

"Hey, glad you made it," her mom said as she caught sight of Natalie out of one eye and didn't lower the camera.

Natalie sidled up next to her and leaned her arms on the railing of the arena. "Wow, what a beautiful horse. Such a gorgeous deep brown color." She gasped a little when the horse reared up near the man. He had to move fast to avoid getting kicked. "Whoa, he's kinda wild, huh?"

"The horse or Moses?" Her mother chuckled but kept the camera on her shoulder.

"The horse, Mother." Natalie rolled her eyes, then took in her surroundings—the small house, horse arena, barn with horse stalls, field of hay, and windmill. "This place is amazing."

"If you like the country life, I suppose."

Natalie chuckled. "Are you filming a movie with that big thing, or what?"

Moses ran his hand along his neck, as if to say "cut." Natalie's mom lowered the camera and gently set it on the ground. "That's an ancient video recorder." She spoke in a whisper since Moses was almost within earshot. Natalie vaguely recalled seeing him in the small crowd at Levi and Mary's house a couple weeks ago.

"You must be Natalie." The guy held out his hand between the fence boards.

She nodded and shook it. Moses was a nice-looking Amish man, even for an old guy.

"I've been recording Moses as he tries to green break that fellow, but the horse hates that saddle. He still hasn't been able to get on him." Her mother had dark circles underneath her eyes, which Natalie suspected were from lack of sleep, but something else was different about her. After a few seconds she realized that Cecelia Collins barely had on any makeup. Natalie couldn't think of a single instance when her mother left home without perfect hair and tons of makeup.

"You look pretty without as much makeup," she whispered.

"Doesn't she?" Moses smiled at Natalie before he turned to her mother and winked.

Natalie cut her eyes in her mother's direction just in time to see her wave a dismissive hand before she giggled.

Natalie gave her head a shake as she wondered if things could get any more bizarre. Her mother had been correct. *Moses is a flirt.* It was kind of cute to see her mother get giddy, especially since she'd been so distraught about the flowers from Dad. But this seemed to confirm that Moses was the reason she'd torn up the card. Maybe she really was trying to move on, but it shouldn't be with Moses.

"I know your *mamm* is scared of most animals, but she said you were going to school to become a veterinarian, so I'm guessing you must have a fondness for them." Moses pushed up the rim of his straw hat, smiling. He had pretty hazel eyes.

Natalie and her mother exchanged looks before Natalie responded. "I love animals, especially horses." She pointed at the one in the arena. "And that one is gorgeous." She lifted her hand to her forehead, blocking the sun again as the horse reared up from where he was pacing on the other side of the arena.

"*Ya*, he's a beauty, but he's got fire in him. I'm not sure I'll get him calmed down enough to take him to auction." Moses looped his thumbs beneath his suspenders and shook his head, scowling. "I was telling your mother that the prior owner didn't treat him properly, and the horse isn't very trusting."

"Can I try to pet him?" Natalie kept her eyes on the animal, who seemed to be watching her too.

"Don't you dare go in there with that crazed horse," her mother practically yelled.

Natalie handed her purse to her. "I meant from the other side of the fence, not actually go inside." She raised an eyebrow as she looked at Moses. "Is that okay?"

"*Ya*, sure. He will probably run from you. A couple of the boys next door have tried to pet him, but he won't even let them get close."

Natalie wondered if Lucas was one of the boys, but she shut down the emotional meltdown that was sure to follow at the thought of him. It would come later, but hopefully in the privacy of her apartment.

"I have to head to town in a little while. You okay out here if your *mamm* and I go look at this video before I leave?"

"Sure." Natalie started making her way around the arena as her mother and Moses walked back to the house. The horse lowered his head and snorted as she approached. When she was close enough to reach out and touch him, he ran the other way, then reared up on his hind legs and whinnied loudly.

Natalie leaned her arms on the railing, feeling suffocated by regret. About Lucas and the realization that she might not be cut out to be a vet. "Hey there, fella," she whispered as she rested her chin on her hands.

The horse jerked his head up and down and dug at the ground like a bull.

"Oh, I bet you're not as fierce as you think you are." She spoke softly as she slowly reached out toward him with one hand. "What's your name?"

The horse tossed his head from side to side, then stopped and stared at Natalie. "I bet I can outstare you." She widened her eyes behind her sunglasses as she extended her other arm over the railing, both palms up. "I bet it would feel good if you let me scratch your nose."

She stood quietly, her thoughts drifting back to Lucas despite her best efforts. It had taken every bit of willpower not to run to him earlier. But what would she have said? *I'm sorry that I love you?* It would have been a lie. She wasn't sorry she loved him, but she was sorry she'd hurt him and that her own heart had been left a tattered mess.

She was pulled from her thoughts when she felt soft skin and whiskers rub against one of her hands. Slowly, she touched the horse's nose, only to have him back up and shake his head, his mane whipping in the wind.

"See, you're not a monster," she whispered, smiling. She kept her arms where they were, and the horse slowly came back toward her. Finally she was able to scratch his nose.

❧

Cecelia stood in the den while Moses paced. They'd watched the video at least a dozen times.

"I can't figure out that animal. He's better if I try to mount on the left side, but once my leg touches his right side, he bucks me off." Moses stroked his beard as he stared at the fireplace.

He grunted and threw his head back. "I'll be right back. I hear the commode running again upstairs, the way it was the other night when you were here." He rushed across the room wearing his boots. Moses didn't seem to care about tracking mud through the house. Cecelia wondered if it had always been that way, or if his wife had requested that he take his shoes off before entering. She also wondered what his wife looked like. Was she pretty? She shook away the thought. What did it matter?

A few minutes later, Moses returned. She wasn't sure how many times he'd carried the lantern upstairs last Friday night to mess with that toilet. It didn't just run—the pipes made a horrible sound when it happened. He'd eventually turned off the valve when he couldn't get it fixed.

"I guess I better stop at Kirby's Hardware while I'm in town and get the parts to fix that thing. I need to go to Gallion's for a few things too." At some point, he'd lowered his suspenders to his sides, and as he pulled them up, Cecelia figured he was about to leave. "Do you need anything?"

She shook her head. Gallion's Supermarket and Kirby's in Orleans wasn't far from here by car, but in a buggy, she was sure it would take Moses a few hours to run his errands. "Besides, it's probably around two by now. I'm going to write checks for some of those bills, and then I'll head home. But I'll see you tomorrow."

Moses tipped his straw hat at her and grinned. "I'll be looking forward to it."

Cecelia's stomach swirled a little, but the flirty gesture actually took her back to thoughts of Tom.

"*Ach*, look at that." Moses stopped at the window on his

way to the front door. "Come here." He didn't turn around but motioned to Cecelia with his hand.

She rushed to his side. "Oh, my." Natalie was petting the wild horse.

"That's a first." Moses leaned closer to the window, which was partially open, a light breeze drifting into the room.

"She's had some experience with horses. She took riding lessons when she was younger. I was against it. Horses are so big and dangerous. But she talked her father into it. She even won a barrel racing contest at a fair." Cecelia cringed. "I kept my eyes closed the entire time."

Moses chuckled. "She'll make a wonderful vet someday."

He was still watching Natalie, so he couldn't have seen Cecelia's expression change. She'd been so proud of her daughter's ambitions, about going to college and becoming a vet. Now all of that seemed to be up in the air. She couldn't even blame Natalie's hesitations on Lucas—she'd always known about her daughter's aversion to blood and needles.

Having her children was the best thing Cecelia had ever done, and she was determined to put her life back together, with or without Tom. She'd relied on her daughter too much throughout the divorce. Now, she just wanted Natalie to be happy, whether that included college or not.

They watched Natalie stroking the animal's mane for a few minutes before Moses left to run his errands and Cecelia retreated to the sewing room office. She picked up one of the checkbooks and grabbed the first bill on top of the pile, but she couldn't focus.

She reached into her purse, took out her cell phone, and stared at the text message from Tom. Then she punched in

Thank you for the flowers. Love, Cecelia. But she deleted Love, Cecelia, and this time she hit Send. She picked up the checkbook again, took a deep breath, and got to work.

Helen carried another load of wet clothes out to the line. With the girls gone, all the washing fell on her this afternoon. Monday was laundry day, and she should have taken that into consideration before she said her three daughters could go to the bake sale. But she knew Sarah, Hannah, and Miriam could use the extra pocket money. Eli and Jacob had come down with whatever Isaac was suffering from, mostly congestion and a low fever, so they were in bed. She figured they would all end up with the illness before it was over.

Before the girls left, Miriam had told Helen that Lucas wasn't spending time with Natalie anymore. Apparently, he had confided in his sister the day before. Helen assumed that was why he'd been moping around and moody. She disliked seeing any of her children in pain, but if things had continued with Lucas and Natalie, they'd have suffered even more later. It was for the best.

Lucas was still on Helen's mind when he came across the yard carrying his toolbox. "Fence all done?" She pinned a towel to the line, then glanced his way.

"*Ya*, it's fixed." He kept walking in the direction of the barn.

Helen waited until he passed her again on his way to the house before calling out. "Lucas, wait, *sohn*." She took a few steps in his direction, her hip crying out with every step. "One of the girls told me you aren't spending time with Natalie anymore."

"*Ya*, that's right." He folded his arms across his puffed-up chest as he grimaced, probably itching for a confrontation to release some of the hurt. Helen decided not to push too much.

"I'm sorry."

He lowered his hands to his sides and took long strides toward Helen. "*Nee*, I don't think you are. But you were right. We care for each other more than either of us wanted to admit, and I realized that parting ways now would be easier than later."

Helen hung her head and scratched her forehead before she looked back at him. "I am sorry you are hurting." It sounded like Lucas made the decision. Maybe that had lessened the blow for her son. At least Natalie hadn't stomped on his heart. But she couldn't recall ever seeing Lucas this miserable.

"I'll be all right." He continued his trek to the house, and Helen wished she could wrap her arms around him, pray away his pain, and comfort him the way she had when he was a young boy. Only Abram was still at that age. Helen picked up a towel and reached into the pocket of her apron for a clothespin. She couldn't coddle Lucas, but she could still try to pray away his pain.

⁓

Lucas poured himself a glass of iced tea and took it out on the porch to sit and think. He should probably help his mother with the clothes. He should probably join whoever was in the barn hammering something. He should probably do something other than just sit and drink iced tea. But his thumb still hurt, and he was worn out, although repairing the fence wasn't the cause of his exhaustion. Natalie was.

He'd watched her for almost an hour. First, she'd talked with her mother and Moses, and then she'd spent time getting to know that crazy horse Moses had. It was mind boggling that she was able to pet the animal. Neither Lucas nor any of his brothers could get near him. But Natalie had leaned over the railing and slowly seemed to earn the animal's trust. It started with a scratch on the nose, then she rubbed his mane, and with an abundance of patience, she'd stuck with it until she actually nuzzled that horse's nose with her own.

He looked toward his mother and caught her flinching, so he set down the glass, shuffled across the yard, and reached for a towel.

"I can finish this, *Mamm*. Go rest your hip." Lucas pinned one end of the towel to the line as he eyed what was left in the basket. It was almost full, but his mother had likely been doing laundry since daybreak. Lucas doubted his thumb hurt anywhere near as much as his mother's hip.

"*Nee, nee.*" She waved him off. "I got this, *sohn*."

"Let me help, *Mamm*. I don't have anything else to do right now." He sounded pitiful. Maybe he needed a little motherly love, even if she'd been against him seeing Natalie.

His mother turned to face him, then cupped his cheek. "You will recover from this, *sohn*. It will just take time." She patted his cheek before she reached for another towel.

Lucas stifled the urge to tell her he would never get over it. But maybe his mother was right. She'd been right about him getting too close to Natalie. Everyone had been right. Except for him and Natalie.

They didn't say anything for a while. Lucas welcomed the quiet time with his mother, a rarity in such a large family. The girls would be back from the bake sale shortly, and Abram was due home from school any minute. Things would be bustling soon enough.

A few minutes later, sure enough, Lloyd and Ben came out of the barn carrying a large rocking chair. They loaded it on a small trailer. After they readied the horse and hooked the trailer to the buggy, Lloyd hollered, "We're taking this to Reuben. Be back soon."

Lucas was tempted to abandon his mother to go with them, but he didn't have the heart to leave her with the rest of the laundry. He was hanging the last towel when he heard a loud scream. He froze. It took him two seconds to figure out what he'd heard, then he sprinted across the yard. "Natalie!"

He ran across the field as fast as he could. That horse was dragging Natalie around like a mop, her blonde hair flying every direction in the dirt, her foot caught in the stirrup. He jumped the barbed wire fences he usually walked around—he'd never thought he could get over them. Then she screamed again as he reached the arena at the same time as Natalie's mother, who was crying hysterically right along with Natalie.

Lucas pushed Cecelia out of the way and opened the gate. He moved slowly, his palms held up and facing the horse.

The horse bucked, and Natalie screamed again, covering her face as a hoof landed right beside her.

"Natalie, be quiet." He spoke in a firm whisper. "You need to relax."

She was shaking so badly, he didn't know if that was possible.

As he moved toward the beast, it became more agitated and swung Natalie around again, causing her to cry out. Lucas saw blood on her arms and face but couldn't tell how bad her injuries were. He had to get her foot free.

"Hey, fella." Lucas spoke softly and inched closer to the horse.

"Lucas, Lucas." Cecelia spoke through her sobs in a loud whisper. "Look behind you."

When he turned, he saw his mother in the field. She held up her right hand and circled it three times. Lucas knew exactly what that meant. He positioned himself so he would be ready to grab Natalie before the horse fell. He'd have less than ten seconds to free her foot.

His mother took the shot, and Natalie and Cecelia screamed. Lucas bolted toward Natalie, praying for strength—and a few extra seconds to wiggle her foot out of the stirrup. She wailed in pain as he struggled to free her, the horse about to drop. He yanked her foot again, freed it, and pulled her to safety—and not a second too soon. The horse fell with a loud thud, causing dust to cover them.

She jumped into his arms, knocking him to the ground. When he sat up, she clung to his shirt with both hands and buried her head against his chest.

Lucas grabbed both of her shoulders and pushed her

away. "Where are you hurt?" Her lip was swollen and bleeding, and there was blood in her hair.

"I don't know," she said as she curled up in his lap. He wrapped both arms around her and held her as she sobbed. Cecelia was on the phone with a 911 operator. In the distance, he saw his mother limping toward them.

"Is the horse dead?" Natalie whimpered though her tears.

"*Nee*, he's not dead. It's a tranquilizer gun." He tried to ease her away again so he could see if her ankle was broken or if she was bleeding anywhere else, but her hold on him indicated she wasn't letting go anytime soon. He kept his arms around her as she cried, one hand cupping the back of her head as her face remained buried in his shirt.

"Natalie . . ." Her mother had ended the call and come into the arena. She laid a hand on her daughter's back. "Honey, come here."

Natalie clung even tighter to Lucas. He saw his mother out of the corner of his eye holding the tranquilizer gun, and in the distance his father, Eli, and Jacob were yelling, asking if everyone was okay as they rushed across the field.

Lucas remained sitting in the dirt, rocking Natalie in his lap. "I love you. I love you so much." He kissed the top of her head, then each temple, and when she finally looked up at him, tears pouring down her face, eyes still wild with fear, he kissed her tenderly on the side of her lip that wasn't bleeding. "I love you. I love you." He couldn't seem to tell her enough as he rocked her, gently pushing hair away from her face.

He heard sirens in the distance. Cecelia had squatted down next to them, but Natalie wouldn't let go of Lucas.

And he would never let go of her again.

CHAPTER 11

Helen perched on the edge of her bed and wished she had more of the ibuprofen Cecelia had given her. Eli had brought over a buggy and driven her home from Moses's house, but her trek across the field left a pulsing pain in her hip the rest of the afternoon and into the evening.

"So, the girl will be okay?" Isaac lifted himself to a sitting position and yawned.

Helen twisted to face him as she took off her *kapp* and began removing the pins in her hair. "*Ya.* The paramedics said she has a lot of bruising, a busted lip, and a sprained ankle. It's nothing short of a miracle that she wasn't hurt worse." She began to run a brush through her hair. "But we have lost Lucas to the *Englisch* world." Her voice cracked as she forced herself to say the words aloud.

Isaac groaned as he shook his head. "*Ach*, Helen, you can't be sure of that."

"*Ya*, I can." She placed her brush back in the drawer and crawled beneath the covers. "You arrived not long after I did, and you saw the way they were together. I'm sure the child was in shock, but she stayed curled up in Lucas's lap. She wouldn't even have anything to do with her mother. Lucas told her over and over again how much he loved her, right in front of Cecelia and me. And that girl clung to him, trembling. I felt sorry for her, but I felt even more despair knowing Lucas will be stepping off the path *Gott* chose for him."

Isaac was quiet for a while before he gently nudged her, and in the dim light from the lantern, she saw the corners of her husband's mouth crinkle as he grinned. "Had you ever shot the tranquilizer gun before?"

Helen snuggled up against him until she found a position with the least amount of pressure on her hip. "*Nee*. But I'd seen you and the boys use it, and it was in the barn. I knew I could get there the fastest even though my hip slowed me down." She laughed a little. "After I took the shot and the horse fell, I couldn't move for a while. I just stood there in the field shaking all over, thinking how I could have hit Lucas, the girl, or her mother." She paused. "If it had to be someone, I'd have chosen the mother, I think."

Isaac chuckled. "She would have been sore and had a nasty headache when she woke up, but she would have been all right."

"Cecelia demanded to ride in the ambulance with her daughter, but Natalie wanted Lucas to go instead. She pleaded with the paramedics to allow him to do so. Cecelia actually stomped her foot and yelled at Lucas to move, telling the paramedics that she was family." Helen shook her head. "Lucas said, 'I'm her family too,' so firmly that Cecelia shut up, and the paramedics agreed to let him go because Natalie's blood pressure was rising. His love and need to protect that girl is strong."

"Then we can't fight it, Helen. Lucas isn't baptized. He won't be shunned from the community, so we will still see him." Her husband eased an arm around her and pulled her closer. "What did Moses say when he got home and saw his horse laid over?"

"He didn't see a thing. Cecelia followed the ambulance in her car, and I offered to wait at Moses's *haus* until he got home so he wouldn't think someone killed the horse or call a vet or Big Rudy. I waited two hours, and Moses still wasn't home. The horse was back on its feet, so I filled a bucket with oats and left it some water."

"I guess Cecelia will give Lucas a ride home?" Isaac reached for a tissue by the bed and blew his nose.

"*Ya*, I guess. I didn't hear which hospital they were taking Natalie to. Probably the one in Bedford, so Lucas might call a driver." She looked at Isaac and lifted his chin closer to the flickering light. "You've got some color back in your face. Are you feeling better?"

He coughed a little. "*Ya*, I just needed a little rest to fight off whatever bug I picked up. Eli and Jacob said this afternoon that they're feeling better too."

"That's *gut*." Helen kissed Isaac on the cheek. "I think I need a warm glass of milk and a sugar cookie. I'll try to be quiet when I come back to bed." She picked up her robe, then turned on her flashlight and extinguished the lantern so her husband could sleep.

"Helen . . ."

"*Ya*?" She slowed her pace, shining the light at her feet.

"I've been married to you for a long time. I know when you are trying to hide your feelings. But Lucas must make his own way."

Helen felt like she'd been to battle and lost. "I know," she said softly as she made her way to the kitchen. She sat at the table and stared into the darkness, then let the tears spill.

Natalie woke up the next morning in an unfamiliar bed, feeling like she'd been in a car accident. She lifted herself up on her elbows, looked around, and remembered she'd slept in her mother's bed. She'd insisted on taking Natalie home with her when the hospital released her. Lucas had called a driver.

The events of the day before rushed into her mind. The ordeal with the horse, Lucas, the ambulance ride, and finally getting released from the hospital around midnight. She lifted her arms out from under the covers and eyed the bruises. As she touched her swollen bottom lip, she wondered how bad the rest of her looked, but she wasn't ready to crawl out of bed yet.

Closing her eyes, she thought about Lucas. There should be no doubt in her mind that they would stay together. He'd told her repeatedly that he loved her and wanted to be with her. He said he would give up his Amish life to have a life with her, willingly and without regret. Natalie believed Lucas loved her, but she had doubts about him giving up the only life he'd ever known, without regrets. Maybe he meant it now, but what if he regretted it later?

Her cell phone was on the nightstand, and her mother had even plugged it in. She picked it up and saw that she had seven texts. The first one was from her father late last night.

Nat, I love you, and I'll be there first thing in the morning. Mom says you're okay, but I'm coming anyway.

There were two texts from Mary this morning. The first one read, Lucas let us know what happened. We love you. The second, Please come to supper Friday if you feel up to it.

The last four texts were from Lucas. She'd been loopy from the pain medicine last night and fell right to sleep when she got into her mother's bed. In succession, the texts read, I love you so much, but I'm sure you are still sleeping, so I won't call this early, then, I'll call you later when I can talk, next was, I'm crazy in love with you, and finally, You are the only person for me. I love you.

She wrote back, I love you too. Library Wednesday at three?

In less than a minute, her phone dinged. Can't really talk right now, but ya, I will be there. Love you.

Natalie forced herself to sit up, even though her head was spinning. She was wearing one of her mother's night-gowns, but she didn't even remember getting out of her bloody clothes, which were already laundered and folded on the dresser. Was her mother up all night, or did she get up early to wash the clothes? She glanced at the time on her phone, and her eyes widened when she saw it was nine thirty. The moment she stood, she realized she wouldn't have been able to go to class today anyway. Putting pressure on her ankle hurt, and when she lifted the nightgown, she saw bruising up and down both legs. Her knees were weak as she hopped on one foot to her mother's bathroom and looked in the mirror. "Wow," she said softly.

Her lip was super swollen on the right side, but at least there weren't any stitches. She had a bruise on her cheek and the beginning of a black eye. *Thank You, God, for not letting it be worse.* She'd been so stupid to get on that horse. She'd thought if she could do something successfully involving animals, or face a fear, maybe there was still a way to become a veterinarian. She was so unsure about school and what her future held, but knowing Lucas would be a part of it gave her comfort.

Natalie heard voices coming from somewhere, but they were muffled. It took awhile for her to get dressed. Every movement caused an ache somewhere on her body. Once she had clothes on, she hobbled down the hallway, then into the living room.

"Hey, baby." Her mother hurried over to hug her.

"Ow, Mom." She wiggled out of the embrace, and her mother stepped back and made room for Natalie's father.

"I'm not going to manhandle you the way your mother just did." He smiled and kissed her on the cheek. "Do you feel as bad as you look?"

"Thanks, Dad." She tried to smile, but her swollen lip wouldn't allow it. "I hurt everywhere."

"What in the world made you try to ride a horse that a

professional couldn't even stay on?" He frowned. "You could have been killed."

Her mother let out a heavy sigh. "That's what I asked last night. You scared me to death, Natalie."

"Well, it wasn't a picnic for me either. It was a dumb thing to do, but I'd gotten the horse to trust me a little bit, and he actually did let me get on his back. Then he went nuts." She eased herself onto the couch as she reached up and touched her swollen eye. "I think I'm going to have a big ol' shiner." Groaning, she laid her head back against the couch. Her parents stood next to each other and stared at her. It was the first time in a long while that they were in the same room together without yelling or her mother crying.

Her dad finally sat down beside her, but her mother stayed standing, hands folded together in front of her. *Uh-oh.* They had talked, come up with a plan, or made a major decision about something. She'd seen these looks on their faces before. *Natalie, your mother and I don't want you seeing that boy in your math class. Natalie, please don't dye your hair purple. Natalie, your mother and I are separating. Natalie, your mother and I are getting a divorce.* And the list went on. Now, would it be, *Natalie, your mother and I are getting back together?*

"Nat . . ." Her father took a deep breath.

Here it comes. She closed her eyes.

"Your mother said she's been concerned about your relationship with Lucas. I mean, you do come from two entirely different worlds."

Natalie lifted her head and opened her eyes, although the right one didn't want to cooperate due to the swelling.

"Everyone has been worried about it, Lucas and me included. We tried to walk away from each other, but it only lasted three days." Pausing, she realized that wasn't entirely accurate. Lucas had actually walked away from her.

She glanced back and forth between her parents. "We don't want to be without each other, so we will go back to trusting God's will for us." In the back of her mind, she wondered if Lucas had acted out of duress.

"What if Lucas isn't willing to leave his people to be with you?" Her father narrowed his eyebrows into a frown. "Then what? Are you going to become Amish?"

"He said he would leave the Amish world to be with me, without any regrets. And he won't be shunned because he hasn't been baptized yet." Again, she wondered if yesterday's event had brought forth emotions Lucas was trying to bury. But all of his follow-up texts . . . "Dad, Lucas and I will figure it out. Right now, I feel like I've been run over by a train."

Her father grinned. "It was a horse."

"Ha-ha. I know." Natalie held his hand when he reached for hers.

"You're right. Take today to rest." After he squeezed her hand, he let go and stood. "I just had to lay eyes on my little girl and make sure she was in one piece."

"Banged up, but in one piece." She eased her bare feet onto the coffee table.

"I'll talk to you later." He turned to Natalie's mother, gently held both of her upper arms, and kissed her on the cheek. "And I'll talk to you later too."

Natalie waited until he was out the door before she

crossed her bruised arms over her chest and stared at her mother, whose face was as red as the blouse she had on today. "What was that about?"

She shrugged. "I'm sure he'll call me later to check on you."

"I won't be here. I'll be at my apartment, and he can call me on my cell. I'm not a child." She lowered her head and shook it. "Are you getting back together?" At least Natalie didn't live here to witness any fighting that might be forthcoming.

"We haven't discussed that. Your father and I thought it might be best if you stayed here for a while, just until you're feeling better." Her mother smiled, as if their entire world hadn't been turned upside down over the last couple of years, as if they were back to being a family again.

"I wasn't planning on staying here." Natalie glanced at the clock on the mantel. "It's after ten—don't you need to go to work? You're going to be late."

Her mother gasped a little. "Yes. You're right. I do." She paused, eying Natalie up and down. "But my hours are flexible. I feel like I should stay home with you."

Natalie shook her head slowly. Even that simple movement hurt, but she tried not to cringe so her mother wouldn't decide to babysit her all day. It was a sweet offer, but Natalie would be more comfortable in her own bed. "Go to work, Mom. You need the money, and I'll probably go back to my apartment." Then she realized there was a problem. "Where's my car?"

"Oh, it's still at Moses's house." Her mother quickly turned toward the hutch behind her and picked up her purse and keys.

"Wait, then. You can take me to get my car." The thought of being stuck here all day and possibly even tomorrow and not being able to see Lucas gave her the strength to lift herself off the couch.

"No way." Cecelia pressed her lips firmly together as she slapped her hands to her hips. "You're in no condition to drive. I'll take you to get your car when I get home this afternoon."

"That doesn't even make sense. It's almost forty minutes from Montgomery to Orleans as it is." Natalie found her purse. "Please just take me, or you know I'll call someone to come get me."

Her mother growled. "I think you should give yourself more time to rest, but come on."

Natalie hobbled to the car, and the drive to Moses's house was quiet as she drifted off to sleep. When she opened her eyes, her mother was nudging her. "Honey, we're here."

She blinked a few times, thinking that, for once, her mother might be right. She was hurting all over. Natalie couldn't control her flinching, and her mom was suddenly around the car and opening Natalie's door. After she helped her out, she kept an arm around her. "Maybe I could lie down on Moses's couch for a while before I go home?"

"Of course you can. He has an extra bedroom, too, but it's upstairs."

Natalie leaned into her mom's hold and curled an arm around her. "I love you, Mom."

"And I love you."

They took a few more steps. "Moses isn't even here. His buggy is gone."

"Okay." Natalie was ready to lie down on the grass and couldn't get to the couch fast enough.

∽

After Cecelia got Natalie settled on the couch, her daughter was asleep within minutes. Cecelia shivered every time she thought about that horse dragging Natalie around the arena. Lucas had probably saved her life. He seemed like a nice young man who really cared about Natalie, but to be with her, he'd have to make a lot of sacrifices.

Cecelia heard horse hooves approaching, so she tiptoed across the den, gently opened the door, and closed it quietly behind her. She wanted to let Moses know Natalie was asleep on the couch. Then she'd fill him in on everything that happened. But it wasn't Moses who stepped out of the buggy. It was Helen and one of her sons. Cecelia walked toward them.

"How is Natalie?" Helen brushed off what looked like flour from her black apron.

"She's pretty banged up." Cecelia nodded over her shoulder. "She's actually asleep on the couch inside."

Helen nodded before she turned to the young man next to her. "I don't know if you remember *mei sohn* Jacob."

"Hello, Jacob." She turned back to Helen. "Moses isn't here, if you were wanting to speak to him."

Helen pointed toward the arena and spoke to her son. "After you check on that wild horse, go ahead and check on the other animals."

Jacob nodded before he walked off, and Helen turned back to Cecelia. "*Nee,* I knew he wasn't home. After you left and followed the ambulance last night, I waited for about two hours so I could tell him that his horse was sleeping and not dead or sick, but he never showed up. He still wasn't home at four o'clock this morning." She shrugged. "I figure he must not have come home, which isn't like him since he has these animals to tend to. *Mei* boys take care of their three horses, but Moses has about a dozen of his own."

"Hmm . . . He said he was going to town for errands when he left yesterday, and I had the impression that he wouldn't be gone very long." Cecelia tucked her semi-blonde hair behind her ears.

"I'm glad Natalie is recovering well. It will probably take awhile for her to feel back to normal." Helen started to walk in the direction her son had gone.

"Helen . . ." Cecelia was barefoot. She'd kicked off her shoes in the house so they didn't click against the wood floor and wake up Natalie. As she stepped across the pebbles on the driveway to get to Helen, she cringed. "Ow, ow, ow." Then she glanced at Helen's bare feet, chafed around the edges. *Nope. Natalie would never live like that.* But Cecelia wanted absolute assurance that Lucas didn't think she might consider it. "I guess you saw the way Lucas was with Natalie yesterday."

Helen raised her chin, the way she often did when they spoke about their children. "*Ya.* And I saw the way Natalie was with Lucas . . . after he saved her life, that is."

Cecelia brought a hand to her chest. "And I will be forever grateful to Lucas for that. But . . . aren't you worried about where this is going now? It looked more serious than

I could have imagined, especially since they recently decided not to see each other anymore. Lucas would have to make a lot of changes to be with Natalie."

Helen cut her eyes at Cecelia, that chin of hers lifted even higher. "I am well aware of that." She turned to walk away.

"Wait. Helen." Cecelia scratched her forehead as she tried to think of a way to let Helen know she wasn't happy about the relationship either. But she didn't want to hurt Helen's feelings. The woman had tranquilized a horse that could have killed Natalie, and she was kind enough to ask how Natalie was doing. "I'm not in favor of this relationship either. I'm sure Lucas is a fine young man, but Natalie is going to college, and I don't want anything—or anyone—to derail her plans."

Cecelia wasn't even sure if that was the case, but Lucas would still have a strong influence on Natalie's decisions, whether she realized it or not. "We're on the same side when it comes to Lucas and Natalie. What if this thing with them goes the distance and they decide to get married? What kind of a job can Lucas get in the outside world with only an eighth-grade education?"

Helen's face turned bright red. "Is that what is at stake for you, Cecelia? That your daughter will marry beneath herself? What is happening to *mei* family is every parent's nightmare—one of our children leaving to go live in a world where we can't be sure they are safe. To live in a world with people who are unequally yoked with us. Temptation, crime, and a host of worldly things will threaten our Lucas and everything he has been taught and stands for."

Cecelia pressed her lips into a thin line, then took a deep

breath. "Careful, Helen. You make it sound like your people are better than us, and that doesn't seem very Christian to me."

"Isn't that what you just implied when you said Lucas only has an eighth-grade education?"

"Okay, I probably shouldn't have said that." She did regret it. Cecelia knew lots of people who had dropped out of school and gone on to have successful careers. "I think we are just going to have to call a truce and accept what is happening. They're young and haven't been spending time together all that long. This could fizzle out, and we could be worrying for nothing."

"I hope you're right. Natalie is the last thing Lucas needs."

Cecelia's jaw dropped. "There are tons of men who would love to have Natalie in their life. Lucas should count his lucky stars."

Helen hung her head for a few seconds, and when she looked back up, a fire blazed in her eyes. "Lucas will probably give up everything that is important to him to be with Natalie. We will pray that he stays true to his faith if and when he chooses to be with your daughter. But your world is filled with temptation, and Lucas would be living a lifestyle we don't approve of."

Cecelia's mouth fell open again. "You make it sound like our way of life will influence Lucas's choices for good or bad, but how he was raised will play a large factor in the choices he makes. And I'm sure your community has plenty of crime, sinners, and people who make bad judgments just like everywhere else."

"Of course we have sinners, but the most important part of our detachment from the outside world is that we are unequally yoked with the *Englisch*." She shook her head. "You wouldn't understand."

"Try me." Cecelia spat the words.

"We are certain of those in our district, of their belief in God and their commitment to the *Ordnung*, the rules we follow and know by heart. *Ya*, we have sinners among us. We are *all* sinners. And for that reason, we try to stay as detached as we can from others—those we don't know, those who might think they know the Lord but who are not living by His standards."

"Helen, you don't know anything about me. Or Natalie. How do you know that our faith in God isn't as strong as yours?" Cecelia was reaching, but it made for a good argument.

Helen offered a sad smile. "That's just it. We don't."

Cecelia scratched her head. "Okay, well . . . I guess we could go on like this all day, but I've got work to do."

Helen faced off with her. "I will be hoping and praying that this is an infatuation that will pass."

Cecelia clenched her fists at her sides before she took a deep breath. This wasn't worth it. "I will be hoping and praying the same thing." She turned to go inside and eased the door open, her stomach clenching when she saw Natalie standing by the open window. Cecelia's heart pounded. She sighed. "How much did you hear?"

A tear rolled down Natalie's swollen cheek. "Enough."

CHAPTER 12

Natalie had slept on Moses's couch most of the day Tuesday, despite being upset about the conversation between her mother and Helen. She hadn't had the energy to leave until later in the afternoon.

Moses never came home. Her mother's concern was evident by the time Natalie left around three. She'd told Natalie repeatedly how sorry she was that she overheard the conversation with Helen. Natalie wished she hadn't heard it. When people were in love, it was usually important for the couple to have their families' blessing. Lucas and Natalie weren't going to have it from either side.

She'd slept better in her own bed last night, but she woke up as sore as she'd been the previous day, and she looked like someone had punched her in the face. Her eye was more swollen and blacker, and her lip wasn't looking any better. She'd called Lucas last night, but they hadn't talked for long since Natalie was groggy and hurting. This morning, she sent him a text asking if they could meet somewhere else so the people at the library didn't see her looking like this. To her surprise, he texted back and said he would come to her apartment. Maybe this was his first step toward a different kind of life.

As she waited for him to arrive, the conversation between her mother and Helen played over and over again in her mind. It was going to devastate Lucas's entire family when he left. And would her mother and her Amish in-laws ever see eye to eye on anything? Or was Natalie jumping the gun by thinking about such things?

Her talk with Mary kept replaying in her mind as well. Everyone assumed Natalie could never make the changes necessary to be in Lucas's world. *But could I?* She rolled the thought around, picturing herself driving a buggy instead of a car. At first she couldn't imagine traveling that way. But as she closed her eyes and thought about the wind in her hair, the aroma of freshly cut hay, and the possibility of owning a horse of her own, she reconsidered that maybe giving up a car wouldn't be as devastating as she'd thought.

Then there were the clothes. No more blue jeans, T-shirts—or even haircuts. She tossed that thought around for a few minutes. Then she looked beyond the material aspects and focused on what the religion stood for—a powerful, loyal relationship with God without the distractions that were so abundant in her world. That was one thing she would hold on to no matter how she lived her life. Did those who knew her doubt her convictions? Their assumptions that she wasn't capable of such a conversion began to bother her.

When she heard a knock, she hobbled across the floor in her gray sweatpants. She paused to glance at the decorative mirror on the wall and shook her head at her reflection before opening the door.

"I know I look awful." She lowered her head.

Lucas stepped inside and closed the door behind him. "You look beautiful." He kissed her on the side of her face that wasn't bruised. The right side of her body had taken on the brunt of the injuries.

She pointed a finger at him. "Now, that's a lie." She'd been resting in her bedroom, but lying on her bed, however innocent, would be awkward for Lucas. And it was a huge step for him to be here. She pointed to the couch. "I need to sit if that's okay." She reached for his hand and led him to the couch, where they sat side by side.

"I don't want you to be uncomfortable here with me, like this. You know, us alone together in my apartment. I know the rules." She avoided his eyes until he spoke.

"*Ya*, it's a rule, I guess. But my not wanting to be alone with you was more about temptation. We were trying to stay friends, and I didn't want to add any more challenges to our relationship." He squeezed her hand, his own trembling. She wondered if the temptation had grown worse for him since they'd kissed. It had for her. She felt a strong desire to show Lucas how much she loved him. But she knew it would be wrong if they were physical and not married, so she made a mental note not to let things travel to a place that would cause both of them remorse later.

When Lucas brought her hand to his mouth and kissed it softly, she had a better understanding of the not-being-alone rule and reminded herself that temptation could sneak up on them easily.

"I didn't realize how much I loved you until I thought I might lose you." Lucas stared into her eyes. "I want to be with you, no matter what."

Natalie clung to his words, the one solid reality in a world that was shifting beneath their feet. "I feel the same way." She paused as she remembered the conversation between her mother and Helen again. "I overheard your mother and mine talking yesterday." She sighed. "It wasn't pretty. Neither of our families wants us together, Lucas."

"It's not up to them. I've prayed about this a lot, and I thought I could walk away from you since everyone thought that was best." He maintained eye contact, unflinching, still holding her hand. "It's too late for that now."

Natalie's eyes filled with tears. "I feel the same way, but . . . I don't want you to have regrets about this decision later." She didn't want to use the words "when you stop being Amish," even though that was exactly what had to happen for them to have a life together.

Maybe she was being too forward. They loved each other, but it wasn't like he'd asked her to marry him. She couldn't help but wonder if there was some better compromise somehow. Was there a way for them to be together without him having to make all of the sacrifices?

When he didn't respond to her comment, his silence seemed to speak volumes to Natalie. How could he *not* have regrets about leaving his family, his lifestyle, everything he knew—and how would that affect them down the line?

Lucas's life plan was changing. He was going to marry Natalie someday. He had waited until he was twenty-two years old to find the right person, and he never could have imagined she would be someone outside of his community. If being without her for three days caused him so much grief, what would the rest of his life have been like without her? She made him feel like a better version of himself.

Even so, giving up the life he'd always known and the future he'd dreamed of ripped at his insides. He wouldn't be shunned, but he wouldn't be raising a family the way he'd always assumed he would. His chest tightened. He didn't even know if Natalie wanted children. They'd been so dead set about staying friends that he'd never asked. His pulse sped up as he considered what her answer might be. What if she didn't want a large family? What if she didn't want kids at all?

Lucas eased his arm around her. "Am I hurting you?"

She shook her head. "No. Not any more than I'm already hurting." She leaned her head on his shoulder. "That was such a stupid thing to do—thinking I could ride that horse."

"*Ya*. Don't ever do something like that again." He scowled as he thought about how much worse things could have been. "Why did you try to ride him, anyway?"

She stared into space for a couple seconds before she met his eyes. "I wanted to do something no one else had been able to do, to prove to myself that I did have something to contribute when it came to animals. I thought if I could ride him, maybe it would make up for the other areas I'm having trouble with." Shrugging, she said, "I rode horses when I was younger, but that was a long time ago. I should have known better."

She nudged him with her elbow. "Are you still with me? You look like you're off in another world."

Lucas gathered up his emotional loose ends and refocused. "*Ya*, I heard you. I'm just glad you're all right." His mind had been guilty of drifting. He couldn't get the question about children off his mind.

"I've never been in your apartment." He eyed the red couch they were sitting on, the abstract paintings on the wall, and the weird coffee table that looked like it had giant talons for legs. He swallowed hard as he wondered how Natalie would decorate their home someday. Lucas could already see his mother's face if she came to visit and it looked anything like this. Yet everything about the place seemed to represent Natalie.

"Can I lay my head in your lap?" Her face twisted in pain. Lucas eased his arm from around her and scooted to the end of the small couch, wishing he could take away some of her discomfort.

"Of course you can. Do you want me to leave so you can rest?"

She readjusted, laying her head on his leg as she got settled on her back. "Not yet."

Natalie closed her eyes, and they were quiet for a while.

"What's wrong, Lucas?"

He'd thought she was asleep. "Nothing. Why?"

"You're tapping your foot, and you haven't been still since you got here."

He cringed. "Sorry. I didn't realize I was doing that. I

guess I just . . ." He was terrified to ask, but he had to know. Would her answer devastate or thrill him? "I want to know . . . if you ever think about us having a family?" There. It was out. He kept his eyes on her and wasn't going to look away until she answered—that way he would know if she was being completely truthful.

"Is that why you've been squirming around?" She playfully poked him in the ribs.

It wasn't the only reason he'd been squirming around, as she put it. A lot of things were making him nervous and anxious, but this was the biggest right now.

"Lucas . . ." She said his name softly, her smile fading and her expression turning serious. "I know the Amish have big families." She leaned up and kissed him on the cheek. He couldn't breathe. "And there is nothing I want more than to have all the babies you want." She smiled. "After we're mar—" She stopped abruptly and cleared her throat. "I mean, when it's the right time, of course."

He stroked her head, his hand gliding through her soft blonde hair as relief washed over him. He hadn't asked her to marry him, but it was clearly assumed since they were discussing having a family. "I wonder what color hair our children will have."

She closed her eyes, yawned, and said, "I hope they all have different colored hair."

Lucas looked around the apartment again. *Diversity.* That was Natalie, with her home furnishings and even her children's hair color. But she wanted children, and Lucas hoped the Lord blessed them with a large family. He was quiet again in case she wanted to sleep.

"You're still fidgeting." She reached up and touched his cheek. "What else is on your mind?"

When they got married, they would likely live in her apartment with electricity, air-conditioning, television, a microwave, and other conveniences the *Englisch* enjoyed.

"I guess I just have a lot of questions." He forced his foot still when he realized he was tapping it again. "I-I was wondering if someday we would live here, in your apartment." He looked around and tried to envision himself sitting on this couch and watching television, dining at the small bar that faced the tiny kitchen, and even sleeping in bed with Natalie, holding her as they drifted off to sleep.

"We might have to, at least for a while." She kept her eyes locked with his. "Is that going to be okay?"

"*Ya*, sure." He scratched his head. "I'll need a job, maybe doing construction work." He wondered where he would find work outside of his community. Could he ever own his own furniture store, or at least build furniture part-time with his brothers?

"You're talented, Lucas." She reached up and cupped his cheek. "You won't have trouble finding a job."

"I-I wonder where we'd go to church." That part probably stung the worse. He wouldn't be allowed to attend worship services with his family.

"I want to find a church home, so that's something we can explore together . . . when the time is right." Again she avoided mentioning marriage. Lucas would need to pose the question, and his thoughts echoed Natalie's words, *when the time is right.*

He had guided Natalie on a spiritual path to God, but

what he'd thought was only a season with her had turned into a lifetime. He waited for fear and regret to take hold of him, but despite the questions spinning in his mind like a tornado, he felt a calm within the storm.

"Lucas . . ." She smiled up at him as best she could. "We don't have to figure out everything right now. I want to continue trusting God and listening to Him. He will show us the way. We can do everything in baby steps." She waved one of her bruised arms around the room. "This isn't you. I know that. If it was up to me, we'd live on a farm out in the country somewhere and have tons of animals."

His heart was full as she dozed off to sleep. He leaned his head back against the couch and closed his eyes. There wasn't anywhere else in the world he wanted to be except here with Natalie. There was freedom in being able to express how he felt about her. They were still getting to know each other in many ways, yet Lucas felt like he'd known her forever.

❦

On Wednesday afternoon, Cecelia stood in the middle of Moses's house with her hands on her hips. Should she call the police and report him missing? He left Monday afternoon to run errands and didn't appear to have been home since then. She'd paid the bills and taken them to the post office since Moses didn't have a mailbox outside. After that, she'd returned and snooped a little. It didn't look like the bed had been slept in, though she had no way to know for sure. There were no dishes in the sink, the pipes still rattled from the toilet running upstairs, and Helen hadn't seen him as of yesterday.

Helen. Every time she recalled their conversation and the look on Natalie's face after hearing it, she wanted to cry. Natalie had left shortly after. She was upset, but at least she'd been answering Cecelia's calls, letting her know she was okay.

Cecelia sank into the worn cushions on the couch and crossed one leg over the other, kicking her foot nervously. Jacob came by earlier. He was alone this time, and he'd gone straight to the barn, presumably to feed the animals and make sure they had water. If he hadn't come by, Cecelia had already decided she would brave it and check on the horses herself.

Maybe she should go ask Helen if she'd heard anything. Doubtful, since none of them had phones, except Lucas, she presumed. She didn't relish another run-in with Helen anyway.

Then there was Tom. She could use this time to consider her ex's intentions. When they talked yesterday morning, he said he was going to leave Olivia. Tom seemed to think he could waltz back into her life as if the past few years hadn't happened. Every time she pictured him moving back in, she remembered the fighting, the heartache, and the blow to her self-confidence. Not to mention what they'd both put Natalie through. Then Moses's face flashed in her mind when she began to contemplate a possible reconciliation with Tom, which didn't make sense. Was it the flattery Moses often threw her way that caused her to feel better about herself? She hadn't received such attention from Tom. Not until recently anyway. He'd thrown it on pretty thick the past couple days. Perhaps Moses was just a safe crush because she knew they could never be together. Or was Cecelia slowly changing into a person who would no longer be compatible with Tom—or tolerant of his behavior?

She jumped when her phone buzzed, and even though she usually didn't answer calls from numbers she didn't recognize, she hoped it might be Moses, and answered.

"Well, hello there. I'm alive and well." It *was* him.

"Moses, where in the world have you been? I've been worried sick!" She uncrossed her legs, stood up, and began to pace.

"I was at the store getting the parts to fix the upstairs toilet when I ran into a man who told me about a horse, a purebred black stallion. I took a bus to Bloomington, bought the horse, and have been trying to find a way to get this beauty home. I borrowed a phone to call and let you know." He drew in a breath. "Anyway, I've paid a man to deliver the horse."

"Don't do that again, worry me like that." Cecelia quit pacing and sat on the couch again.

"Aw, did you miss me?" He drew out the words in that sensual voice he was able to turn on at a moment's notice.

Cecelia tried to stop the grin taking over her face. "That flirty voice doesn't excuse you."

"I really am sorry. And it won't happen again." He paused. "There is one bill I was wondering if you paid. It was a biggie to a fellow named Frank Jones."

Cecelia had hesitated to pay such a large amount, almost ten thousand dollars, but it was in the pile, so she'd written and mailed the check. "Yes, I paid it, but I'd forgotten to ask you if it needed to be recorded as relevant to the horses or house expenses. I dropped several payments at the post office today."

"It was the purchase of a horse. Glad you got that one in the mail. And I've got cash to pay you when I get back."

"Will you be back by Friday?"

He chuckled. "I *do* think you've missed me. And, hey . . . I've missed you."

Cecelia had gone from zero to a hundred when it came to men's affections recently. It was hard not to be flattered, even if it left her confused too. She decided to sidestep the comment.

"Did you take *gut* care of the horses while I was gone?"

Cecelia grunted, unintentionally, and not very ladylike. "Did you just assume I would tend to the horses in your absence?" She would have, but Moses knew she was afraid of them.

"I'd hoped you might face your fears and see what lovable animals they really are."

Sighing, she said, "Actually, one of Helen's sons has been taking care of them."

"They're *gut* kids."

Cecelia stayed quiet. She wasn't going to ask him again when he was coming home since he took the question to mean she missed him.

"You still there?" he asked.

"I'm here."

"Hey, Cecelia."

She grinned. "What? I'm here."

"I'll see you Friday." He couldn't have sounded more seductive if he'd tried.

"Okay, see you then." She pressed End right away so she could answer another incoming call.

"Hi, Tom."

"How's Natalie?"

She raised a hand to her forehead. It was such an abrupt transition from one man to the other. She laughed on the inside at the thought. "She's mad at me about a conversation she overheard between me and Lucas's mother, but she's answering the phone and letting me know she's okay."

Cecelia briefly filled him in about her chat with Helen.

He was quiet for a few seconds. "You don't think she'd ever consider converting, do you? I mean, become Amish?"

"Of course not. Can you picture Natalie living that kind of life? I don't care how much she thinks she loves this guy, it wouldn't happen. If they take things to the next level"—she touched her throbbing temple—"and it sounds like they already have, then it is Lucas who will be making some major lifestyle changes."

"Yeah, I guess so."

Cecelia dropped her hand to her side as she thought about how odd it was to have a normal conversation with Tom. They were just two parents, discussing their child's future.

"Have dinner with me tonight?" There was a desperation in Tom's voice that Cecelia treasured, but she was tempted to say no, to inflict an inkling of the hurt he'd caused her. But she wanted to see him.

"Okay, I suppose. Where?" She tapped a finger to her chin.

"Anywhere you want to go." More sultriness from her other suitor. "I'm still staying at Stan's. There's a new place down the road I think you'd like."

Cecelia didn't care for Stan. He'd covered for Tom many times while Tom was having his affair with Olivia. At least he wasn't asking to stay at her house—*their* old house.

She agreed on the restaurant, and after ending the call, Cecelia left to go get ready for her date with bachelor number one. *Or is he bachelor number two?* He'd been around longer than Moses, so he was bachelor number one, she supposed.

She called Natalie while she drove. "Hi, honey. I'm about halfway home from work, but I wanted to call and check on you."

"I'm okay, Mom. Just sore."

"Do you need anything?" Cecelia eased around an Amish buggy and tried to picture Natalie sitting beside Lucas in one. The vision disappeared in a cartoonish poof.

"No. Lucas was here most of the day, and I slept a lot."

Cecelia bit her tongue. "I'm sorry, again, that you overheard Helen and me. But we both have valid concerns."

"The whole conversation made me sad, but at the end of the day, it's my and Lucas's decision. He told me repeatedly all day that he wants to be with me, no matter what."

"I know, but, Natalie, he'll be giving up the life he was born into. That's a lot of change." When her daughter didn't respond, she said, "I'm having dinner with your father tonight."

There was a lengthy silence before Natalie spoke. "I love Dad, and you know that, but I watched how badly he hurt you. I don't know if it's healthy for you guys to be thinking about a reconciliation, if that's what's going on here."

Cecelia swerved to miss a car that cut into her lane. "I honestly don't know what's going on. But I guess I need to see what's on his mind. Call or text if you need anything."

After she hung up, she pondered Natalie's comments and recognized the role reversal that had inched into their lives—slowly at first, but it seemed to define their relationship now. As Cecelia thought more about it, she was ashamed to admit to herself that it had been going on for a while.

More than once, Cecelia had heard her daughter talking about prayer. It still felt foreign to Cecelia, but as she drove, she figured she didn't have anything to lose. Since she wasn't sure exactly what to pray for, she asked God to give her guidance and help her make the right choice when it came to Tom.

⁓

Lucas lay in bed with his hands behind his head staring at the rafters. He tried to imagine himself sleeping in Natalie's bed with the wild purple-and-red bedspread. The apartment was small, so even though he'd never gone into her bedroom, he saw the corner of her bed from where they had settled on the red couch.

She slept a lot while he was there, which had given him plenty of time to think about all the life changes he would be making in order to be with her. He was glad she was willing to take baby steps toward the life they wanted.

Lucas would miss hearing the roosters ring in each new

day. Would he hear crickets chirping outside her apartment like he could hear them right now? He turned and faced the only window in his bedroom, marveling at the number of stars out. Natalie lived in an area that was well lit at night. Her apartment complex had security lights in the parking lot, and not far off he'd seen businesses with the lights on, people bustling around.

Would they ever have enough money to buy their own farm? Was Natalie a good cook like his mother? Had she ever witnessed the miracle of a calf being born? And would Lucas ever see that again? Did she understand the satisfaction of tending the land, especially at harvesttime, and then coming home exhausted but with an appreciation for the soil that God gave them to work, for the nourishment of their bodies?

Lucas could come up with a hundred more changes that would be forthcoming when it came to having a life with Natalie, and he was willing to do whatever he needed to so he could be with her. One thing would never change. He would leave here with an unwavering faith. The external changes didn't mean his relationship with God had to change. The Lord would stay in his heart no matter where or how he lived. He was sure of that, although other questions rolled around in his mind like tumbleweeds with no direction, traveling wherever the wind blew. His entire future was going in a direction he hadn't planned on, and he needed a clear mind with organized thoughts.

And then she called.

"I love you, and I miss you already," Natalie whispered.

A fierce wind blew into his mind and cleared the tumbleweeds.

"I love and miss you too."

He closed his eyes and listened to the crickets, then gazed out the window at the stars, knowing he would give it all up for her.

CHAPTER 13

Cecelia allowed Tom to kiss her good night after dinner. When he wanted to come in and stay the night, however, she said no, insisting he go back to Stan's to stay. As it turned out, he was still living with Olivia. He was lying to *her* now about Cecelia, and Cecelia had become the other woman. There was only so far Cecelia could go in this scenario. For the first time ever, she felt a little sorry for Olivia, who was clueless that her fiancé was stepping out with his ex-wife.

She was getting into bed when her phone rang. She saw the name and hurried to answer it.

"Natalie, are you okay?" Cecelia squeezed her eyes closed, praying her daughter was all right. *Praying.* It became easier and felt more natural each time.

"Yes, Mom. I'm fine. I'm going to make a full recovery, remember?" She laughed a little, which was nice to hear. "Eventually. Please don't worry so much."

Cecelia let out a breath. "I will try not to worry so much, but no promises."

"I just wondered how things went with Dad."

Cecelia opened her mouth to tell Natalie about her dinner with Tom, about how she'd turned into the other woman, how Tom had kissed her good night, and how confused she was. But she stopped to consider her options and decided she needed to be Natalie's mother, to protect her daughter from fear and worry. For once, she wasn't going to drag her daughter into a situation that only she and Tom could sort out. "It was a nice dinner. I don't know what will happen, but it was an enjoyable evening."

After a few seconds, Natalie said, "That's good. And I want you to know that I'll support any decision you and Dad make, whether it's getting back together or not."

Cecelia blinked back tears, knowing that Natalie needed to hear those same words from her. She took a deep breath. "And I will support whatever decision you and Lucas make about your relationship."

"Really? I mean, no matter what?"

"Really." Cecelia smiled, happy to be having a normal mother-daughter conversation with Natalie, one without sarcasm or attitude—or, in Cecelia's case, constant whining and crying. Cecelia was Natalie's mother after all, not her best friend. Not that the roles couldn't coincide, but she hadn't been the mother Natalie needed for a long time, and she wanted to change that.

"I just want you to know that I love you very much."

"I love you too, Mom."

Cecelia wished her daughter a good night's sleep, closed

her eyes, and decided she'd try talking to someone she was only beginning to know, but who gave her a sense of peace that she'd never had before. *God, are You there?*

Helen stood at the bottom of the ladder that led to Lucas's room. She'd tackled it once before when she spied on her son, but her hip had worsened since then. As badly as she wanted to talk to Lucas, she decided not to ask him to come down-stairs, even though she could see a faint light beneath his door and knew he was likely awake.

When she went into her bedroom, she tiptoed as she changed into her nightclothes, then started out the door to go to the kitchen.

Isaac cleared his throat. "I know you don't go to the kitchen to eat cookies and have warm milk."

Helen froze. "I didn't know you were awake." She slowly turned around. "Hmm . . . How long have you known that?"

"How long have we been married? That's how long." Her husband lit the lantern, then patted the bed. "Come here, *lieb*."

She shuffled to the bed and collapsed as her bottom lip trembled. "I'm feeling bad about the way I talked to Cecelia. I am heartbroken about Lucas. Miriam's boyfriend broke up with her, and while I think she will get over it, she's upset." Helen swiped at her eyes. "Abram has taken to wetting the bed again, and I thought we were past that." She held her head in her hands as a tear slid down her cheek. "And some-times I don't want to talk to anyone about it. I just want to cry. Not talk. Only cry. It might seem silly, I know, but after holding things in, I feel the need to cry it away. And I pray."

Isaac opened his arms wide, and Helen laid her face against his bare chest and cried while he stroked her hair. "You don't have to carry the weight of the world on your shoulders alone, Helen. I'm here. But you must also try not to worry about the things we can't control."

"*Ya*, if only it was that easy," she said as she sniffled.

"If it was easy, we wouldn't appreciate the fruits of our labor." He eased her away and looked into her eyes. "Now, do you know what I think?"

Helen waited.

"I think we should sneak into the kitchen and have a couple of those sugar cookies and maybe even a slice of that key lime pie you made." He pushed her hair away from her face and kissed her on the forehead. "And there's a box of donuts from the bakery on the counter. You know those will be gone right away in the morning, so we might as well have one. And . . ."

Helen stopped crying and smiled.

Isaac laughed softly. "And . . . I have a root beer hidden in the back of one of the cabinets. We can ice it down and split it."

Helen's mouth fell open. They never bought sodas.

"Sometimes you have to change things up, Helen. Let the Lord do His *gut* work while you're stuffing yourself silly."

She gave a taut nod of her head as a grin overtook her face, and together they started toward the kitchen.

"I love you, Isaac," she whispered as they left their bedroom.

"And I love you, Helen."

~

Cecelia showed up at Moses's house right at ten on Friday. Since she'd paid all the bills—and those had added up to a lot—she wasn't sure what to do until he returned home. She wanted to earn the money he was paying her. After locating some cleaning supplies, she gave the furniture a once-over with polish, then swept the wood floors, and when he wasn't home by noon, she found a can of ravioli in the pantry. She'd already opened the can when she realized she didn't know a thing about operating a wood oven. There was kindling in a metal carrier next to it, along with some larger logs. She'd seen Moses retrieve matches from a drawer by the sink. As she looked back and forth between the oven and the can of ravioli, she opted to eat it cold instead of risk burning down the house. She'd loved the stuff when she was a kid, but not so much now, especially cold.

Afterward, she made a list of things he needed to stock the pantry. Cecelia couldn't afford to buy the food, but if he approved the list, she could at least do the shopping so the man wouldn't starve.

It was nearing three o'clock when she heard a car pull onto the gravel drive, and by the time she got to the window, Moses had stepped out of the car. Whoever was driving cut the engine, got out, and leaned against the vehicle.

"Welcome home," she said when Moses came through the door. He was wearing the same clothes as when he'd left Monday. *Or is he?* The only variance in his wardrobe was the shirts, and she supposed he had more than one gray shirt. But he wasn't holding a suitcase. Cecelia could never take an impromptu trip like that—see a man in a store about a horse, then leave right then to go have a look, and stay for days. But if Moses's checkbooks said anything, it was that the guy had money.

He hung his hat on the rack by the door. "Happy to be home." Smiling, he walked toward her and stopped inches away. "You don't have any makeup on."

Cecelia blushed. She'd slowly been wearing less and less—except when she'd gone to dinner with Tom. "I-I've slowly been eliminating it." She didn't want him to think it was solely because of him, so she added, "It's better for my complexion." Besides, the kind of makeup she'd been using for years was expensive, which reminded her of the purse she found in her closet the day before that still had the tags on it. In an effort to improve her financial situation, maybe she could take it back and get a refund.

"I like it." Moses gazed into her eyes, his lips close enough that he could have easily kissed her. When he brushed a loose strand of hair from her face, Cecelia was afraid he might actually do it. And she might have let him. Instead, he eased around her and walked to his bedroom. She willed her heart to stop pounding so hard, but she was glad he hadn't kissed her. She wasn't ready for that, and she still wasn't sure about her feelings for Tom.

Moses returned to the living room a few minutes later with a wad of cash in his hand. "I think I calculated your hours correctly, but if not, just let me know, and I'll get you the rest."

Cecelia accepted the cash, hoping his calculations weren't off.

"I need to tell you something. I'm afraid there was a situation with one of your horses." She paused when Moses frowned. "The horse is fine. And my daughter will be okay, eventually."

Moses's jaw dropped a little bit. "What about Natalie? What do you mean she'll be okay *eventually*?"

His instant concern for her daughter touched Cecelia. She gave him a blow-by-blow account of what happened, leaving nothing out.

"Anyway, Natalie is pretty bruised up, but getting better." Cecelia squeezed her eyes closed, then looked back at him. "She knows she was foolish to think she could ride that horse. I'm so sorry Helen had to tranquilize it. The entire ordeal was terrifying."

"*Ach*, no worries. I'm just glad your daughter wasn't hurt worse. Thank *Gott* for that." He held up a finger as he walked toward his bedroom. "Don't go away. I'll be right back." He closed the door behind him.

Cecelia waited about five minutes but finally got her purse and walked to his door. She didn't open it or knock. "I'm leaving. See you Monday."

"Wait. I'll be out in a minute."

She sat back down on the couch and counted the money he'd given her. He had calculated correctly, and she supposed that to most people, it might not seem like much. But it would scratch the surface on her highest credit card bill. And, more than that, it felt like a huge accomplishment.

After another fifteen minutes, Moses emerged with two large suitcases.

"You're leaving again?" At least he was packing this

time, but by the size of the luggage, she suspected he would be gone longer than four days.

"*Ya*." He hung his head and shook it. "I hate traveling, but sometimes my job calls for it. There are three horses I need to see, but they're in Springfield."

"Springfield, Illinois? That's about a five-hour drive, isn't it?"

Moses nodded. "*Ya*, the driver is waiting to take me to the bus station." He sniffed the air. "It smells like lemons in here."

"I ran out of things to do, so I cleaned a little. I hope you don't mind." Cecelia folded her hands in front of her and wondered if Moses thought her blue blouse brought out the color of her eyes. *Does it really matter if he notices such things?*

"Mind? Of course, I don't mind, but you can always leave for the day if you run out of things to do."

Cecelia was quiet. She needed the money. Maybe if she worked hard, Moses would increase her hours.

"How long will you be gone this time?" The best part of this job, aside from the money she was making, was spending time with Moses. As friends, of course.

"*Ach*, I'm not sure. Maybe a couple weeks." He walked toward her and handed her a piece of paper with numbers on it. "I made some deposits, and here are the amounts I put in each account." He walked back into his room, then returned with a plastic grocery bag, handing it to her. "And these are the bills I need paid while I'm gone."

Cecelia peeked inside the bag. "Good grief. That's a lot of bills." She'd just mailed the other ones. "It won't take two weeks for me to pay these. Which account should I use?"

"These are payments to individuals, people who have done work for me, like farriers, repairmen, a guy I bought hay from, things like that. So, pay them out of the business account." He winked at her. "Then you can do whatever you want."

Cecelia scratched her head with one finger, frowning. "I'm confused. You're paying me to work from ten to three, basically four and a half hours per day, considering the half hour for lunch. What do you mean do whatever I want? I want to earn my paycheck." *Small as it may be.*

He touched her arm. "Don't worry. I'm still going to pay you the hours we agreed on. But for the next two weeks, if you see a project you feel like tackling, have at it. Or if you want to leave early, I'm fine with that too." He removed his hand from her arm and pointed to the plastic bag. "There's also an envelope with some cash for Helen, so she can pay one of her boys to tend to the horses while I'm gone. Tell her I don't want her doing it." *No arguments from me.* "She's got bad arthritis." He hung his head briefly before looking back at Cecelia. "It's sad, too, because she's so young for that."

"Yes, all right." She thought for a few minutes. "Do you mind if I paint the room I'm working in and maybe store some of the sewing things in the basement?" No need to stock his pantry since he was leaving again.

"*Ya*, sure. That's fine." He raised an eyebrow. "How are things with Tom?"

Cecelia's pulse raced at the mention of her ex-husband's name, but the jolt was also fueled by Moses's interest in her love life. She shrugged. "I don't know. We had dinner the other night, and it went okay."

She searched his face for any kind of reaction, but his blank expression wasn't providing any clues. *It shouldn't matter if he cares or not.* Then his eyebrows narrowed into a frown, just briefly, before the poker face returned.

"Could you forgive him?" Moses kept his eyes fused with hers.

"Could you, if it had been Marianne?"

His face took on a calculating expression as he stroked his beard. "I can't imagine Marianne or me ever cheating on each other."

"I couldn't have predicted Tom would either." Cecelia looked down and sighed.

"Hey." Moses gently cupped her chin and lifted her eyes to his. She could tell by the way he was looking at her that he was going to kiss her if she let him. She didn't move when he pressed his lips against hers, the kiss as tender and light as the early-spring breeze wafting in the opened windows. Cecelia basked in the heady sensation.

CHAPTER 14

Helen walked into her bedroom and closed the door behind her. Abram was home from school having a snack, the girls were starting supper, and Isaac was in the barn with the boys. All except for Lucas, who had gone to Levi and Mary's for supper. Presumably Natalie would be there, but she couldn't concern herself with that right now.

Limping to the nightstand, she took out the binoculars and went to the window. Earlier, she'd taken glasses and a pitcher of iced tea to Isaac and the boys. On her way back from the barn, she'd seen Cecelia's car at Moses's house, after three o'clock, which was when she'd been leaving most days. Helen heard the car start in the distance every afternoon when Cecelia left. There was also a driver leaning against the car that must have delivered Moses home.

As she held the binoculars to her eyes, Helen's hands trembled, mostly because she didn't want Isaac catching her spying on their neighbor, but her arthritis was giving her hands trouble too. Moses's front door opened, and he stepped out with two suitcases. Cecelia followed him to the car. Helen supposed he was off on another business trip. *But he just got home.*

After the driver stowed the luggage in the trunk, he went and waited in the driver's seat. Then Moses turned around and hugged Cecelia. Then he kissed her on the mouth, and Helen gasped and dropped the binoculars.

She saw the barn door open, and Eli walked out with his father, followed by the rest of her boys. She quickly scooped up the binoculars and stashed them back in the drawer of the nightstand. She sat on the bed as disappointment rushed over her. Moses and Marianne had been good neighbors and friends to Helen and her family, and she was sure Moses was lonely now that Marianne had passed. But Helen had hoped she was wrong about her neighbor and Cecelia.

She stood up, sighed, and made her way to the kitchen to help the girls get supper on the table, as Isaac and the boys were surely taking their seats. She passed the window in the living room and saw Cecelia's car pull in the driveway. Helen hurried out the front door and met Cecelia in the yard, not wanting that woman anywhere near her family.

Cecelia handed Helen an envelope. "Moses asked me to give this to you. He has to be gone for a couple weeks, and he was hoping one of your sons could look after his horses while he's gone. He asked that you not tend to them because of your arthritis. There's cash in the envelope."

Helen pushed it back at Cecelia, but she didn't take it. "Moses is a *gut* man, and he lets *mei sohns* keep their horses in his barn." She shook her head. "We won't accept payment."

Cecelia shifted her weight. "You can take that up with him when he gets back. But I'm sure he would prefer that you keep the money."

It felt wrong to accept payment since it was just one neighbor helping another, but Helen nodded. Maybe she'd assign Jacob with the task. He probably needed the money the most.

Cecelia looked down, kicked at the grass with the toe of her white sandal, then lifted her eyes to Helen's. "I said some ugly things to you the other day, especially about Lucas, and I want to apologize."

Helen wanted to apologize, too, for some of the things she'd said, but the words weren't coming. God was surely frowning down on her right now. He was presenting her with an opportunity.

"I will speak with Moses when he returns." Helen kept the envelope, turned around, and started back to the house.

She slowed and again considered apologizing to Cecelia, but each time she opened her mouth, she recalled the kiss she'd witnessed, which caused her pulse to pound against her temples. She turned around and called out to Cecelia.

"I saw you kissing Moses." She pointed a finger at Cecelia and waited for her to take on a snappy tone and defend herself. Instead, the woman tucked her chin and went back to her car without looking at Helen or saying another word.

❧

Natalie and Lucas had shown up at Levi and Mary's at the same time, so they walked into the living room holding hands, a show of unity. It felt good to have their feelings for each other out in the open.

But Mary didn't seem to notice. She took one look at Natalie and covered her mouth with her hand as her eyes welled with tears.

"Don't cry." Natalie let go of Lucas's hand and went to Mary. "It looks much worse than it feels." Her eye was really black now, and the entire right side of her face had swollen even more, despite the ice she kept on it. Her upper lip resembled a platypus on one side. She'd worn long sleeves and jeans, even though she knew it would be warm in the house. "But maybe don't hug me." She grinned. "It's not just my face that took a beating." Chuckling, she said, "I had some explaining to do at school today."

Mary lowered her hand from her mouth, glanced at Lucas, then back at Natalie. "I'm so sorry that happened. I really am." She continued to blink back tears, as she was known to cry when someone she loved was hurting.

"What's for supper?" Natalie lifted an eyebrow, hoping to lighten the moment. "You know how much I look forward to this. It's the best meal of the week, plus I get to see you two." She pointed back and forth between Mary and Levi, then turned to Lucas. "And this guy."

"We're having ham, potato salad, green beans, and, of course, buttered bread and chow-chow." Mary sniffled.

"Yum." Mary always prepared a great meal, and chow-chow was always on the table. Natalie loved the pickled vegetables. She followed Levi and Mary into the kitchen, Lucas trailing behind her.

After they'd bowed their heads in prayer, Natalie was

prepared for a bombardment of questions about her and Lucas, but it wasn't until dessert—a peach pie—that Mary cleared her throat.

"So, word travels quickly." She dabbed at her mouth with her napkin. "I understand you two have officially become a couple. Jacob overheard his parents talking about what happened after the horse incident. He had errands in Shoals, so he stopped in to see us."

Lucas had a mouthful of food, so Natalie spoke up. "We love each other, and not being together was hurting us both more than we were willing to bear."

Lucas looked at his brother. "Levi, I know this upsets the entire family, but I hope Natalie and I will have your blessing."

Levi nodded but cast his eyes down.

Natalie glanced at each of them. Lucas had stopped eating. Levi continued looking at his plate, and Mary looked like she might cry again. Natalie looked at Lucas. "But you're not baptized, so you won't be shunned, right?" She knew it to be true but said it as a reminder to everyone.

"*Nee*, I won't be shunned." Lucas turned to Levi. "Be happy for us, *mei bruder*. We want to be together."

In unison, Mary and Levi smiled, though both of their expressions looked forced. "Of course we're happy for you," Mary said without making eye contact with Natalie or Lucas.

Natalie was aware of the sacrifices Lucas would be making to be with her, but she'd wrongly assumed that it would be hardest on his parents. She looked at Levi, whose face was drawn as he moved food around on his plate. Mary still wouldn't look up either.

But wouldn't Lucas also be gaining things he'd never had? A chance to further his education if he chose to. He'd learn to drive and enjoy air-conditioning during the hot summers. He'd be able to watch television, have a cell phone without feeling bad about it, and listen to music. They could go to the movies together, and so much more. But as she looked back and forth between Mary and Levi, who couldn't hide the sorrow in their expressions, Natalie realized something. Everything she'd just thought of—all the things Lucas would gain or be able to do—were just that, *things*, and all external. What about his heart?

She'd underestimated the transitions Lucas would have to make, including the most important one of all. He wouldn't be able to attend the Amish worship services he loved. He'd asked her if they would go to church, but it wouldn't be the same for him.

After studying each of their faces, she felt like an outsider again, and she excused herself to the bathroom.

She closed the door, put down the commode seat, and sat. Mary still hadn't painted over the pink-and-red floral wallpaper. Natalie was glad because it was a reminder of Adeline. She wondered what advice Adeline would give her right now. Her lip trembled as she began to question her relationship with Lucas again, which usually didn't happen when she was with him. She didn't doubt their love for each other, but everything that went alongside that love was going to be a huge challenge for Lucas.

She asked the One who was guiding her steps. *God, I want to do right by Lucas and all those I love.*

One of Mary's dresses was hanging on a hook on the

back of the bathroom door, along with a black apron. Natalie gingerly removed both items, laying the apron on the toilet seat. She slipped the dark purple dress over her head and over her clothes, then put on the apron. She even pulled her hair into a bun on the top of her head, then stared at herself in the mirror.

When she was able to look past her black eye and swollen face, she imagined herself wearing this kind of clothing every day. Then she put herself in Lucas's place and truly considered how he must be feeling about a complete lifestyle overhaul, just to be with her, and everything he was giving up. Maybe Natalie should be the one to convert to his ways.

As she stared at herself in the mirror, a tear slipped down her cheek. She didn't even like to change the furniture around in her apartment. How could she overhaul her entire life to be with Lucas? Yet, he was willing to do it for her. What would she be giving up if she converted to Lucas's way of life? She knew it would be all the things she'd just thought about—those external *things*—that Lucas would be gaining to be with her. Their hearts, their love and devotion to God, weren't going to change no matter how they lived. Even as she considered giving as unselfishly to Lucas as he was prepared to give to her, fear and worry consumed her. If she'd learned anything lately, it was that fear and worry blocked the voice of God. She needed to hear Him more than ever right now. Perhaps the negative emotions had already taken over because she wasn't hearing Him.

I'm sorry, God. I'm sorry, Lucas. I just can't do it.

Natalie took off the apron and dress and hung the items back on the hook, dried her eyes, and went back to join the others.

❧

Cecelia lost sleep Friday night, ignoring calls from Tom, and glad Moses didn't have a phone. How was it that she was mildly involved with two men who weren't right for her?

By the time she woke up on Saturday, she'd decided she wasn't going to spend time with Tom anymore, not as long as he was living with Olivia. And she knew being kissy-kissy with Moses was playing with fire and would never work out. How familiar her advice to herself sounded. Natalie and Lucas had let things build to a point of no return. For once, Cecelia was going to do the right thing and tell Moses she was happy to continue working for him, but they could only be friends. Then she recalled how Natalie and Lucas started out as friends.

She got out of bed, shuffled to the kitchen, and pulled a bottle of vodka from the cabinet. Then she got a glass and filled it one-third full of orange juice. It wasn't something she normally did, at least not recently. But these weren't normal times.

After several long moments of staring at the bottle, she twisted off the top, then poured it down the drain. She wanted to turn her life around, and even though she was doing it slowly, she wanted to keep her stride moving forward, not backward.

She called Tom back Saturday afternoon and told him she had a migraine. They agreed to talk later, so Cecelia spent most of Saturday and Sunday in her bedroom with the blinds drawn.

Thankfully, by the time Monday came around, the

headache was gone, and she was ready to get to Moses's house. She needed to occupy her mind, so she set to writing checks for the people in the grocery bag after she recorded the deposit amounts Moses had written on the slip of paper. They were even more than the last deposits. She'd take the payments to the post office when she left.

She didn't want to abuse her time at Moses's house by being a slacker, so she rummaged around in the basement and found two cans of paint. She wouldn't have been comfortable being paid for leaving early. Taking note of that, she smiled. A year ago, she was in such despair, she probably would have done just enough work to get by, left early, and taken the money.

As it neared three o'clock, she'd finished painting the small sewing room office and moved the things she could lift to the basement, giving her more space to work. It was a hot task, though, without any air-conditioning. She walked outside to get some fresh air, her jeans and white T-shirt splattered with the tan-colored paint. Cecelia wasn't sure what she was going to do to stay busy for the next two weeks.

Jacob walked by in the distance and waved.

She went back inside and poured a glass of iced tea, then walked to the barn.

"I thought you might be thirsty." Cecelia offered the glass to Jacob, glad she'd thought to bring him a drink. The boy was dripping in sweat. He finished filling a bucket with oats and accepted the tea.

"*Danki*," he said after he caught his breath. "I mean, thank you."

Cecelia knew what *danki* meant, but she just said, "You're welcome."

He gulped it all down at once. "I should have brought you a bigger glass." She smiled. "There's a pitcher on the counter in the kitchen and some ice in a cooler nearby. Just help yourself whenever you want."

"Thank you." He handed the glass back to Cecelia. "Looks like you've been painting."

She looked down at her paint-splattered clothes. "Yeah, I have. I'm a messy painter."

"Moses has been gone a lot lately." Jacob leaned over to fill the next horse's bucket with feed.

"More horse deals, but this time in Springfield, Illinois."

Jacob stood and smiled. He was a cute kid, maybe about Natalie's age. Although, several of Helen's children looked to be about Natalie's age. She must have stayed pregnant for years straight.

"That's a long way to go for horses. How's he gonna get them back here?"

"He didn't say, but I guess he'll have to rent one of those horse trailers and hire a driver who knows how to pull it." Cecelia could feel sweat running down the back of her T-shirt. "I'm about done for the day, but help yourself to more tea if you'd like. Moses keeps his doors unlocked."

Jacob nodded.

Cecelia went back to the house, closed the paint cans, and washed the brushes outside under water she had to pump. After she was back inside, she observed her work for the day. Tomorrow she'd do the trim.

She got her purse, reached around until she found her

keys, and looked at her phone. No messages or texts from Tom. That was probably a good thing. At least for now. Not so long ago, Tom had consumed all her thoughts.

There were no lights to turn off when she left, and it always felt odd not to lock the doors, but Cecelia didn't have a key anyway, and she supposed that was how it was done around here. Apparently, Helen kept a watchful eye on the place since she'd caught Cecelia and Moses's little kiss outside.

It was good that he was gone for a while too. Cecelia needed this time to think. As she drove home, she wondered how Natalie was doing. Her phone was almost dead from not having a place to charge it at Moses's house. She'd call her daughter later this evening.

≈

Lucas went back to Natalie's apartment Wednesday night. His visit before felt justified since she had been injured, and he'd wanted to make sure she was okay. But as she moved around the small kitchen, Lucas couldn't get comfortable on the red sofa, and he could hear the TV on low in her bedroom. If he was going to be with Natalie, he would have to start getting used to it. But he was enjoying the air-conditioning.

"The chicken casserole is in the oven. It's my mom's recipe." She sat next to him and covered her face. "Don't look at me. I know I still look awful."

He eased her hands away. "I fell in love with the person you are, not your looks. But you've always been beautiful. And your eye is starting to turn yellow, so it's getting better."

She reached up and touched her mouth.

"Your lip is better too."

"I guess." She rolled her eyes. "I love horses, but I won't be getting on one again for a while."

Lucas glanced at the framed pictures Natalie had hung on the walls. There was one with her mother at the beach and one with her father in the mountains somewhere. When they were married, Lucas would be able to record his life in photos too. Although, the word hadn't come up yet, it seemed assumed for both of them. Maybe she was waiting for him to properly propose. When an *Englisch* man asked a woman to marry him, he gave her a ring, which was unlike how it was done in his community. He didn't have the money for a ring, and he didn't foresee having it for a while. He wondered how much that token of love meant to Natalie.

"My brother called today." Her face lit up. "Remember, I told you Sean is in the army."

Lucas nodded. "*Ya*, I remember."

"I don't hear from him very often. Mom talks to him more than I do, but this time he was calling to ask about her. He said she'd sounded different on the phone recently, better. I told him I thought it had a lot to do with her having a job and a sense of purpose." She shrugged. "It's only part-time, and I know she is still struggling for money, but it's a start, and I'm proud of her."

Lucas was glad Natalie and her mother were finding their way back to each other after her family went through the divorce, but he felt like he was losing his family. His mother barely spoke to him, and his siblings had distanced themselves—everyone but Hannah. At sixteen, Hannah had started her *rumschpringe*, and Lucas wasn't sure much could get her down right now. Every teenager looked forward to that rite of passage when they would be allowed to venture out into the world a little.

Lucas wondered if he would always feel like an outsider within his own family. As he looked around Natalie's apartment, he couldn't imagine himself living here, but it would surely be all they could afford. He wondered again if they would ever have a farm. Would Natalie be happy tending to the land Lucas loved so much? And how much did it matter, as long as they had each other? They'd tried to stay apart, but only for three days. Lucas's head started to throb.

"Are you okay?" Natalie touched his arm.

"*Ya*, sure." He kissed her gently on the cheek. They'd talked about having a family someday, and her desire to do so had eased his mind, but there were still so many questions scrambling for answers in his mind.

⁂

Natalie looked at the man she loved, the man who had saved her life, the man she would hopefully be with forever. She couldn't help but wonder if he would be happy with his new life when they married. She wondered if that was a worry they even needed to have right now. They hadn't been seeing each other that long. Would they ease into the life they'd talked about by building the foundation, then adding to it over time?

"I can see the worry all over your face, Lucas." She reached for his hand and squeezed. "I know we both have a lot to think about, but maybe we'd both feel better if we talk things through."

He brought her hand to his lips and kissed it. "*Ya*, I have a lot on *mei* mind, about how this is going to work, but I'm committed to do whatever I need to because I can't picture my life without you in it." He paused. "But I bet you have questions racing through your mind too."

Natalie was in love with Lucas, and she didn't have any doubts about that, but she recognized that she was only nineteen. Mary and Levi hadn't dated for long when they got married. Both told Natalie separately that they were one hundred percent sure of their commitment to each other, and they were both Natalie's age. Was the fact that she was questioning their ages and how long they'd known each other a sign? Or was it because of all the restructuring in Lucas's life that was forthcoming? Would he be able to adapt to the modernization without resenting Natalie down the line? Was their love strong enough to weather such a transition?

"How does a person know if they have the right kind of love that will last a lifetime? And, don't say anything yet, because I don't want you to think I doubt how much we love each other. But . . ." She gazed into his eyes. "I thought my parents had that kind of love and look what happened."

Lucas leaned his head back against the couch, then scratched his chin. "I think that in an Amish family, since divorce isn't allowed, there isn't ever an escape route. You have to make it work through the good and the bad, no matter what. So, once you remove divorce as an option and accept that you will love your spouse forever, it makes you work harder to have a *gut* relationship."

Natalie smiled. "Then, let's take that wisdom into our own"—she paused, making note that they were still avoiding the word *marriage*—"into our own relationship. A never-give-up, work-hard-at-it, no-matter-what attitude."

Lucas nodded, and they were quiet for a while.

"I sleepwalk." He turned to her and grinned.

Even though Natalie knew about this from Mary, she smiled. "I hope you don't go too far."

He laughed. "Only if I'm sleeping somewhere besides *mei* own bed."

Natalie wondered what Lucas's bedroom looked like. Was it plainly decorated, like the rooms in most Amish homes? She knew he had converted the attic into his bedroom so he could have some privacy. What color was the quilt on his bed? How many lanterns did he use? Was he ever concerned about a fire starting?

From there, the questions filling her mind became even more random. She'd never heard him say he drank coffee. *Does he?* Would he do construction work when they got married? Would he build furniture with his brothers, even after he'd moved out? And when would that be? She knew they would never live together unless they were married. How was this going to work? *Baby steps.*

"I can see the wheels in your head spinning." Lucas nudged her with his elbow. "But we can't figure out everything right now. I think we will have to be like Mary and Levi and compromise."

Natalie lowered her chin and sighed. "I feel like you will be making most of the changes, and I don't ever want you to regret anything." She thought of the way her parents had looked at each other toward the end of their relationship, and she didn't think she could bear for Lucas to ever look at her that way. But this was the second time she'd told him she didn't want him to regret anything. The first time he hadn't responded. She held her breath, needing to hear a response.

"The only thing I would regret is not being with you." He spoke softly and with a tenderness Natalie had come to rely on. Lucas kept her grounded.

Lucas was scooting around the biggest issue, and for a future with Natalie to feel within his grasp, he wanted her to know how serious he was about being with her.

"What's wrong? You're fidgeting again." She leaned her head against his shoulder.

He kissed her temple. "Just hungry."

Lucas had a lot on his mind. He was overwhelmed by everything he would face to be in Natalie's life. But being without her wasn't an option. He swallowed hard. "I want to marry you, Natalie." As his pulse calmed down, he felt like God was reaching out to him, pulling the fear from his heart, and telling him he was where he needed to be—even if it was in Natalie's wild apartment with the red couch, TV, and electricity. "So, will you marry me? I don't have a ring or—"

She squealed so loudly that Lucas's ears rang.

"Yes, yes, yes!"

Lucas burst out laughing. Then she did too. Everything was going to be okay. God wouldn't have led him down this path otherwise.

CHAPTER 15

Cecilia closed the paint cans and once again washed the brushes at the pump outside. It had been almost two weeks since Moses left, and she had repainted most of the inside of his house. It needed it, and it was the same color as before, so she hadn't broken any Amish rules.

Moses had called twice from borrowed phones, and during their last conversation two days ago he'd said he might be gone a little longer than he thought. To Cecelia's surprise, distance wasn't making the heart grow fonder toward Moses. Tom was working hard to win back her heart, and it was almost working until he mentioned he'd fallen on hard times financially. Based on the way he told her, Cecelia believed Olivia was about to kick him out, and he would need a place to live. And apparently his buddy Stan wasn't interested in a roommate.

She didn't think he had expected her to read between

the lines. She'd turned him down twice since he'd asked her to dinner. He'd gotten mad, and Cecelia remembered the way their marriage ended. After all this time, she was able to see Tom's true colors a little clearer.

Back in Moses's living room, she wondered why in the world he hired her when he clearly didn't have enough for her to do. But he had a freshly painted house, and Cecelia had been able to get her head straight. Maybe she needed to take up painting as a full-time job. She chuckled at the thought. But she did need to find a job that was forty hours per week, and she would talk to Moses about it when he returned. She'd been searching online for bookkeeping jobs in the evenings since that was something she knew how to do. She'd also returned some of the more luxurious items she'd bought recently. She lost money on some of the jewelry, but it gave her some quick cash. She returned the purse to the boutique where she'd purchased it, and the clerk gave her a full refund. Those items felt less important to her these days.

She started closing the windows in the house. Not that it mattered. If anyone wanted to steal anything, they could walk through the unlocked door. If she left the windows open, it would help with the paint smell, but after thinking about it, she closed them. She'd open them back up tomorrow.

When she couldn't find her keys in her purse, she sat on the couch and rummaged around, finding them just as her phone started to buzz.

"I wanted to tell you this in person, but I can't wait any longer." Natalie sounded breathless. "And, I'm sorry. I told Mary. Maybe I should have told you first. I don't know."

"Goodness, what is it?" Cecelia stiffened as her pulse picked up. "Nothing bad, I hope."

"Nope. Nothing bad. Guess what?"

Cecelia grinned. "Um . . . I have no idea."

"Guess."

Leaning back against the couch, Cecelia took a deep breath and wondered if this was a trivial matter or something huge. Natalie tended to approach the big and little things with an exaggerated level of excitement. Cecelia would be happy for her daughter no matter what it was. "Just tell me."

"Lucas asked me to marry him, and I said yes!"

Cecelia sat straight up, blinking a few times. Her first inclination was to say that it was way too soon, that Natalie hadn't thought things through and she was too young. But in her efforts to reclaim her life, Cecelia was trying to control only the things she could. Controlling Natalie had never been an option. She did what she wanted, and she'd always been a good kid and made mostly good choices. But this was more than just deciding whether to go to college or buy a new car. Marriage was a lifelong commitment. *At least, it's supposed to be.* "Oh," she finally managed to say. "When?"

"Um . . . about a week ago. And I need you to be happy for me because I'm thrilled. You know how much I love Lucas."

Cecelia had talked to Natalie on the phone almost every night over the past week. She suspected her daughter was afraid to tell her, fearful Cecelia wouldn't be happy for her. She took a deep breath and tried to choose her words carefully. She and Natalie had managed to work their way back to a good mother-daughter relationship, and Cecelia didn't want to mess that up. "If you're happy, I'm happy, sweetheart. It-it's a lot to think about. Mostly for Lucas and how it will . . ." Cecelia's heart began to hammer as she realized Natalie hadn't said which one of them would be conforming to the other person's way of life. "Are you, uh, or is he, um . . . someone will have to change their life if you two are going to get married."

"Breathe, Mother. I'm not converting to Amish. Lucas is willing to make the changes so we can be together."

Cecelia relaxed her shoulders and closed her eyes as relief flowed through her. This might not be the ideal situation, but she was going to trust her daughter's decisions. Or at least try to. "Have you set a date?"

"No, not yet. We're going to gradually work toward the type of life we think will suit us both. Even though Lucas will be making the most changes, I want the transition to be easy on him, so I'll be making some adjustments too. We haven't gotten into the details yet, but we are in love, and we can have God in our hearts no matter how we choose to live."

It sounded logical, although Cecelia suspected her daughter was so caught up in being in love that she hadn't thought much further. She would have to keep reminding herself that this was in God's hands, not Cecelia's.

"Sweetheart, I want to hear all about this, and we can talk more later, but a car just pulled into the driveway." *A sheriff's car.*

Cecelia knew Natalie was okay. But Sean? *Dear God, please don't let anything have happened to my son.* She didn't want Natalie to worry, so she told her goodbye without mentioning what kind of car had pulled in.

Her lip trembled as she walked to the door, which was open. On the other side of the screen two sheriff's deputies were walking up the porch steps. "What's wrong?" she asked as she brought a hand to her chest.

"Can we come in, please?" The taller of the two men spoke.

Cecelia pushed open the screen door and stepped aside. "Is my son, Sean, okay? What's wrong?" Even though Sean wasn't in active military duty, that status could change. Maybe he was being sent overseas. But they didn't send sheriff's deputies to your place of work for that.

"Are you Cecelia Collins?"

She nodded as tears built in the corners of her eyes. The moment she opened the door, she could tell by the solemn expressions on the men's faces that this was more serious than a traffic violation.

"Your son is fine, as far as we know." The taller deputy pulled loose a set of handcuffs attached to his belt. "Can you turn around, please, and put your hands behind your back? You're under arrest. You have the right to remain silent . . ."

Cecelia was in a fog, not understanding what the man was saying as the handcuffs clicked behind her back. "What did I do? What did I do?" She'd never been in jail. She had never even visited someone in jail. "Why are you doing this?" Somewhere in the process, she'd started to cry. "What am I being charged with?"

The quiet deputy gently turned her around and spoke to her. "Do you seriously not know?"

Cecelia was shaking so badly, she couldn't speak.

The deputies exchanged a glance, both scowling. "You've bounced checks in excess of one hundred thousand dollars, for starters. But you are also being arrested for writing checks to known drug runners."

Cecelia struggled to catch her breath, then said, "Wait. Wait. Wait. You have the wrong person. I can see where the mistake has been made. I am only a bookkeeper. I wrote those checks for Moses Schwartz. I sign on his accounts as a convenience. I was just following his instructions." She couldn't imagine Moses being involved in something like this, but stranger things had happened. Still trembling, she could at least see the bigger picture. "It's Moses you want. This is his house."

"Ma'am, we've never heard of Moses Schwartz, and this house is in your name."

Cecelia went weak in the knees and almost fell. "I-I need to call my daughter."

"After you're booked and processed, you'll get a phone call." One deputy guided her out the door, and the other picked up her purse.

What is happening?

❧

Helen folded her hands across her stomach as she stood in the barn with the rest of her family. Lucas waited until everyone was present before he said he had an important announcement to make. The barn had been their meeting place for family gatherings for as long as Helen could remember, weather permitting.

There were bales of hay for her children to sit on, though Jacob usually perched atop the workbench, and Isaac had a special chair in the corner. It was an unspoken rule that meetings in the barn were not to be missed, as they were reserved for important topics.

Today, fear wrapped around Helen's heart and squeezed so hard that she almost felt faint. Isaac had offered her his chair, but she wanted to stand, even if she stood on wobbly legs. What was Lucas about to tell them? In Helen's heart, she knew, but she prayed steadily to God that she was wrong.

"*Danki* for coming." Lucas addressed his family with a formality that confirmed to Helen that the news wasn't going to be good. "Normally, this kind of announcement would be published and there wouldn't be a need for this meeting."

Helen placed a hand over her heart and leaned against the workbench next to where Jacob was sitting. Her son rested a hand on her shoulder, as if he knew what was coming too. Helen glanced around at all of her children, and then at her husband. Each person in the musty barn was solemn, their expressions filled with dread. Miriam even had tears in her eyes.

"But this news won't be published, and I wanted you to hear it from me." Lucas paused, took off his hat, and wiped sweat from his forehead. He held on to the hat, dangling it at his side, and his eyes found Helen's. "I've asked Natalie to marry me, and . . ." Her son's voice cracked only slightly. No one might have noticed, except for Helen. "And she said *ya*, and I won't be baptized into our faith." He kept his eyes on Helen, whose bottom lip was quivering now. "I need you all to be happy for me."

Helen wanted to run to him, throw her arms around her son, and beg him not to do this, but she pressed her lips firmly together. Her children began to congratulate their brother with an empty enthusiasm that was less than genuine, an emotion Helen couldn't summon as she looked down at her bare feet atop the soft dirt.

Slowly, his siblings either shook Lucas's hand or hugged him briefly before they left the barn. Isaac didn't rise from his chair. When everyone was gone, Helen slowly made her way to Lucas and wrapped her arms around her much taller son, burying her face in his chest, wishing he was a child who had to be obedient. But Lucas was a grown man.

Helen held on to her son for a long while before she released him and left the barn. She couldn't bring herself to congratulate Lucas, which she might regret later, but right now, she wanted to be alone. It wouldn't be in the kitchen, where some of her children would gather. She would go to her bedroom and hopefully have time to gather herself before her husband joined her. She left the two men alone, knowing Isaac would want to talk to Lucas privately.

～

Lucas's heart was breaking, and he didn't know what to expect from his father, but seeing his mother's expression and feeling her disappointment had almost been too much to bear. Lucas was sure his siblings had expected this, and maybe his parents had, too, but family was everything to Lucas. He was going to hold out hope that his father had at least one positive thing to say about his proposal to Natalie.

His dad slowly stood up, walked to the workbench, and leaned against it, facing Lucas a few feet away. "You had to know this wouldn't go well," he said as he stroked his long beard. "And I know by the look on your face that this has been a difficult choice for you, no matter how much you *lieb* the *maedel*."

Lucas looked up at his father because he knew he wouldn't continue until he had Lucas's full attention.

"I will ask you only one question, *mei sohn*."

Lucas waited, praying he would answer his father truthfully no matter what the question was.

"Love presents itself in many forms, and often in many layers. Each layer must support the others. As a person ages, weathering over time, the layers of our skin become thinner and dependent on the other layers to be supportive, strong, and resilient. A person in love must also make sure the depth of his emotions is strong and supportive enough to sustain him throughout the layers of life." His father paused and locked eyes with Lucas. "Is this the kind of love you have for Natalie?"

"*Ya*." Lucas didn't hesitate, but after he'd answered, he wondered if he understood his father completely, but maybe some things could only be deciphered with time. All Lucas knew for sure was that he loved Natalie, and he never wanted to be without her.

His father nodded. "Then go in peace with *mei* blessing."

Lucas was grateful for his father's words but wondered if he would ever have his mother's blessing.

Helen didn't know she could still run at all, but she ran toward the barn as fast as she could, her hip on fire the whole time. "Cecelia was just arrested!" She made the announcement to Isaac and Lucas, who were leaning against the workbench. "She was taken away in handcuffs. I saw it out of our bedroom window." She glanced at her husband, knowing he would be unhappy that she was spying on the neighbors again, but surely it would be overlooked this time.

Lucas's jaw dropped as he walked to his mother. "Why was she arrested? Does Natalie know?"

Helen held up her palms. "I have no idea. I just saw her hauled away in a sheriff's car, handcuffed!"

Lucas pulled a cell phone out of his pocket.

Helen had wanted to ask him how long he'd had a cell phone ever since she found the cord in his drawer. He'd never pulled it out in front of anyone. But now wasn't the time to question him about it.

Lucas walked around her, the phone to his ear.

Isaac gently took Helen's arm, and they followed Lucas out of the barn. By the time they caught up to their son, who was standing in the middle of the front yard, he was talking to Natalie.

"*Nee, nee.* I don't know anything," Lucas said. "*Mei mamm* just saw it happen." He listened for a few seconds before turning to his father. "*Daed,* when someone is arrested here in Orleans, where would they go?"

Isaac stroked his beard. "To Paoli."

Lucas turned away briefly for a few seconds, then ended his call with Natalie. "I have to go." He looked back and forth between his parents. "I need the buggy."

Isaac nodded, and after Lucas had run to ready the horse and buggy, Helen groaned. "I knew that woman was trouble."

෪

Natalie sat in the small waiting area of the Paoli jail, waiting for her mother to be released. She'd paid the ten-thousand-dollar bond, filled out the paperwork, and was trying to ignore the curious stares from people coming in and out—officers, visitors, a maintenance guy carrying a weed eater, and a mailman. Maybe she was just overly self-conscience about her black eye and busted lip.

Her mother had lucked out. Today happened to be the day cases went before the judge, and she wouldn't have to spend the night.

Natalie turned when the door opened again. Lucas walked in and sat beside her. "What's going on?"

"Thank you for coming," she whispered as two deputies came in. One actually snickered.

"You don't see that often—an Amish guy in here." The men disappeared behind a door that read Authorized Personnel Only.

Lucas didn't seem to notice, or if he did, he ignored it.

"She was charged with writing bad checks—like a ton of them for a lot of money—and apparently being involved somehow with drug dealers." Natalie struggled to maintain her composure. "I know this can't be true. My mom has never been in trouble. She probably has a few creditors calling, but she'd never do anything like this. *Never*."

A door to their left swung open, and Natalie's mother

came out, shaking and crying, followed by another woman who handed her purse to her. Natalie rushed to her and threw her arms around her. Her mother cried on her shoulder for a few seconds before she lifted her head and looked at Lucas.

"Your neighbor did this to me. Moses set me up." She stomped a foot, crying harder. "How could he do this?"

Natalie motioned for Lucas to follow them outside and kept an arm around her mother, guiding her to the door.

Once they were outside, her mother completely broke down, bending at the waist and sobbing. "I only did what he told me to do. I only signed checks he approved." She straightened as her eyes blazed with anger. "His house is in my name! And it's not like I can keep it. He's so far behind on the mortgage that it's about to go into foreclosure." She tossed her head from side to side, wild strands of hair slapping at her face. "Why would he give me a house? Why is this happening? And where is he?" She looked up at the sky. "I've had enough!"

Natalie glanced at Lucas. His jaw hung low, and his eyes bulged.

"And how did *his* house get in *my* name?" Her mother asked again as she dropped her purse. Lucas quickly picked it up and handed it back to her, then looked over his shoulder when his horse neighed. His buggy was tethered to a pole at the far side of the parking lot.

"I don't know, Mom, but we will get it figured out." Natalie looped an arm through her mother's and coaxed her toward the car. She told Lucas she would call him later. She felt bad that he'd traveled the eight miles in his buggy, only to turn around and go home, but right now, Natalie's mother needed her.

"I'm going to need an attorney. I heard someone say I'll have to pay back the money." She sobbed harder. "Where would I get a hundred thousand dollars when I can't even pay my mortgage or credit card bills?" When they got to the car, she swiped at her eyes and looked at Natalie. "Why would he do this?"

Natalie blinked back tears of her own. "I don't know, Mom, but yeah, I guess we need a lawyer. At least I have enough money for that." After the ten-thousand-dollar bond she'd paid, Natalie tried to mentally calculate what she had left from the sale of Adeline's piano. She'd bought a more reliable car with the money, paid for this semester's tuition and books, and given some to her mother when she needed it. She was sure her mother would be found innocent, but at what price? Lawyers were expensive. Would she have enough left to finish four years of college—*if* she chose to keep going? These were questions she didn't have answers to, but she was going to do whatever was needed to clear her mother of this horrible injustice.

"Let's get you home." Natalie finally got her mother in the car, but no matter what Natalie said, she just cried.

"Mom, this is a huge mistake, and we will get it straightened out." Natalie heard the shakiness in her voice. Neither she nor her mother knew a thing about the legal system. They'd never been caught up in anything like this before.

"I'm going to get a court-appointed attorney so you don't have to spend your money. It's your money, whether you choose to stay in school or not."

Natalie blinked back tears as the knot in her throat grew. She had watched what divorce could do to a person, the bitterness and ugliness of it all. Now, she was witnessing another transition in her mother. She was putting her daughter first, which made Natalie want to help her even more. "No, we'll get you your own lawyer."

Her mother cried harder. "I will find a way to make this up to you." She took a tissue from her purse and blew her nose. "I should have known better than to blindly trust a man I barely knew, but he's Amish. They're supposed to be honest and good."

"I guess there are bad people in every walk of life." Natalie thought for a while. "Maybe Dad can help us."

"Ha. No way. Your father is apparently overextended himself. Olivia is about to throw him out. I think he was only trying to start up things with me because he was going to need a place to live soon."

Natalie's mouth fell open as she glanced at her mother. "You're kidding!" Her heart hurt, and she was angry that her father would try to worm his way back into their lives under false pretenses. Especially since her mother had been working so hard to take back her life. Natalie feared this might be a big step backward.

⁂

Lucas didn't get home until almost ten, and by the time he got the horse in the barn, his legs felt like lead as he shuffled across the front yard. His parents were on the porch sitting in the rocking chairs. Lucas didn't want to talk about this now, but it was going to be unavoidable.

His mother stood. "What did Cecelia do to get arrested?"

Lucas believed Natalie about her mother's innocence, but he was having a hard time believing Moses would set up Cecelia. There had to be another explanation, but until one presented itself, he'd have to go with what he knew. "It sounded like Moses set her up by putting her name on his checking accounts and telling her there was more money in the accounts than there actually was. Whatever happened, a lot of checks that she signed bounced."

His mother grunted. "Moses wouldn't do that." She raised her chin and folded her arms across her chest.

"Then where is Moses? He didn't come back when he was supposed to. And why would he put his house in Cecelia's name?"

His mother's eyes widened. "What?"

Lucas took off his hat and sat on the top porch step, twisting slightly to face his parents. His mother had sat in the rocking chair again. "Natalie said her mother has never been in any kind of trouble before, and by the way Cecelia was crying and carrying on, I'm sure she didn't do what she's being accused of." He rubbed his tired eyes. "Can we talk about this tomorrow?"

His mother shook her head, but his father said, "*Ya*, we will talk about it tomorrow."

"And what about the proposal—"

"That can be discussed later also." His father spoke firmly, and Lucas was grateful.

He got up and trudged into the house. Everyone was in his or her room, and he was relieved. He didn't want questions. He just wanted to talk to Natalie. But when he called, it went straight to voice mail.

His head was spinning with so many questions, and he needed to know if the odd feeling in the pit of his stomach was all in his mind. Or had Natalie seemed distant? She was understandably preoccupied with her mother, but something else felt off to Lucas.

⁂

Helen kicked her rocking chair into motion as she chewed on her bottom lip. "You don't think that's true about Moses setting up Cecelia, do you?" She looked at her husband, who shrugged.

"I don't know. Maybe."

Helen frowned. "How can you say that? How many times did we have Moses and Marianne over for supper? Probably not nearly as many times as they had you and me as their guests for a meal. They were always the first to volunteer for a project or assist anyone who needed help." She lowered her head and folded her hands together before she looked back at him. "I don't believe it."

Isaac was quiet, yawning as he stroked his beard.

"Maybe it's a big misunderstanding that Moses will clear up when he returns." Helen unfolded her hands, brushed away strands of gray hair that had fallen from beneath her prayer covering, and pondered what Cecelia had to gain by writing checks that wouldn't clear. Was it some kind of effort to get Moses's house, and if so, how?

"*If* he comes back." Isaac scratched his cheek before his hand found its way back to his beard.

"Of course he'll come back. He has thousands of dollars'

worth of horses over there. And I don't care what Lucas said, Moses wouldn't give Cecelia his *haus*."

"Moses and Marianne weren't here that long. They'd only moved here a year or so before she died a few months ago." He stilled his hand and turned to face Helen. "How well did we really know them?"

Helen's jaw dropped. "They were our friends. Moses is *still* our friend. Even if he did make a bad choice by getting involved with Cecelia."

"Do you remember, after Marianne died, Moses bought a kitchen set from us?"

Helen nodded. "*Ya*, he said he didn't need the big dining room table they had anymore. He sold it and bought the one you and Jacob made."

"*Ya*, but the check he gave me wasn't *gut*. I needed cash for something that day, so I went to the bank it was drawn on, and the teller said there were insufficient funds to cash it."

Helen scowled. "You never mentioned that."

Isaac shrugged as he dropped his hand to his lap. "His *fraa* had recently died, and I figured he forgot to make a deposit or something. I never said anything and neither did he. I tried to cash it again a week later, but there still wasn't enough money in his account."

"Why didn't you confront him? It wasn't that long ago, only a few months." Helen remembered the time and craftsmanship Isaac and Jacob had invested in the project. "Didn't you sell it to him for five hundred dollars?" They could have used that money. They lived hand to mouth most days.

"*Ya*. But like you said, he was our friend. I was waiting for him to make it right."

Helen closed her eyes and leaned her head back, trying to rationalize Moses's actions. "He was grieving, and like you said, he probably forgot a deposit. I'm sure that was an isolated incident."

"*Nee*, I don't think it was."

Helen yawned. This was the second time she and Isaac had stayed up past their normal bedtime recently, and four o'clock was going to come early. "What makes you say that?"

"Joseph Zook told me in private that Moses owed him some money, that a check he'd given him for hay didn't clear the bank. At that point, I figured the poor fellow was having financial troubles we didn't know about. Folks gossip, so I didn't tell him I'd also gotten a bad check from Moses."

Helen was quiet.

Isaac stood. "I'm going to bed. You coming?"

"*Ya*." But Helen didn't budge.

Isaac leaned down and kissed her on the forehead. "I see your wheels spinning, *mei lieb*, but consider what Cecelia would have to gain from this. It does sound like maybe she is taking the fall for Moses."

Helen recalled the things she'd said to Cecelia the day they'd had words. If what her husband said was true, then Helen owed Cecelia even more of an apology than before. Helen had practically come out and said her people were better than the *Englisch*. It had been an awful thing to say, but Cecelia had put down Helen's family and fueled her words. That still didn't make it right, though.

She reached for the lantern on the table beside her, pushed herself up, and with a hand on her hip, began to make her way into the house.

After she closed the front door, she hobbled to the bedroom but slowed in the middle of the living room, then turned to go to the kitchen. She placed the lantern on the table, then sat and held her head in her hands, wondering how she'd ever get to sleep. Her body was exhausted, but she couldn't turn off her mind. Their friend and neighbor apparently wasn't who he'd seemed to be. And one of her children was choosing marriage to an *Englisch* woman instead of being baptized into their faith.

She put a hand over her mouth to muffle her cries. Then she prayed for God to somehow make everything all right.

CHAPTER 16

Natalie sat beside her mother on one side of a large oak desk. A small man with silver hair and thick black glasses sat across from them. It had taken two weeks to get an appointment with Roger Livingston, the best criminal attorney in the area, according to Natalie's mother. Natalie had asked around as well, and Mr. Livingston's name kept coming up. She hoped he would be worth his high-dollar retainer.

Between school and helping her mother, Natalie had less time to worry, and Lucas's proposal had gotten lost in the shuffle. When she talked to him in the evenings, a sense of calm fell over her, and she felt strong enough to get up the next day and do what she needed to do. As she nodded off to sleep each night, she'd picture her life with Lucas. For now, she needed to stay focused on her mother's situation.

After introductions, Mr. Livingston had sat and opened a folder on his desk. "Before our meeting today, I did some checking around based on what you told my paralegal on the phone." He pulled out a sheet of paper with handwritten notes. "First of all, Moses deeded his house to you." He looked over the rims of his thick glasses. "And you signed the deed."

"No, I didn't." Natalie's mother pressed her lips together and shook her head.

Mr. Livingston pushed a piece of paper toward them. "This is a quitclaim deed." He pointed to the bottom of the page. "Is this your signature?"

Even Natalie recognized her mother's handwriting.

"Yes, but . . ." Her mother paused, her lip trembling. "He only asked me to sign forms for the bank so I could sign checks on his accounts. I signed a couple of other documents, but . . ." She pulled out the reading glasses she always complained about, put them on, and studied the paper in front of her. "I might have signed a few things without my glasses on, but I-I . . ." She took off the glasses. "Yes, that's my signature, but I assure you I didn't know what I was signing."

Natalie believed that. Her mother hated those glasses and didn't wear them unless she was alone.

Mr. Livingston leaned back in the oversize leather chair and rubbed his clean-shaven chin. "Any idea why he'd want you to have his house? Were you two involved in a romantic relationship?"

Her mother glanced at Natalie, then back at the lawyer. "No."

Mr. Livingston took off his own glasses and grimaced. "If I'm going to be your lawyer, you're going to have to be honest with me. A neighbor said she saw you kiss Moses not long ago. Carrie, my paralegal, asked around about him.

Apparently, the district attorney also did some digging and was told the same thing by the same woman."

Natalie's jaw dropped. "Mom, is that true?"

Her mother's face turned as red as her fingernail polish. "We kissed a couple times, but there was not a relationship, or anything else, for that matter. I planned to tell him when he returned that I wanted to remain friends. I was also planning to look for another job that was full-time."

"Well . . ." Mr. Livingston slipped his glasses back on and studied his notes. "The fact that someone saw you kissing, and the fact that he deeded his home to you, makes it look like the two of you were involved—and in collusion."

Natalie leaned her head back and closed her eyes. *This keeps getting worse and worse.*

"Furthermore, Moses wasn't a signer on the bank accounts, only you."

"That's not true. He had me sign two signature cards. One had his name at the top and was for household expenses, and the other was his business account."

"A business *you* own." Mr. Livingston pushed another piece of paper toward Natalie's mother. "You signed this transfer of ownership, too, but it wasn't from a man named Moses. It was from a man we haven't tracked down yet, possibly this Moses using another name. We aren't sure."

Natalie's mother lifted a hand to her quivering lip as she blinked back tears. "What about the account I paid the household expenses out of?"

"The name on that account was Marianne Schwartz, not Moses Schwartz." Mr. Livingston sighed. "I know that's his deceased wife, but the checks from that account cleared the bank. Only the ones from the business account in your name bounced."

Natalie's stomach churned.

"Look, it's fairly easy to see that this guy set you up pretty good," Mr. Livingston said. Natalie's mother lowered her head and covered her face as her shoulders shook. "The tricky part is that we will have to convince a jury that you didn't know what you were signing, specifically the quit-claim deed and transfer of ownership for the business. And that you were paying bills that Moses—we'll call him that for now—instructed you to pay."

Natalie reached an arm around her mother's back. "Mom, it's going to be okay."

Mr. Livingston closed the file and stood. "There will be a preliminary hearing, and the judge will decide whether or not there is sufficient evidence to warrant a trial."

Natalie rose from her chair on shaky legs, her mother following suit, as she dabbed at her eyes and nodded.

"My paralegal is going to keep researching, but I might need to hire a private investigator to find out more information about Moses, or whoever he is. That's not included in my retainer. This isn't a big enough crime for the police to put at the top of their list. Hopefully, we can find out about Moses before the hearing."

Natalie's mother sat back down, covered her face again, and cried. Then she looked at Mr. Livingston. "No private investigator."

Natalie sat and patted her mother's leg. "Yes, Mom. If he thinks you need a PI, we'll hire one."

Her mother offered a weak smile. "No. You're already

spending too much money on this. And I'm going to pay you back."

Natalie didn't see how her mother was ever going to pay her back, but she would not let her go to jail for crimes she didn't commit, at least not intentionally.

Mr. Livingston cleared his throat. "Let's see what we can find out before the preliminary hearing, and then we can readdress the issue of a private investigator if necessary."

They stood again, and through her tears, her mother thanked Mr. Livingston and shook his hand.

After they left the lawyer's office, Natalie stopped at the first restroom she saw and pointed at the door. "Do you need to go?"

Her mother shook her head and leaned against the wall. "I'll be right back."

Natalie closed the stall door behind her and threw up.

⌘

Before supper, Lucas told his parents that Natalie was coming over to talk to the three of them afterward. She hadn't said much on the phone, and Lucas was nervous about the meeting. Over the past couple weeks, he had talked to Natalie every night, and twice they'd met at the library, but he'd felt distance growing between them since Natalie's mother was arrested.

Their meeting with the lawyer had been earlier today. Lucas asked her on the phone earlier how it went, and she said she would explain everything tonight. *But why come here?* And why involve his parents?

He'd only had a brief conversation with his family about marrying Natalie. Cecelia's arrest had temporarily overshadowed their engagement, but Lucas knew that when the dust settled, there would be more discussion.

After supper, Lucas and his parents walked outside when they heard a car pulling in.

"I don't understand why she needs to talk to us." His mother sat in one of the rockers, but Lucas and his father remained standing and waited for Natalie to reach them. She stopped at the bottom porch step.

Lucas could tell right away that she'd been crying. Her black eye was almost completely healed, but both eyes were puffy.

"Thank you for agreeing to meet with me." Natalie paused, and Lucas thought she sounded oddly formal. "As you know . . ." Her lip quivered. Lucas wanted to hug her, but it would only further upset his mother if he showed affection toward Natalie in front of them.

"As you know," she began again, "my mother has been charged with a crime. Today we met with an attorney, and we will have to go to a preliminary hearing in May." A tear slipped down her cheek, and again, Lucas resisted the urge to go to her. "My mother has never been in any trouble. She has no history of criminal activity. And she is devastated beyond words that this is happening—that she trusted a man she believed to be good and honest."

Her tears were glazing over into a glare as she found his mother's eyes. "Moses Schwartz, or whatever his name really is, intentionally set up my mother. She is being accused of bouncing a lot of large checks. He also had my mother unknowingly sign a quitclaim deed to his house, although we have no idea why, except to make it look like they were in collusion. He also coerced her to sign a transfer of owner-ship for his business. We don't know why he did that either.

"So, Mom now owns his company and is the only signer listed on his checking account, which has no money in it. Mom never saw a bank statement. Moses told her the amounts of the deposits he said he was making." She paused, snif-fling. "I know Lucas has told you some of this. And maybe we could have proven it all as a setup, but because some-one saw my mother and Moses kiss, it adds strength to the case that they were in collusion. And they weren't!"

Natalie was sobbing now and covered her face with her hands briefly. Lucas walked to her side, but she stepped away from him, locking her eyes on his mother.

She lowered her head, and Lucas suspected she was the person who offered up the information about the kiss. His father held a stoic expression but kept his eyes on Natalie.

"We believed Moses to be who he said he was." His father spoke with authority, and Lucas prayed things didn't get ugly. Natalie was overwhelmed with emotion, and right-fully so, but his family had nothing to do with what had happened. Natalie had seemed calm and rational during their visits at the library and phone conversations, even though he'd felt some distance between them. This meeting must have been more difficult than she'd expected.

"Helen . . ." Natalie blotted her eyes with a tissue she had crumpled in her hand. Lucas prayed again that Natalie didn't attack his mother verbally, because Lucas was sure his father would defend her. "I know you and my mother have had words in the past, and you both live different lives. But my mother has been through a lot. She is a good person and has been working hard to put her life back together after her divorce from my father. I don't know you very well, but I do know you are against Lucas and me getting married." She looked at Lucas's father. "And you too," she said. "But this man was your friend."

Natalie looked at Lucas with the saddest look he'd ever seen, her eyes swollen, tears streaming down her cheeks, her mouth trembling. "I love you with all of my heart, Lucas. And I wanted more than anything to be your wife."

Lucas heard her speaking in past tense and felt his own lip beginning to quiver as his heart pounded like a jackhammer in his chest.

"But I think we should put any plans of marriage on the back burner for now. I need to focus on this situation with my mother."

Lucas took the steps necessary to get close enough to hold her arms. "Don't do this, Natalie. Forget about everyone else for a minute, even *mei* parents." He waved a dismissive hand in their direction. His father stepped forward and was about to say something when his mother stood, put a hand on his father's chest, and shook her head, signaling him to wait.

"It's us. You and me. I love you with all of my heart too." Lucas tried to keep the shakiness out of his voice. "I'm willing to change everything about my life to be with you."

She reached up and cupped his face with one hand. "And you shouldn't have to. Don't you think I see how uncomfortable you are at my apartment? Your family is so hurt that you won't be baptized into the faith you were born into, even

Levi, and it's devastating to your parents." She paused, sniffling. "This is going to be all-consuming with my mother for a while, and she needs me. Maybe we need to step back for a while and see our situation the way everyone else does."

Lucas lowered his head as she moved her hand from his cheek, mostly because he didn't want her—or his parents—to see the tears in his eyes. "Don't do this, Natalie. We aren't everyone else." He looked at her. "No one is forcing me to leave my community. It is a choice I made because I want to be with you."

She looked at Lucas's parents. His father's expression hadn't changed, but his mother had tears in her eyes as she looked at Lucas.

"I am my mother's only support system. I'm all she has. And she has been wronged because she trusted whoever lived in that house—someone she met through your family." She pointed toward Moses's house.

"I'm not blaming you." Still crying, she looked at his mother. "I'm not blaming anyone." But it sounded like she was blaming them, even if just a little. Natalie lowered her head for a few seconds, and when she looked up at Lucas she whispered, "I can't marry you. At least not right now."

She turned around and ran to her car.

Lucas ran after her but stopped when she slammed the car door as tears poured down his face. She said "not right now," but he feared she was backing out of sharing their lives together at all. "Don't go!"

But, in his heart, he knew she was already gone.

Helen reached for Lucas as he passed her on the porch, but he jerked away before he went in the house and slammed the door.

Helen brought a hand to her mouth, but it was impossible to stifle her cries.

"Let him be." Isaac came up behind her and wrapped an arm around her waist. "I know you want to go to him, but you can't change any of this."

"I've never seen Lucas like that before." She turned to face her husband.

He gently brushed away her tears with his thumbs. "He is in *lieb*. And his heart is broken. But it will mend with time."

Helen wasn't so sure about that. She wanted to be happy that Lucas wasn't marrying an outsider, but happiness wasn't what she felt about any of this. "I was quick to tell the official person who came out here that I saw Moses and Cecelia kiss, that they were carrying on in an improper way. I told the young lawyer lady the same thing. Both times, I offered up the information on my own."

Isaac sighed. "I assumed you did. But this situation is not of your making."

Helen began pacing the porch, even though her hip rebelled. "I can't believe Moses did this."

"If that's even his real name," Isaac interjected.

She stopped pacing and lowered herself into the rocker, then looked up at her husband. "Do you think Marianne was involved in anything illegal?"

Isaac shrugged. "I don't know. But setting up another person to pay the price for a crime you committed . . . That is about as low as a man can go."

Helen took a deep breath, thought for a few minutes, then said, "I practically told Cecelia that our people were better than the *Englisch*. It sounds wrong and silly now, but that's more or less what I told her. And I think Moses must have been Amish, baptized into the faith. Otherwise, he wouldn't have spoken our Pennsylvania *Deutsch* so well. And that makes what I said to Cecelia even worse." Helen's stomach clenched as she remembered her unkind words to Natalie's mother.

Isaac dropped his suspenders and untucked his shirt, then sat down in the other rocking chair, sighing. "Our community has sinners like everywhere else, but I am surprised about Moses."

Helen shook her head and was quiet for a short while, her thoughts drifting back to Lucas. "I guess I should be happy that Natalie broke things off with Lucas, for now anyway." She looked at her husband. "So, why do I feel so awful?"

"Because our *sohn* is hurting." Isaac stroked his beard. "I'm going to go see the other elders and the bishop tomorrow. We need to have a meeting about this thing with Moses. In the meantime, let's not push Lucas into conversations he might not be ready to have. Let him work through this in his own way."

Helen nodded. There was someone she needed to have a meeting with too.

CHAPTER 17

Cecelia tightened the belt on her white robe, opened the bottle of vodka, and added it to her glass of orange juice. She'd found another bottle this morning that she'd forgotten about. It had been awhile since she'd felt the need to drown her sorrows with alcohol. And most of those times, she ended up pouring the drink down the sink, like she had recently.

After staring at the glass for several minutes, she brought it to her lips and downed the entire thing in a few large gulps. Natalie would be disappointed in her. Cecelia was disgusted with herself. But she poured another one anyway.

Tom had reconnected with Olivia via text message from Mississippi. *Coward.* And he hadn't called Cecelia since he'd gotten word of her legal issues from Natalie. And that was fine. In addition to helping her see how he'd tried to play her, his cowardly actions had enabled Cecelia to view the situation as someone looking in from the outside. Her ex-husband would always be Natalie's father, and once the dust settled, Cecelia hoped Natalie would make an effort to be closer to her father, but that was up to her. Cecelia was done pining over the loss of her marriage. She also didn't care if she ever saw Moses or heard his name again.

Halfway through her second drink, she flipped through the bills on the counter, then sorted them by the most demanding, and the mortgage company landed on the top of the pile. She didn't even open it. What was the point? She still didn't have the money to pay it, and she wasn't asking Natalie for another dime. Her daughter was blowing through her college money in an effort to keep Cecelia out of prison. A knock at the door interrupted her thoughts.

She scooted across the floor in her fuzzy white slippers, dotted with orange juice she'd spilled, and wondered who would be knocking so early in the morning. After glancing at the clock on the mantel, she decided ten wasn't really that early to most people.

"Oh, perfect," she said after she opened the door. "Helen, if you've come to rub my nose in my own poop, this isn't a good time." Cecelia raised the glass to her lips and took a sip.

"Can I please come in? I want to talk to you, and I've asked the driver to wait." She nodded over her shoulder, then looked back at Cecelia. "I found your address in the phone book."

Cecelia didn't know anyone even used phone books anymore. She tossed hers every time a new one showed up in the mail or on the doorstep. Cell phones and Google had made phone books obsolete. Apparently, not for the Amish.

She moved aside and waved an arm. "Sure. Why not? Come on in, Helen."

She closed the door and motioned to the couch. "Have a seat." She raised an eyebrow. "Can I get you anything to drink?"

Helen sat on the edge of the couch, her little black purse in her lap. "*Nee.* I'm fine."

Cecelia sat in the chair across from Helen, keeping her eyes on the woman, and took another drink. Helen would surely dub Cecelia as an alcoholic, even though Cecelia hadn't had a drink before noon in a long time.

"So, what brings you to my neck of the woods this fine morning?" Cecelia crossed one leg over the other and kicked her fuzzy slipper into motion, willing it to fly off and smack Helen in the face.

"I wanted you to know that none of us knew about Moses." She lowered her eyes, sighed, and looked back at Cecelia. "We are so upset about this. Isaac is meeting with the bishop and elders right now."

"Oh, I wouldn't give it too much thought, Helen. I'm sure everyone in your little community will survive. And look at the bright side. I now own Moses's house. I'll be your neighbor." She let out a fake gasp. "Oh, wait. No. Let's see." She tapped a finger to her chin. "I won't be living there, even though this house is probably going to foreclose soon, because I don't have the eleven thousand dollars needed to catch up on the mortgage, so that property will likely foreclose too. I guess I'll be homeless." She let out a louder gasp. "Ha! I almost forgot. Who needs a house when you're in prison?" She chugged the rest of her drink.

"Cecelia, we are sorry for your troubles. We really are. We believed Moses to be a *gut* man." Helen looked down.

"Well, okay. You've come to clear your conscience, so, mission accomplished." Cecelia wondered if she was slurring since she wasn't used to drinking, and she suspected she wasn't going to feel very good about herself later. She stood, empty glass in hand. For now, she wanted to be alone. "As you said, your driver is waiting."

"Did you know Natalie called off her marriage to Lucas? Or, at least, put things on hold."

Cecelia sat back down. "No. Are you sure? I just talked to her last night." Thinking back, Natalie hadn't sounded like herself, but Cecelia assumed it was because of this legal stuff.

"*Ach*, I'm sure. She told Lucas in front of me and Isaac." Helen lowered her eyes again. "Lucas is heartbroken."

"I'm sure Natalie is too. She loves Lucas." Cecelia tried to picture how the scene must have unfolded when Natalie told them there wouldn't be a wedding anytime soon. "Well, we got our wish." Although, Cecelia felt worse than ever now.

Helen dabbed at one eye with a tissue she'd pulled out of her apron pocket. "*Ya*, I guess we did. But I can't stand to see Lucas so upset. Maybe I didn't realize how much he really loved her. I've been so caught up worrying about him leaving us that I couldn't see past that. But, seeing them together last night, and all the tears . . ." She wiped her eyes again.

Both women were quiet for a while.

"Did she give a reason?" Cecelia set her glass on the

end table, resolved not to have any more. She rubbed her temples, hoping a migraine didn't come on.

"She gave several reasons. She was upset that Moses was our friend. She's upset about what happened to you, but she also said she'd be asking Lucas to give up too much." Helen tipped her head to one side. "It was so sincere, so giving, to make such a sacrifice. But now I worry if Lucas will ever love anyone as much as he loves her."

Cecelia was quiet.

Helen stood. "Thank you for allowing me to come in. Isaac and our family—actually, our entire community—is saddened by what Moses did. We feel sure the truth will come out and you won't go to jail." She tucked her chin and limped toward the door.

This was a Helen that Cecelia had never seen. *Humbled.*

Cecelia stood, walked her to the door, and opened it for her.

After Helen stepped across the threshold, she turned to face Cecelia, her eyes filled with tears. "*Mei* family will be saying extra prayers for you—and Natalie—each and every day."

Cecelia stared at the woman, then said, "Thank you for coming, Helen. I'm going to talk to Natalie to make sure that any decision she made wasn't influenced by my situation." Even though Cecelia knew it was.

Helen nodded before she hobbled down the sidewalk.

Cecelia closed the door, went to the kitchen, and poured out the bottle of vodka. Then she went to call her daughter, who obviously needed her but probably assumed Cecelia had already checked out emotionally.

That was the old Cecelia, she reminded herself as she

got dressed. *There's a new gal in town, one who wants to be a better mother.*

❧

Natalie shoved a spoon into the container of chocolate ice cream, her feet propped up on the coffee table. As she savored the bite, she ran her hand along her red sofa and wished Adeline was here to comfort her.

Natalie had been questioning God all morning. She'd worked hard to be a good person, to get to know Him, and she couldn't understand why He was letting all of this happen. Her thoughts returned to the fact that maybe she wasn't worthy. And every time she thought about Lucas, she started to cry again. He'd sent her several texts and called twice since last night. She hadn't answered.

And then it hit her. *This is why God is letting this happen. Lucas isn't meant to be with me, and he'd never have the heart to break things off.* Natalie might not have had the strength to end things either, if all this business with her mother hadn't happened. Maybe she needed an excuse to end the relationship. She loved Lucas enough to let him go lead the life God had planned for him. While they'd been discussing things like his learning to drive, where they would live, and a whole bunch of other transitions, maybe they had overlooked the more important issues, the ones that revolved around the spiritual aspects of their being together.

She stood when there was a knock at the door. Squeezing her eyes closed, she hoped it wasn't Lucas. After a few seconds, she looked though the peephole. It was her mother. She wondered how she would summon up enough energy to comfort her mother when she couldn't even eat enough ice cream to lessen her own pain.

With the spoon hanging out of her mouth, Natalie eased the door open and stepped aside.

Her mother swooshed past her into the living room, then turned to face Natalie before she sat on the couch and patted the spot beside her.

After she took the spoon from her mouth, Natalie closed the door, then lumbered her way to the couch and plopped down with the ice cream in her lap. Her mother gently took the ice cream and the spoon and placed them on the table. Then she pulled Natalie into a hug and rubbed her back.

Within seconds, Natalie started to cry. She sobbed for a while before she eased out of the embrace.

"I sensed you might need a hug." Her mother pushed hair away from Natalie's face, leaned over and kissed her on the cheek, then handed the ice cream back to her. "Although sometimes ice cream is exactly what we need."

Natalie shook her head. "I've had enough." She handed the container to her mother, who placed it on the coffee table again. Natalie waited for her to state the purpose of her visit. A phone call from Dad? Or maybe a call from the lawyer had her worked up.

"Helen came to see me this morning." Her mother slipped her feet out of a pair of black flip-flops. "She said you broke up with Lucas." When Natalie didn't say anything, her mother picked up the ice cream, then eased her feet up on Natalie's coffee table as she leaned against the back of the couch. Natalie got comfortable, too, and stretched her legs out.

Her mother took a giant bite of ice cream. "Do you want to talk about it?"

"No." Natalie waited for her mother to force the conversation, but she just took another bite, then offered Natalie the spoon. This time, Natalie took it and plunged it into the ice cream, pulling out a large spoonful.

They continued to share the ice cream, and eventually Natalie laid her head on her mother's shoulder, and her mom reached an arm around her and held her.

They stayed that way for a long while.

"Today is Good Friday." Mom kissed Natalie on the forehead. "I was thinking maybe we could go to church Sunday for Easter."

Natalie looked to see if her mother was teasing. "We don't have a church."

Shrugging, her mother smiled. "Maybe we should find one. Then after the service, I'll cook a ham, and we can have mashed potatoes, green beans, and whatever else I can dream up."

Natalie nodded as a tear slid down her cheek. "That would be great."

Maybe God was hearing her prayers. Natalie's life was in shambles, but He had returned her mother to her, the woman she remembered before the divorce. And her mother's effort was particularly appreciated since Natalie was sure she was equally distraught.

She smiled. "Thank you for coming, Mom."

"You're welcome, baby girl."

Lucas arrived at Mary and Levi's house at their normal sup-pertime Friday night, not surprised that Natalie's car wasn't there.

"Have you heard from her?" Lucas asked Mary as he followed her to the kitchen. Only three places were set at the table. "I guess you have."

"She stopped by earlier." His sister-in-law hugged him. "Levi and I are both sorry that the two of you are hurting."

Levi walked into the kitchen and also embraced Lucas as Mary stepped away. "*Wie bischt?*"

Lucas went to his usual spot and pulled out the chair. "I miss her so much."

Mary poured tea for everyone before she joined the men at the table. After praying, they were quiet as they filled their plates. Lucas hoped and prayed his brother or sister-in-law wouldn't tell him the breakup was for the best.

After a while, Lucas finally said it. "Maybe this was for the best." If he said it enough times, perhaps he'd start to believe it.

Levi and Mary exchanged glances, but neither said anything.

"I mean . . ." Lucas shrugged. "There's all of this going on with her *mudder*, and I was never comfortable in her world." His voice cracked so he looked down at his plate and pushed his peas around. Mary had made his favorites—pork tenderloin, creamed peas, twice-baked potatoes, and a cucumber salad. Lucas had also noticed the shoofly pie on the counter. He forced himself to take a bite of tenderloin so he wouldn't hurt his sister-in-law's feelings.

Mary cleared her throat. "Lucas, Levi and I would have accepted any decision you and Natalie made, even if it meant you living in the *Englisch* world. It wouldn't have been ideal, but we love you both."

"I didn't make the decision to stop seeing each other. *She* did." Lucas wrangled with the bitterness that kept battling for room in his heart, as if anger could squash the hurt he was feeling. "How was she when she came by?"

"Broken." Mary blinked back tears. "She said she loves you, but she could tell you weren't comfortable away from your community, and once she stepped back and got some perspective, she realized that. Obviously, she is also concerned about her mother."

Lucas excused himself and went to the bathroom. He leaned against the door and closed his eyes. For the hundredth time, he asked God to send Natalie back to him. It was a selfish request, so he forced himself to look at things from a different angle. Even though he couldn't picture his life without her, he prayed again. But this time he prayed for Natalie. *What is best for her,* Gott?

CHAPTER 18

It took almost an hour to get to the Paoli courthouse Monday morning. Cecelia sat next to her attorney in the front row. It was a small room. Natalie was in the second row. They stood when the judge walked in, but the only other people there were the court reporter and Mr. Livingston's paralegal, Carrie.

Most of Cecelia's dealings had been with Carrie over the past three weeks. She'd only talked to Mr. Livingston once, and he'd assured her that the charges would be thrown out. The private investigator Natalie ended up paying for had located Moses in Canada. His real name was David Shingles, originally from New York, and evidently he had been baptized into an Amish community before he married his wife.

It would be up to law enforcement to decide whether to extradite him. Mr. Livingston said it was highly unlikely they would. Apparently, it was an expensive process reserved for people who had committed much worse crimes. Marianne had been Amish too, but she'd broken the law along with her husband, just not to the extent that Moses—David—had.

The logistics didn't make sense to Cecelia. Why not just flee the country? Why leave Cecelia his house? Did Moses assume she had some cash stashed away somewhere to catch up the mortgage? She'd accidentally mentioned her financial problems once, so she doubted he thought that. But, for today, she wanted this business behind her. She spent most of her time trying to figure out a way to make it all up to Natalie. Her daughter had dropped out of college without finishing the first semester, which disheartened Cecelia, but maybe Natalie did need some downtime to figure out what she really wanted. Cecelia still hoped she would continue her education, even if she changed her major. But she was resolved to accept whatever decisions Natalie made.

More worrisome was the fact that her daughter seemed to have lost her zest for life after she broke up with Lucas. The light in her eyes had dimmed, and it broke Cecelia's heart. She planned to keep a close eye on her daughter to make sure the light didn't flicker and go out completely, the way it had for Cecelia throughout the divorce process. Her life became a dark place to live, and she didn't want to see Natalie go down that path.

As if everything else happening wasn't hard enough, the bank foreclosed on Cecelia's house last week. Natalie paid to have most of Cecelia's things moved to a storage unit, and Cecelia was living with her in her small apartment. They had enough money to eat and pay rent for a couple more months, but then they would be broke.

Cecelia couldn't believe how much her attorney and

the private investigator had cost. Natalie had admitted she didn't realize how fast money could slip through her fingers, something Cecelia knew all about. Even though Natalie had quit her job, paid for her tuition and books, and had living expenses, Cecelia knew she was part of her daughter's financial demise as well. And that bothered her more than anything.

The judge read Cecelia's charges, then Mr. Livingston began to present evidence to have the charges dropped. Her biggest saving grace was probably that David Shingles had a record a mile long, and he'd done this sort of thing before. Cecelia had also never been in trouble with the law before, and David left a sloppy paper trail. Her hands were clammy and her chest was tight. What if her attorney was wrong? What if there wasn't enough evidence to exonerate her? What if Mr. Livingston had missed something that would cause her to go to jail? As her head filled with what-ifs, the door at the back of the small courtroom creaked open.

An older Amish man walked into the room, followed by a dozen other men, all with long gray beards and straw hats, whom Cecelia had never seen before. Behind them were Helen and her family, including Lucas. Cecelia hadn't talked to Helen since the day she'd shown up at the house.

Mr. Livingston, Cecelia, Natalie, and Carrie turned to look at the trail of Amish people coming in. There wasn't even enough room for all of them to sit. The judge looked as perplexed as Cecelia felt as he took off his glasses and waited for everyone to get settled. Mr. Livingston turned back around to continue, but the judge waved him off.

"Hello, ladies and gentlemen." The judge rubbed his chin, eyeing the people who had filled his courtroom. "Anyone can be present for these proceedings, but might I ask why all of you are here today?"

The first man who had walked in cleared his throat. "I am Bishop Troyer, and we have come to support Cecelia Collins."

What? Cecelia brought a hand to her chest and tapped a couple of times, hoping to slow her heart rate. Their support wouldn't change the outcome, but Cecelia was touched by their effort.

The judge grinned. He was an older man Cecelia suspected was in his seventies. "Okay. Very well." He rubbed his chin again and motioned for Mr. Livingston to continue.

Cecelia searched the crowd until she saw Helen sitting in the back row beside Lucas. But Helen stared straight ahead, as did Lucas. Cecelia quickly turned her eyes to Natalie and saw that her daughter was staring at Lucas. *Please, dear Lord, help me find a way to make things right for Natalie, whether with Lucas or not, but please, she's been through so much.*

Cecelia had been praying more and more these last weeks. She and Natalie had attended the Easter service at a church they'd both liked and had continued to visit, but there was something else happening with Cecelia, something inside that couldn't be credited simply to attending church. Natalie explained that her heart was opening to God, listening to His love, and finding a peace only He could give her. She'd said the Lord was all that kept her going sometimes. Cecelia was beginning to understand what her daughter meant. Especially now. Even though the ordeal had been devastating, Cecelia found strength through her growing relationship with God.

When the judge dismissed the charges, Cecelia covered her face with her hands and cried. Natalie was quickly by her side, an arm around her. When Cecelia realized the Amish folks were filing out in a single line toward the exit, she dabbed at her eyes and told Natalie she needed to find Helen.

⁂

Natalie's eyes darted around the room until she found Lucas. He was standing in the back corner of the courtroom, his thumbs looped beneath his suspenders, and he didn't look in a hurry to leave since he wasn't moving in the line out the door. She waited until almost everyone was in the hallway before she walked over to where he was standing.

Sniffling, she said, "It's a wonderful thing you all have done, coming here like this."

He shrugged. "We wanted to make sure the judge knew we didn't condone what Moses had done, and that we also believed in your *mudder*."

"You mean, what David Shingles had done." She gazed into his eyes.

He stared back at her with a longing Natalie recognized. She felt it every day. "I miss you," he said softly.

"I miss you too." She wanted to fall into his arms, but nothing about their circumstances had changed. "I have to confess that I was angry at you and your family when this first happened, but it also seemed like a chance to set you free." A tear rolled down her cheek as she waited for him to argue. Not that it would change anything.

"You don't belong in my world, Lucas." She waved an arm toward the few Amish people still moving out the door. "But what you all did by coming here"—she took a deep breath to avoid more tears—"it means a lot to Mom and me." She hung her head before she looked up and locked eyes with him again, offering a weak smile. "I'd better go find my mom." But she didn't move. Her feet stayed rooted to the floor.

Lucas rubbed his forehead, took in a deep breath, then said, "*Ya,* I have to go."

As he walked away, Natalie was sure he took a piece of her heart with him. She trudged toward the exit to find her mother. This was a good day for them both. But all she wanted to do was hole up and cry somewhere. Now that her mother was living with her, she couldn't even do that.

She wanted to stay strong for her mom, who was making remarkable changes daily, seeming to find the woman she was always meant to be, even amid the hardships they were facing. Her mother admitted to a slipup of having a couple drinks, but the fact that she'd been open about it to Natalie was also a stride in the right direction.

&

Cecelia wanted to pull out her phone and snap a picture of the dozens of buggies surrounding the courthouse. Some were tied to the hitching post at the far end of the parking lot. Others were tethered to trees. It was quite a sight to see so many of them, and she couldn't believe they'd all come to support her.

The sun shone brightly today, outside and in Cecelia's heart. She lifted a hand to her forehead and searched for Helen, who was stepping into one of the buggies when Cecelia spotted her.

"Wait," she called out, then edged over to the sidewalk when her heels started to sink into the grass.

Cecelia hadn't thought she could cry anymore, but tears spilled when she reached Helen. "I can't believe you did this." She shook her head.

Helen met her eyes. "I didn't. Bishop Troyer did." She smiled a tiny bit, but her eyes were moist.

Cecelia threw caution to the wind as she pulled Helen into a hug, in front of God, her people, and anyone else who happened to be nearby, and Helen hugged her back. "Thank you," Cecelia whispered. "How can I ever repay you?" Again, she realized the outcome of her case hadn't depended on any of them being there, but she wanted Helen to understand how much it meant to her.

Helen eased away, but then leaned close to Cecelia's ear. "You don't happen to have any of that medication you gave me, do you?"

Cecelia had to search her mind for a few moments. "Oh, do you mean the ibuprofen?"

Helen glanced around frowning, as if they were making a drug deal on the courthouse lawn. "*Ya*," she whispered before she pressed her lips together.

Cecelia dug around in her bag for a coin purse she kept various medications in, like Tylenol, ibuprofen, and migraine meds. She pulled out six ibuprofen tablets. "This is all I've got on me."

Helen held out her hand. "*Danki.*" She dropped two in her mouth and swallowed them without anything to drink. "I know God is the worker of miracles, but I think these pills are too."

"Why haven't you gotten more since I gave you what was left in that bottle?" Cecelia was sure the Amish frequented places like Walmart and used modern medication, but then she remembered that Helen's family wasn't like most Amish. They were much more conservative. Before Helen responded, Cecelia whispered, "They have them at Walmart. I'll get you some."

"Are they expensive?" Helen's eyebrows drew inward.

"No. They're not." Cecelia smiled. "It's the least I can do for this incredible show of support." She motioned with her arm at all the buggies, some already untethered and pulling out onto the road.

Helen shifted her weight and placed a hand on her hip. "How is Natalie?"

"Sad. What about Lucas?"

"The same." Helen grimaced. "I might have been wrong in my thinking. As painful as it would be if Lucas chose the *Englisch* world, I think it's more painful to watch him suffering the way he is now."

"I think Natalie doesn't want him to have to change his way of life." Her daughter had finally opened up to her about feeling the need to set Lucas free.

"That says a lot about Natalie." Helen smiled as her husband finished talking with another man and joined them.

Cecelia thanked him as well, then said goodbye to Helen, promising to bring her the ibuprofen soon. Then she set out to find Natalie.

~

Later in the evening, Natalie received a text from Lucas.

It was *gut* to see you today.

Her finger hovered over the screen to type a message. She finally did.

It was nice to see you too.

She waited, her heart aching at the thought of never being with Lucas, but she and her mother needed to get their lives in order, and Natalie was hoping that staying busy would help her heal. They'd spent the evening searching online for jobs. Natalie had some experience in retail management from her time working at Rural King. Her boss had been understanding when she quit her job to go to college full-time, but he didn't have any openings for her right now. Her mother was looking for an administrative or bookkeeping job of some sort. Montgomery was a small town with fewer than five hundred people, so they'd both broadened their search to include the surrounding towns. It would be a longer commute, but they needed jobs.

She received another text from Lucas.

In *Redeeming Love*, Angel has to find her own way
before she's free to be with Michael. I'm going to wait
for you to find your way. I'm not going anywhere. I'm
called to marry you.

Natalie stretched her neck to see if her mother still had
her head buried in a book in the bedroom, and she did. Her
lip trembled as she blinked back tears, and then she wrote
him back.

No, Lucas. You were called to help me find my way to
God, and you did that. Now, you have to go on with the
life God planned for you.

A tear trailed down her cheek, and she tried to fend off
the meltdown that was threatening to take hold of her. She
didn't want it to happen in front of her mother.

The time on her phone showed that it was almost midnight. By twelve thirty, Lucas hadn't texted back. Yawning,
she got into bed. Her mother had fallen asleep with a book in
her lap, so Natalie moved it and turned off the light. Tomorrow, they were going to go see if anything of value was in
her mother's new home. Maybe they could sell a few things
before the mortgage company foreclosed. The dozen horses
Moses owned weren't worth as much as they'd hoped since
most were still untrained. Natalie hated to part with the
animals, but she wanted them to have good homes. Helen's
sons would have to find a new place to stable their horses,
unless new owners agreed to let them stay.

Natalie's thoughts kept leading back to Lucas. She saw his face when she finally closed her eyes to sleep.

◈

Cecelia woke up before Natalie and started some coffee. She wanted to kick-start her brain for the day ahead. First, she needed a job and a cheap place to live. Even though Natalie said it was fine for her to live in the small apartment as long as she chose to, Cecelia wanted to continue her trek on the path to independence. She'd lost hope in men. Tom and David Shingles had seen to that. In addition to getting her life in order, she wanted desperately to help Natalie in that regard. Her daughter had given up everything for Cecelia—school, her independence, and almost all the money she had. There had to be some way Cecelia could make it up to her. She poured herself a cup of coffee, then prayed that Natalie would have the life she deserved, whether it ended up being with Lucas or not, whether it was returning to school or landing a good job. *I just want her to be happy, God.*

Natalie slept for another hour, then they got ready and headed to Cecelia's new house, smack-dab in the middle of Amish country. It had no electricity, a delinquent mortgage, and a dozen horses that she now owned. The bank accounts in her name were empty.

"Can you pull into that dollar store?" Cecelia pointed to her right. "Since we'll be next door to Helen, I want to get her some ibuprofen."

Natalie nodded. She'd been quiet all morning. Probably because she would be so close to Lucas when they arrived.

Cecelia went into the store and picked up several bottles of the generic brand of ibuprofen and two bottles of water for her and Natalie. It would be hot in that house while they took inventory.

She handed a bottled water to Natalie when she got back in the car.

"Thanks." Natalie twisted the top open as she put the car in reverse, then took a long swig before they got on the road.

When they pulled into the driveway, Natalie looked long and hard toward Lucas's house.

"Do you want to take the ibuprofen to Helen?" Maybe she would see Lucas.

But Natalie shook her head. "No, I'll let you do it."

They got out of the car and walked slowly to the front porch. Cecelia inspected the yard. Someone had mowed recently, and she was sure it must have been one of Helen's boys, who was probably still taking care of the horses too. Natalie was gazing at the arena and barn, and she was actually smiling. Maybe they could keep one of the horses, although Cecelia trembled at the thought of Natalie getting back on one of the feisty animals. But she knew her daughter would. It was only a matter of time.

As they approached the front door, she saw an envelope taped to it with "Cecelia" written on it. She stared at it for a few seconds before she pulled it free and slid her finger along the seal to open it.

"What is it?" Natalie glanced back toward the horses while Cecelia pulled out and unfolded a single piece of paper. She studied it, and it took her a minute to figure out what it was.

"Mom, what is it?" Natalie leaned closer now, eyeing the paper.

"Good grief." Cecelia brought a hand to her chest. "What have these crazy Amish people done now?"

Natalie leaned closer, also studying the piece of paper. "*Wow!* Oh wow." Her daughter's eyes bugged out, surely the same way Cecelia's had.

"Go on in," Cecelia said. "I'm sure the door is open. You might want to open the windows and get a breeze going." She couldn't take her eyes off the document in her hand. "Start looking around for things you might want or that we can sell. Obviously, I need to go talk to Helen. Can I take your car? I could walk, but . . ." She pointed to the sandals she was wearing. "I'm not sure these are good shoes to traipse across a field in."

Natalie nodded before she went inside. Cecelia had the ibuprofen in her purse, but it was the other item, the piece of paper, that had her heart racing.

CHAPTER 19

Helen took two loaves of bread from the wood oven, then asked the girls to stay in the kitchen while she went to talk to Lucas. She'd seen him earlier staring out the window, and he hadn't even noticed her walk by him.

She crossed through the den and placed her hand on his back. "*Wie bischt, sohn?* Are you all right?"

He turned to her briefly but then peered out the window again. "*Ya,* I'm okay."

Natalie's car was at Moses's house—David Shingles's old house, which now belonged to Cecelia. Helen would never get used to the fact that Moses wasn't Moses, but a dishonest Amish man from New York. She was, however, adjusting to the possibility of Cecelia being her neighbor. Except, she worried about Natalie's visits to see her mother. Would seeing her push the knife further into her son's heart? Maybe Cecelia would choose to sell the property.

"Maybe you should go talk to her," Helen said softly, but he shook his head. A few weeks ago, she would have been jumping for joy that wedding plans were no longer on the table. She hadn't expected to feel such empathy for her son.

"*Nee*. I have to give her time." He kept his eyes focused on the house and car in the distance. When the car pulled out of the driveway and headed their way, Lucas said he had to get back to work and headed to the barn. "*I have to give her time*." But would time change anything?

Helen rubbed the back of her neck. Natalie was probably bringing her the ibuprofen from Cecelia. Helen wanted to pay for it even though Cecelia had said not to worry about it, but she wasn't sure she had enough cash.

Her heart hurt for Lucas. She recalled how hard she'd resisted the idea of him and Natalie being together, and now a part of her wanted to beg the girl to reconsider. But it was Cecelia who got out of the car—alone—and came up the porch steps. Helen met her at the door, and Cecelia handed her a bag from the dollar store. "How much do I owe you?"

Cecelia burst out laughing. "Are you kidding me? I'm going to owe you for the rest of my life." Her expression sobered as she pulled a piece of paper from her purse, unfolded it, and handed it to Helen. "I honestly have no idea who I should be thanking, but I know it had to be someone in your community who came up with the money to catch up the mortgage. I will pay back every cent when I get a job and get on my feet." She hung her head, sighed, and looked back up at Helen with tears in her eyes. "Now we can sell the house instead of having another foreclosure on my record." She wrapped her arms around Helen, which Helen was starting to get used to, if only a little bit.

"No thanks is required. Everyone chipped in." Helen eased out of the hug.

Cecelia chuckled. "This is a game changer for Natalie and me, to be able to sell the house." She looked up. "Praise God, and please thank everyone."

Helen wondered if selling the house would bring finality to this entire situation. Eventually a new family would move in, and hopefully they would all forget about David Shingles. Helen wished Marianne were alive so she could ask her why she'd allowed herself to become entangled in such a mess. Marianne had grown up Amish, and the man they knew as Moses was handsome. Maybe Marianne had been taken in and gone against the Lord by committing crimes for her husband, whether he was truly Amish or not. Even if he had been baptized into their faith, he'd disrespected them, the Lord, and Cecelia. Helen shook her head, deciding she'd never know for sure.

Cecelia waved as she left. Helen closed the door, then hobbled over to the couch, thinking about how no one could really know a person at all. Moses wasn't who she'd thought he was. And neither was Cecelia. Helen almost felt like she and Natalie's mother could have become friends and learned things from each other.

Cecelia's opinion had changed about Helen's people. And Helen had to admit that her opinion of Cecelia had changed. She loved her daughter as much as Helen loved her own children. And the woman seemed to be trusting God and trying to put her life back together after her divorce.

Helen couldn't imagine going through such a thing with Isaac.

She stood and stretched, then popped two of the ibuprofen into her mouth.

∽

Natalie went from room to room in the small house. She'd opened the windows like her mother suggested. There was a nice cross breeze, but it was hot. And the house smelled like fresh paint. There was a living room area and a small kitchen with a wood-burning oven and a vintage refrigerator that used ice blocks to keep food cold. There was also an ice chest set off to one side. A small kitchen table with two chairs was against one wall. Off to one side was a master bedroom that wasn't very big. The one bathroom had an entrance from the den and bedroom. She went upstairs and down a narrow hallway where she found another modestly furnished bedroom and small bathroom. The property's value hinged mostly on the hundred acres, not the small farmhouse. She went back downstairs when she heard her mother pull the car in the driveway then come inside.

"Mom, there's not anything of real value in here to sell, but now that you have the mortgage caught up, you can sell the house and include everything in it. That would be easier than trying to sell this stuff. The horses are worth money too." She eyed the worn couch, old coffee table, and two chairs in the den. The furniture in the master bedroom looked like it was from another era.

She peered out the window at the horse arena and barn

and sighed. "I love this place, everything about it, except that the man who lived here framed you." She turned to face her mother, who had taken a seat on the couch. "Are you going to try to sell the horses yourself or hire someone to do it?"

"I'm not sure yet. I'm hoping I can get some advice from Helen's husband to help me decide what to do." Cecelia took a tissue from her purse and dabbed at the sweat on her forehead.

"What did Helen say about the mortgage being paid?"

Her mother smiled. "She said that they all chipped in." She shook her head, still smiling. "Amazing that they did that. So generous."

Natalie almost said, "I told you they were good people." But her mother had learned that on her own.

Natalie looked back outside. "There's so much I would do with a place like this. I'd make flower beds in the front on either side of the sidewalk. I'd paint the barn with a fresh coat of red." She turned to her mother. "I'd groom animals to make money. I'd rent out the stables too. She shrugged. "It's a moot point, but someday I hope to have a place like this in the country."

&

Cecelia smiled. "Those are lovely thoughts, but don't you think you'll want to go back to school at some point?"

Natalie shrugged. "Maybe." After a few seconds she said, "But I'd take this life over school any day of the week."

Cecelia could never live this life. Even with electricity and air-conditioning, it was too secluded for her liking. "Even if you had to see Lucas in the distance?"

Natalie looked over her shoulder at her mother, then turned back to the window. "Maybe I'd feel differently some-day, but I'd settle for seeing him from afar as opposed to never seeing him again." She shrugged. "Doesn't matter anyway." She turned and walked over to Cecelia and put her hands on her hips. "So . . . where do you want to start? Box up the junk that won't be included in the sale?"

Cecelia's heart was full, but suddenly there was room for it to become even fuller.

"Mom?" Natalie waved her hand in front of Cecelia's face. "Hello, earth to Mother. Where do you want to start?"

Cecelia tipped her head to one side. "Hmm . . . I think the first thing I'll do is have new locks put on the doors so you'll feel safe."

Natalie's eyes widened. "What?"

Cecelia stood and placed her hands on her daughter's shoulders, then kissed her on the cheek. "I want you to have the house. I will take over your apartment until I find a job. We will sell the horses. We should have enough money to pay the mortgage on this place and your apartment rent for a couple months, but we'll both need jobs *soon*. I could move in here with you for a while"—she cringed—"and even endure the summer heat, but if you break your lease it will go on your credit record, and you don't want that." Cecelia began to pace, tapping a finger to her chin. "The payments for this place are rather hefty, but I think we could refinance and get it to a more affordable monthly payment for you."

Natalie took a step backward. "Absolutely not." She

threw her arms in the air before slapping them to her sides. "For whatever reason, that weirdo left you his house." She shook her head. "Odd, but a blessing. And you will use the money to get another house, a job, and get back on your feet. Maybe he knew you'd have help getting caught up on the mortgage. Or maybe he felt bad about what he'd done to you. But the money from the house is yours."

Cecelia sat in one of the chairs, crossed one leg over the other, and kicked it into action. "Nope. I'm not selling the house. You love it, and I want you to have it. Please let me do this for you. I know it doesn't make up for everything you've endured, but . . ." She paused, wanting to reiterate her biggest concern. "Do you think you could live next to Lucas and see him from afar—as you put it—without it ripping at your heart constantly?" Cecelia suspected they might have unfinished business, but her daughter needed to think this part through carefully.

Natalie turned to the window for several seconds before spinning around to face Cecelia again, a stern expression on her beautiful face. "Yes, I could do it. Maybe we'd even find our way back to being friends someday. But it doesn't matter, Mom. It wouldn't be right for you to give me a house that was meant for you."

"Sit down, Natalie." Cecelia's heart sang loudly, and she wanted her daughter to understand her reasoning. After Natalie finally sat, blowing out a huff as she did so, Cecelia continued. "When Adeline died, she wanted you to have money to go to college. She didn't realize she didn't have much money left. Your friends Levi and Mary couldn't keep a fancy piano, so they sold it and gave you a bundle of money to go to college to become a vet. Now you don't want to be a vet, but you love animals. A man I don't know gave me a house."

She chuckled. "At first, it all seemed bizarre for me to own this house. But now I know why. Everything happens for a reason, according to God's will. And I know in my heart that this is where you are meant to be. Here, in this house. You've already mentioned ways you could make money. And if you choose to go back to school down the line, hopefully I'll be in a position, at some point, to help you pay for it."

Natalie stared at her as her jaw dropped. "Mother, have you been drinking?"

Cecelia frowned. "I'm having an epiphany and you're accusing me of drinking?" She pointed a finger at her. "Bad you."

"Mom, you can't do this." Natalie was smiling, though, and Cecelia knew she was considering it. "Can you?"

Cecelia nodded. "Let me do this for you."

Natalie stood and actually jumped up and down. "I want it!"

Cecelia rushed to her, cupped her face, then pulled her into a brief hug before she stared into her beautiful daughter's eyes. "This is where you're meant to be. And I want to start my life from scratch, taking with me the things I've learned from you."

Natalie rolled her eyes. "Like what?"

"You are unselfish, uncompromising when you believe strongly about something, and strong in your faith, and I'd like to think I'm growing in these areas, thanks to you. I want to be a better person. Take the house, sweetheart. Make it your sanctuary." She kissed her on the cheek. "Because that's what I'm going to do. I'm going to rebuild my life and become the person I want to be."

Natalie rushed to the window and stared out at the fields, the barn, the arena, then turned back to her mother in tears. "I love you, Mom. And I'm so proud of you."

Of all the things Cecelia had ever been told, her daughter's words touched her more than anything. "I'm proud of you, too, Natalie. I always have been."

⁊

By Friday, Lucas's curiosity was piqued, but he had to believe the voice in his head that kept saying, *Be patient, My son.* He'd been watching Natalie arrive at the house next door every morning since Tuesday. Sometimes her mother came for a while, and other times Natalie was there by herself.

Lucas would have thought they were readying the house to sell, but it was hard to miss Natalie's red couch being moved in by two men. Was she going to live there? Lucas would be tormented for the rest of his life, having to see her all the time without being able to love her the way he wanted to. But maybe seeing her from afar was better than not seeing her at all.

"Go to her."

Lucas spun around to see his mother standing behind him. "You peer out that window every day." She touched his arm. "Your *daed* and I were wrong not to support you in your decision to live a life that is dictated by God, not us. I can't stand seeing you unhappy."

He kept his eyes on Natalie. "I would if I thought she wanted to be with me right now." She was hanging clothes on the line outside the house. "I wonder if she's ever done that before, hung out clothes."

"I imagine she's always lived in a place that had a washer and dryer. But even some of the *Englisch* hang their sheets outside to dry, so who knows."

Lucas glanced at his mother before he returned his eyes to Natalie. "Yesterday, she rode one of the horses." He recalled the way her ponytail bounced up and down as she sailed across the pasture, and the way he'd held his breath, praying she didn't fall off. "Isn't the old saying that if you fall off the horse, you get back on?"

"*Ya*. It is." His mother paused. "Are you going to your *bruder*'s house for supper tonight?"

"*Ya*, like always." Although it wasn't the same without Natalie. Maybe tonight Mary and Levi would tell him what Natalie and Cecelia's plans were, if they knew. Lucas had seen Mary at the library recently. He still went, hoping to bump into Natalie. Mary said she still visited them, but usually on Saturdays.

"That's *gut*. I wish some of your siblings would visit Levi and Mary more often, but I know it's a lengthy trip by buggy."

Lucas didn't mind the ride, and he enjoyed the visits. But he always held out hope that maybe Natalie would show up. Even Levi and Mary seemed to feel the void every Friday night.

"*Ach*, well, you have a *gut* time and send our love to Levi and Mary." His mother headed toward the kitchen, and Lucas noticed something. "*Mamm*?"

She turned around. "*Ya*?"

"You aren't limping." Lucas smiled as he raised an eyebrow.

His mother chuckled. "I know. It turns out there's a pill called ibuprofen. It's not a cure-all, but it sure does help." Smiling, she said, "I think I'll take the buggy out for a drive later."

Lucas couldn't remember the last time his mother drove the buggy. They all believed she'd had a near accident and quit driving herself after it. Plus, she didn't go anywhere in the buggy that she didn't have to because of the pain in her hip, which she'd had for as long as Lucas could remember. "Do you need a ride somewhere?"

She smiled. "*Nee, sohn*. I think change is in the air."

⏤

Natalie was excited to see Levi and Mary tonight. She'd bowed out of the Friday night visits when she and Lucas stopped seeing each other. Levi was Lucas's brother, and it seemed only fair that Natalie should be the one to opt out, despite Mary's urging that they switch off Fridays. That reminded Natalie too much of her parents' divorce, alternating weekends whenever it had been convenient for her to visit her dad. But she'd been seeing Mary and Levi whenever she could, although she'd missed the fabulous meals. Tonight, Natalie was excited about dining with her friends and anxious to tell them about her plans for the house. She was still overwhelmed by what the Amish community had done for her and her mother, but she was even more blown away by her mother's generosity.

Helen had stopped by earlier in the day and said she had visited with Mary the day before. She said Lucas wouldn't be able to attend the Friday night meal, and Mary had asked Helen to extend the invitation to Natalie. The relationship between Helen's family and Natalie and Cecelia had softened, but Natalie wondered if she would ever get past not being with Lucas. The void was huge, no matter how busy she kept herself working on the house. She'd even planted a small garden.

She arrived a little late, even though she'd left early. Several cows had wandered onto a road along her route, and it caused a traffic backup. So, she raced up the porch steps, knocked, and then opened the door. "It's me!"

She walked through the living room, a wonderful aroma wafting up her nostrils, but it was quiet. She let out a small gasp when she entered the kitchen. "Lucas."

He stood next to a table set for two. Natalie had been so worried about being late that she hadn't taken notice of the buggies outside. She wasn't sure if she would have been able to tell Lucas's from the others. Would she have left? She didn't know. But seeing him standing in front of her, she was reminded of everything she'd given up. Their friendship, budding romance, and hopes and dreams of a life together. As blessed as she was with a new home and visions for her future, the pictures weren't clear in her mind without Lucas included.

"We've been set up." Lucas rubbed his chin.

Natalie couldn't take her eyes off him. "What?"

He handed her a lined piece of paper, and Natalie recognized Mary's nearly perfect cursive writing.

Dear Natalie and Lucas,

We regret that we can't be here this evening. Maxwell wasn't feeling well, so we thought it best to get him checked out. Please enjoy the meal. Everything is warm in the oven.

Much love,

Mary and Levi

"I'm sorry." Natalie shook her head. "Your mother came over and told me you wouldn't be here, and that Mary had extended an invitation for me to come."

Lucas looped his thumbs beneath his suspenders. "Did she now? I hope she asked the Lord to forgive the lie, because she did know I would be here."

"It seems odd that your mother would be trying to set this up. She didn't want me in your life."

He shrugged. "*Mamm* hasn't mentioned your name, but she made the comment that times were changing. She even drove the buggy for the first time in a long while."

A meow came from underneath the table, and Natalie leaned down in time to see Maxwell stretching. "Uh, if the cat was sick, they sorta forgot to take the patient with them."

Lucas chuckled as Natalie set the note on the table. "I guess Mary was in on it, too, since she wrote, 'Dear Natalie and Lucas.' She'll need to ask *Gott* for forgiveness too. But since we're here, let's see what she cooked." He opened the oven. "Looks like pork chops smothered in mushroom sauce."

Natalie folded her arms across her chest. "I'm not leaving. That's my favorite thing that Mary cooks."

Lucas faced off with her, also folding his arms. "I'm not leaving either."

Natalie shrugged, even though she wanted to rush into his arms. "Then let's eat."

After praying, Natalie was surprised at how easily they fell into conversation. *Like old times.* And the not-being-alone rule seemed to have flown out the window since they spent time together at Natalie's apartment after her accident. Even under the circumstances, Natalie was as comfortable with Lucas as she'd ever been. She wondered if he would bring up their separation and the way things had ended. Natalie was avoiding the subject, telling him of her plans for the house, but intentionally omitting anything that had to do with them.

"Yeah, it was so crazy, and then for my mom to give me the house . . ." She sighed. "I couldn't believe it. She's made so many changes in her life. She even got a job today as a full-time bookkeeper for a law firm in Bedford. Her lawyer knew the guy and recommended her. She starts Monday."

"I saw two men moving in that red couch, and I wondered what was going on." Lucas finished chewing a bite of pork, swallowed, and then gazed into her eyes.

Natalie wondered how she'd ever gotten the strength to let him go and whether this surprise setup was only going to make things worse for her—seeing him, talking to him, reflecting on what might have been.

"And I saw you hanging clothes on the line. Was that a first?"

"Yeah." She tried to smile in an effort to keep things light. The food was amazing, as always. "I don't have air-conditioning or electricity, but it's cozy with the lanterns, and I love hearing the crickets at night."

"I saw you riding."

Natalie's cheeks warmed. "Lucas Shetler, have you been spying on me?"

He stared into her eyes. "Every chance I get."

She felt herself blush. "I'm keeping one horse, the tamest one." She lowered her head, then looked back at him. "How did everything get so messed up?"

"You dumped me. That's how." He sent an exaggerated scowl her way, then shook his head. "Not a nice thing to do to the guy who's in *leib* with you."

Her cheeks felt even hotter. "I can't pull you from the life you know. But it doesn't mean I don't love you." She lowered her eyes as tears threatened to fall. She didn't want to cry. She was having a good time. "Excuse me. I'll be right back."

She rushed to the bathroom, reached for a tissue, and dabbed at her eyes before any tears escaped. She hadn't bothered with makeup tonight, knowing Mary wouldn't have any on. As she thought about it, she realized she hadn't worn makeup all week.

Closing the commode lid, she sat down and thought about her grandmother. Mimi Jean would have loved her new home too. Her thoughts drifted to Adeline, again making her imagine her grandmother and Adeline were somehow together and smiling down on her. Mary still hadn't replaced the red-and-pink wallpaper. By the time she and Levi moved into this house, it was as if God had designed it specifically for them. What appeared to be coincidences—no phone, lack of electricity, modest furnishings—had been an orchestrated plan. Only God could have known that Mary and Levi would end up living in this house.

Natalie thought about the plan for her life. The one she'd laid out—to be a vet—hadn't turned out to be what she truly wanted. Instead, she'd been gifted with a farm. She wasn't missing television, electricity, or even her hair dryer. Eventually, she might have to get a job, but she'd groomed three dogs and was hoping it might catch on. She'd also been busy making her new house her own.

Her mother had turned into a horse broker. She'd sold four of the horses this week, insisting that Natalie keep one for herself. That left seven more to sell. Jacob came by daily to feed their three horses, and Natalie had assured him that it was fine for them to stay.

So many things had changed over the last few months. Mostly, her relationship with God had changed *her*. She knew Him personally now. He might not always reveal His plans, but as she stared at Mary's dark green dress hanging on the hook, along with her black apron, she wondered if it would fit this time.

She slipped out of her blue jeans and T-shirt, which she hadn't done the last time, then pulled the dress over her head. As she tied the black apron strings behind her, the clothing felt different up against her body, without her clothes underneath. It felt like a perfect fit, and it wasn't the feel of the material she was talking about. This time, there was also a prayer covering tied on the hanger. The last time she was in here trying on Mary's clothes, there wasn't one. She pulled her hair into a bun on top of her head, secured it with a rubber band she found in a drawer, then put the prayer covering on.

Smiling, she realized she'd been on her own spiritual

quest, and maybe someday she would be ready to commit to the kind of life God seemed to be offering her. Was there still a possibility that she could be with Lucas?

Her heart thumped wildly against her chest as she looked in the mirror. She'd thought about the things she would have to give up to be with Lucas and assumed she couldn't do it. But those were material things. In the back of her mind, she also feared she wasn't as spiritually mature as Lucas. Her relationship with God had grown, and maybe that had to happen before she was ready to nurture a relationship with Lucas. Perhaps that was part of her pilgrimage she hadn't realized until now. God was involved in her life, directing her steps, and this felt like a path she could walk down.

"Do I need to send a search party?" Lucas hollered from the kitchen.

"No. I'm coming." Natalie gingerly pushed the door open and walked into the kitchen in her bare feet, still wearing Mary's clothes. She battled her fear and the feelings of unworthiness that still threatened to take hold of her and pushed forward until she was standing in front of him.

Lucas stood, blinking eyes that were growing moist. "God told me to be patient."

"And He told me that I belong with you." She looked down at what she was wearing, then slowly touched the prayer covering on her head. "I'm not sure I'm ready for this."

Lucas walked closer to her, his expression unreadable. "You can't convert for me."

"I know." Natalie looked into his beautiful eyes. "The journey is mine. It's a lot to commit to." But even as she said the words, visions of a future with Lucas flooded her mind, clearer than ever. "I love you as much as I ever did, but I know the importance of what these clothes represent, and you're right, I can't do this for you. It has to be for the right reasons."

Natalie thought back a few months, to a time when they weren't even supposed to be alone together, fearful that temptation would get the best of them. But they were under God's protective roof now, and everything felt right. She couldn't keep her eyes from Lucas's lips, recalling the feel of his mouth on hers and the love she'd felt being in his arms.

Lucas kissed the tip of her nose, pushed back strands of hair Natalie hadn't tucked beneath the *kapp*. Then his mouth found hers.

"I love you," he whispered between kisses.

"And I love you."

Listening to love was the right thing to do. Because God *is* love. Natalie was determined to keep trusting her heavenly Father and His plans for her life.

EPILOGUE

Cecelia slipped her pale green dress over her head, then fumbled around in her jewelry box for earrings to match. She slipped into a pair of ivory-colored kitten heels she'd bought just for this occasion. Over time she had adjusted to Natalie's apartment, but she did miss a bigger closet and whirlpool tub. But the price was right, and for the first time ever, she earned her own spending money and was making her own choices.

She was almost out the door when she noticed her pile of mail on the kitchen bar. Cecelia was still getting caught up on bills, but she was also waiting on a refund for the first dress she'd purchased online, instead of trying it on first like the one she was now wearing. She knew better than that. The dress had been almost two hundred dollars, so she was anxious to receive the credit.

Something caught her eye—an envelope with international stamps on it. From Canada. Her heart skipped several beats before she ripped open the letter and read.

Dear Cecelia,

It's your old friend "Moses." I figured deeding you my house was the least I could do for putting you through such agony. Hopefully, you can find a way to get caught up on the mortgage. Sorry I didn't have the funds for that. You must think I'm quite the jerk, but I knew they'd drop the charges against you. It was a clear setup. I had some really bad guys after me, and I needed them to believe they'd been paid so I could get out of the country before they realized the truth. I knew they wouldn't go after you, and you were never in danger. You just bought me some time.

Cecelia squinted as she pressed her lips together. *Yes, you are a jerk.*

Everything I said to you, I meant. Well, of course not everything, lol, but the things that matter. You truly are a beautiful woman. And kindhearted. Probably a little too much. Oh, and maybe wear your glasses when you sign things from now on.

She could almost feel the steam rising from her head.

I've got to tell you, even all these months later, kissing you still lingers in my mind. Seriously, you're a class act. Wish things had turned out differently.

Fondly,

David (Moses)

Cecelia grinned. *The Cecelia you knew is long gone, buddy.* She ripped the letter into pieces and tossed it in the air. She had a wedding to go to. Natalie would be fit to be tied if Cecelia was late.

She took a deep breath. Right now, she was going to go watch her Amish daughter get married. Natalie and Lucas had been baptized together and were ready to commit to each other for life. They'd spent six months dating and being neighbors, but they'd worn a path going back and forth between their houses. During that time, Natalie had several visits with the bishop and took the necessary classes before she could be baptized.

Tom and Olivia had gotten married and would be at the wedding. Cecelia had accepted that, and mostly wanted Tom and Natalie to have a good relationship. Her ex was working toward that, but he still had trouble seeing his daughter living an Old Order Amish lifestyle. But the transformation suited Natalie, and Cecelia had never seen her daughter happier. Tom would eventually see and accept that too.

Cecelia arrived at the wedding feeling overdressed. With the exception of Olivia, who looked absolutely stunning in a tasteful maroon dress. Not all that long ago, Cecelia would have wanted to claw the woman's eyes out. But she couldn't blame Olivia for the dissolution of her marriage. It took two to tango. And looking back, her marriage had been over way before Tom stepped out on her. Her ex looked worn out with dark circles under his eyes and a few more crow's-feet branching out toward his temples. Cecelia had come a long way, but she wasn't perfect.

She grinned a little on the inside. *It must be difficult for Tom to keep up with someone so much younger than he is.*

The wedding at the Shetlers' home was unlike anything Cecelia had ever experienced. Furniture had been moved out of the main rooms, replaced with chairs lined in rows. Tables and chairs were set up outside.

Cecelia didn't understand most of the service since the deacons and bishop spoke in Pennsylvania *Deutsch.* But the fellowship was present, and Natalie glowed as she took her vows with Lucas. It was going to be a new and different world for her daughter. Near the end of the ceremony, the bishop bestowed a holy kiss on Lucas's head, and his wife did the same with Natalie. Cecelia was sure she'd never felt the Lord's presence more than at that moment. At least two hundred people were gathered in His name, and Cecelia was sobbing by the time it was all over.

Emotionally drained but hungry, she quickly learned that the food at an Amish wedding was an event all its own. After the ceremony, women scrambled to take dish after dish of piping hot food out to the tables where the couple and their attendants would be seated and fed first. Normally, Cecelia would have offered to help, but she was afraid of being trampled. These women were like a fine-tuned machine.

"Hi, Mom."

Cecelia turned to her left, dabbed at her eyes, and smiled. "Well, it wouldn't be a wedding without tears, now would it?" She stared into her daughter's eyes. "You look more beautiful than I've ever seen you. And I'm so proud of you."

Natalie's moist eyes twinkled as she reached for Cecelia's hands and squeezed. "You look beautiful too. And I'm equally proud of you."

Cecelia wasn't as far into her newly found spirituality as her daughter, but in so many ways she felt like she'd taken the first step onto a path that would lead to a destination unknown, but one guided by God.

By the end of the long day, which had started at eight o'clock in the morning, Cecelia was as worn out as Tom looked. She'd made nice with both Tom and Olivia, wishing them both well as they left. She stayed to help clean up afterward, along with at least twenty other women, and managed to outlast them all. Eventually it was only Cecelia and Helen in the kitchen.

Cecelia leaned up against the counter. Helen stood next to her kitchen table, a hand on the back of one of the chairs. The two women were becoming friends, another mind-blower for Cecelia. They didn't see each other all that often since Cecelia now had a full-time job, but she had grown to enjoy the time she spent with Helen.

Helen crossed the room, and when she got to Cecelia, she wrapped her arms around her neck and squeezed. It was the first time Helen had ever initiated a hug, and it produced a new round of tears for Cecelia. No words were needed. Cecelia and Helen were joined together in a new way now, as family.

If anyone had asked Cecelia a year ago where she and Natalie would be now, this would not have been the outcome she would have predicted. But as she'd come to learn, God sometimes had a much bigger plan for His children than they could possibly dream up for themselves. Some days, Cecelia felt like she was living a rough draft of her life, but it was coming together, and she couldn't wait to live the final version.

ACKNOWLEDGMENTS

Each book I write continues to be a team effort, and I am grateful for all of the people on my team.

Sharon and Sam, it is a pleasure to dedicate this book to you. Southern Indiana has become a special place for me, a second home. It incorporates so many things that I love into one package—the two of you, CJ, and the rest of my Indiana family are a large part of that package (waving to Linda!). I'm also among an endearing group of Amish folks whom I enjoy writing about, stories that I hope entertain and glorify God. And I can't forget our little cabin on the river, which gives me a peaceful place to write and enjoy all God has blessed me with.

To my husband, Patrick, thank you for being the kind of husband who can fend for himself when I'm traveling. Even though you don't know how to cook, and things don't run as smoothly when I'm not there, you never complain. Thank you for just being you. I love you with all of my heart—to the moon and back again.

I might have been remiss in the past and forgotten to thank my amazing street team—Wiseman's Warriors. You gals ROCK, and I appreciate each and every one of you! And, of course, our fabulous Janet Murphy keeps on top of things and makes sure we all stay on task. Love and appreciate you, Janet!

To my team at HarperCollins Christian Fiction, thank you from the bottom of my heart for allowing me to be a part of this wonderful journey. Special thanks to my editors, Kimberly Carlton and Jodi Hughes.

Thank you to Natasha Kern, the best literary agent a gal could have. You also ROCK, Natasha. What a blessing you have been in my life. XO

As always, my heartfelt thank you is to God. I wanted to write one story that made a difference in one life. But You have blessed me with more stories than I'll ever be able to write. However, I'm going to get as many out there as I can!

DISCUSSION QUESTIONS

1. In the beginning of the story, Natalie and Lucas are convinced that they can be friends without becoming romantically involved, even though they are attracted to each other. Were they being naive? Do you know of couples who have maintained a friendship without bringing romance into the relationship?

2. Everyone around Natalie and Lucas notice signs of their relationship blossoming into something more than friendship. What are some of the things that Cecelia, Helen, Levi, and Mary see that Natalie and Lucas don't?

3. Cecelia is a broken and bitter woman following her divorce and financial problems. What are some of the changes—internal and external—that Cecelia goes through in her effort to be the woman she hopes to be?

4. Helen wants to micromanage Lucas's life in some ways, and she surely doesn't want him leaving their community. But Helen changes her tune toward the end of the story. What causes her to change her mind?

5. Out of all of the characters, who do you think is the most levelheaded when it comes to Lucas and Natalie's blossoming relationship? Why?

6. What did you think about Moses? Did you like him from the beginning? Were you surprised by what he did to Cecelia? Did it soften the blow when he ended up giving her his house, even though he was behind on the mortgage? Was there anything endearing about his motives, or was he just a bad guy whom you didn't like?

7. Cecelia and Helen don't care for each other at the beginning of the book. By the end of the story, they are friends. What are some of the ways we see this friendship evolving?

8. What did you think about Isaac, Lucas's father? He plays a small role in the story, but it's an important one. Can you share some of the wisdom that Isaac shares with Helen and Lucas?

9. Which character did you relate to the most? Why?

10. If you could have rewritten any part of the book, what would you have changed? Why?

Don't miss the first book in the Amish Journey series!

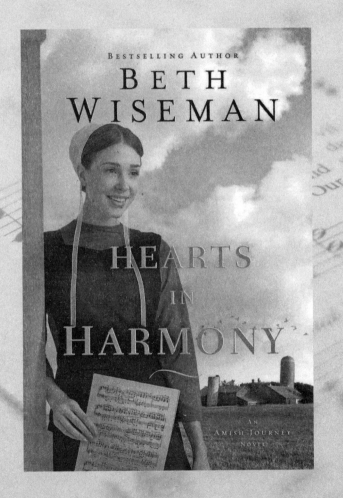

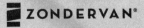

THE AMISH SECRETS COLLECTION

HER BROTHER'S KEEPER

LOVE BEARS ALL THINGS

HOME ALL ALONG

BETH WISEMAN